Truth or Dare

In the afternoon we stopped off and lay in a field just outside Thomastown. I fell asleep while Becka studiously painted her nails with uneven gold and silver stripes. When I woke up again her nails were done and she was grinning from ear to ear. It took a second or two for me to realise what that meant.

'Oh my God,' I said, 'you brought drugs over the border. If they'd found that we'd be in big trouble you know.'

'What, like we will when they find the bodies of those Curran boys?' she parried, passing me the toke.

Becka's so reckless. I suppose that's what I like about her. The lack of pretence. The spirit. The danger. The disloyalty.

SARA SHERIDAN was born in 1968 in Edinburgh. She studied English at Trinity College Dublin and then went on to live in Galway, where she opened and ran an art gallery and restaurant in an abandoned factory beside the River Corrib. She now lives in Edinburgh with her daughter Molly. *Truth or Dare* is her first novel. Her second, *The Pleasure Express*, is now completed, and she is currently working on her third, and an original screen play.

Sara Sheridan

Truth
or
Dare

ARROW

Published in the United Kingdom in 1998 by
Arrow Books

1 3 5 7 9 10 8 6 4 2

Arrow Books
Random House UK Ltd
20 Vauxhall Bridge Road, London, SW1V 2SA

Random House Australia (Pty) Limited
20 Alfred Street, Milsons Point, Sydney,
New South Wales 2061, Australia

Random House New Zealand Limited
18 Poland Road, Glenfield
Auckland 10, New Zealand

Random House South Africa (Pty) Limited
Endulini, 5a Jubilee Road, Parktown, 2193, South Africa

Random House UK Limited Reg. No. 954009

A CIP catalogue record for this book is available from the British Library

Papers used by Random House UK Limited are natural,
recyclable products made from wood grown in sustainable
forests. The manufacturing processes conform to the
environmental regulations of the country of origin

Typeset by Deltatype Ltd, Birkenhead, Merseyside
Printed and bound in the United Kingdom by
Cox & Wyman Ltd, Reading, Berks

ISBN 0 7493 2690 9

To Gemma, who moved to Belfast and gave me ideas
(brave on both counts).

Lest We Forget

In their eagerness for Peace
the dead were all forgotten
the lies were all forgiven
and someone said
'Let's pretend it never happened,
all those people never died,
the crippled and maimed can now all walk,
the blinded can now clearly see.
I never really meant to kill –
well – just a bit.'
And those of us who remember what Peace was really
*   like*
and had always been Irish
must wait to see this 'Promised Land'.

Jack Pakenham

Prologue

It had been a constipated day from the start. Something was waiting to drop. Lorna had woken up in a state of anticipation. It made her mad and it made her clumsy. She had banged her ankle on her way to the kitchen and then she had poured premium-quality breakfast milk all over the worktop. The milk was 5p more expensive than normal milk. This was the sort of detail that Lorna McLeish knew. She bought the milk because of it. It was only six o'clock in the morning, and it was shaping up to be a bad day already. Lorna mopped up the milk, threw the soggy cloth into the sink and decided not to go to the gym. She didn't mind the gym – if she had hated it more she probably would have made herself go, but, as it was, she enjoyed it as much as she could enjoy anything. Bastard.

She walked through to the bathroom and turned on the shower. It took a while to get hot at this time of the morning, so she went back to the bedroom and made the bed, carefully balancing her sundry tiny soft toys in a neat pyramid on the pillows. Then she laid out her clothes. They were expensive and anonymous; all the more senior management could wear what they liked – black or navy suits, that is. She went back to the bathroom and stood under the steaming jets of the shower thinking about him. Bastard.

She knew it had been a mistake. She was not in the

habit of taking such risks, but he was very good-looking and charming and, well, powerful. The Head of Foreign Exchange. He had been a dealer in the East – he had lived in Hong Kong for years. And now he was back in London and he was the youngest Head of Foreign Exchange ever and he was still dealing because she had seen the papers. Bastard. He was dealing illegally. He was covering something up.

Lorna dried herself on a large, comfortable towel and padded back through to the bedroom, leaving droplets of soap-scented shower water in a trail on the carpet behind her. She sat disconsolately on the end of the bed, a defeated woman, pushed her sopping black locks away from her face and then feathered out the consequent ducktail which stuck out at the back of her neck. She stared at herself in the mirror, pulled up her drooping shoulders, held her head high and then looked directly into her own green eyes. They had always been trusting, placid eyes, but today they looked more like the sharp, knowing eyes of a hawk. She had come to the bank thinking it was a decent place. It wasn't. She might never be able to look at herself straight in the eye again if she did the wrong thing. She pulled on the underwear and the white blouse, the black suit, the tights and the shoes, and sat in front of the dressing-table to blow-dry her hair.

This was very difficult. She would have to report him, but when it came out that they were lovers it would be embarrassing and if she was mistaken about it in some way – well, he was her boss. Anything else was collusion, though, and she had told him as much the night before. She would never be able to keep working with him. She pulled her hair into shape and set it there with the drier. They had gone for drinks in the City. He had looked grave. He had asked her to let him sort it out. He had gone outside and paced up and down the pavement, then he had come back to the table, ordered some food and tried to make a deal. A deal! If she went away for three months he would sort it out. He promised. He'd transfer her. He'd get her a temporary stint in one of the provincial branches. She stared at herself unsympathetically in the mirror and applied her lipstick with care. It was only just seven o'clock and she didn't feel like eating anything. She had been tupped by a fellow of exceeding dishonesty. A lecher. It wasn't fair.

She went back to the kitchen and took the hoover out of the cupboard. She might as well do something useful. At a quarter past seven he rang. The early bird. He had just got back from the gym. Damn him.

'Cardiff,' he said. 'You'll get lots of allowances for going. When you get back I'll have sorted it out. You don't understand,' he said, calmly and deliberately.

'Cardiff,' shouted Lorna. 'David, you have to be joking.'

'No. Seriously. Friday.'

'I'm not going to Cardiff.'

'Yes, you are. It's the safest place.'

'What do you mean?'

'You don't understand what is going on. You have to trust me, Lorna. I love you and I want to look after you.'

'If you loved me you'd quit and take the rap.'

'You don't understand.'

'So you keep saying. Why don't you explain this very difficult thing to me?'

'Go to Cardiff. I'll drive you down myself. I'll set it all up. It's safe there. I'll organise the paperwork when I get in this morning. Lorna, I'm not a bad person. I'm really not a bad person. You said you loved me.'

'I did. Bastard.'

'Well, then. Trust me. Just once. Just now.'

Lorna sized it up. She had thought he was kind. The perfect gentleman. She loved being with him. He'd seemed so decent. The stories he had told her about growing up. His mother. The brothers he now never saw. He'd been so frank. It had touched her. Maybe there was a reason. Maybe there had been a mistake. Oh, how could she ever trust him again once she had doubted him about this? It was so unfair. She had thought he was perfect. It had felt so right. But not to be able to trust someone. Trust. His eyes. There must be something more to it. Something more. She wanted there to be. It could be bigger than she thought. It could involve other people at the Bank. It could involve anyone. Who could she go to? Who would be safe, if not him? Who else could she trust? He had been so perfect. She had to trust him. Give him a little.

'I'll go to Cardiff,' she said slowly. 'But if it's not finished when I get back, I'll spill the beans. I mean it.'

'Good. Do you want to come round here for break-fast?'

'No. I'll see you in the office,' she said and hung up.

The floor had never been so clean. She hoovered it twice. On the second time round the bedroom she knocked the bedside table, her clock fell on to the floor and the face popped out with a crack on to the carpet. Lorna roared with fury. This was not habitual. She kicked the bed. One of the soft toys tottered at the peak of the pyramid, then tumbled drowsily from the pillow and landed on the floor beside the clock. In the clenched-teeth certainty of an all-consuming anger, Lorna hoovered it up. Then, satisfied, she sucked the other soft toys up the tube one by one. Small pink rabbits, bears with 'I love you' on their tiny T-shirts and a little white seal which David had bought for her one day when they had visited the zoo all vanished into a dusty oblivion. Bastard. Bastard. Bastard. Bloody Cardiff. I'll never sleep peacefully again.

First Caledonian's London offices were for prestige. There weren't many clients – most had transferred from regional branches when they moved to the capital. In the main it was a brokerage office and a place to entertain foreign visitors. There were two members of staff who were employed almost exclusively to play golf and talk about advanced economic theory to important guests. The main hallway was paved with flagstones and the walls were painted an impressive royal red. Paintings in oil lined the stairs – mostly past Presidents. Downstairs, behind the handsome entrance hall, with its brass chandelier and leather armchairs, was the branch, which consisted of a few desks and some equipment laid out in what must have been, at some point, a large ballroom. Upstairs there were two dining-rooms and many sumptuous meeting rooms of assorted sizes, as well as some offices. Lorna had worked hard to get a job there. After graduation she had enrolled with First Caledonian in Edinburgh and applied herself to night classes. Her degree in Economics and her postgraduate work in Foreign Markets and Computer Studies had secured her small promotions quickly. Suitably encouraged, she had pushed herself nearly to exhaustion to get an MBA in record time, and from then on she had worked any hours and all hours and applied for every job which came up in London. It was only when she had been offered a place at another bank that First Caledonian had come up with the goods. She had always wanted to work somewhere like this – somewhere opulent and hallowed. Somewhere silent in its halls. Somewhere you were well paid. There had been a couple of chances to move to New York and earn even more money, but she loved London and her flat there. Anyhow, everyone said that New York was hectic. London had been perfect. It had all been perfect. And now Cardiff. Bloody hell.

By the time Lorna got to the office it was raining. It was only a spring shower, but she found to her dismay that her white blouse became slightly transparent

7

where the drops had hit it. She rushed moodily past the security guard who held the door and watched her as she strode upstairs with uncharacteristic bustle. When she got to her office she sat down at the desk and stared at the computer, twitching the rain-spattered coat from her shoulders. She switched on the machine, her fingers cumbersome. Things were dropping slow. Marcia, her assistant, came into the room.

'There are a couple of people off down in the branch. There are meetings planned. They want you to meet with a client. A customer. About her loan. They don't have anyone down there who can cover it.' Marcia laid two fluorescent orange files down on the desk. 'Here are the details,' she said.

Lorna took her coat, shook it and placed it carefully around the back of the chair. 'OK,' she said. At least it gave her the morning away from a console. She leafed through the pages of notes. Loans. Overdue loans. People could be so stupid. This was only a small amount of money, but if the repayments weren't met it would get out of hand. The snowball effect. Stupid.

The phone rang. It was him.

'David,' she said. 'I'm working downstairs in the branch this morning.'

'Yes,' he replied flatly. He already knew. 'You'd better start telling people about Cardiff. It's a twelve-week course. You'll be giving it. Well, part of it.'

'What about?'

'International stuff. Exchange stuff. Stuff you know about. You'll be good at it. We're setting up a department there. I'll fill you in later.'

'How did you fix that?'

'A friend in personnel. I knew him in Hong Kong. Can I take you for lunch?'

'No. I don't want to see you till the weekend. Pick me up at the flat – I'd like you to drive me there. I'll have arrangements to make.'

8

'Don't worry. I'll organise somewhere for you to stay. I'll organise everything. There will be a bonus arranged. For the inconvenience.'

'OK. OK. Pick me up on Friday evening at six.'

After she had hung up, Lorna considered going to the President's office and telling him everything she knew. She doodled on her notepad details of what that actually entailed. Hidden transaction. One hidden transaction unaccounted for in the name of a company upon whose account David was the only signatory. There were no records at the Bank for the company. That was it. Stranger things had passed over her desk before, she thought. But still there was David's behaviour. By law a banking official must report anything they find suspicious. Lorna had a sudden vision of herself in court, being cross-examined by a sharp young lawyer who was trying to prove that she had been suspicious about this.

'Milud, I have a trusting nature. Perhaps I have chosen the wrong profession – I am not a suspicious person and my suspicion was not aroused by this. I hardly took it in.'

Ridiculous rules. Something was surely wrong, though. The account. The connection to David. It wasn't enough, though, she couldn't prove anything conclusively. He was certainly doing something unethical. Probably illegal. But perhaps he had reasons. It could be money he was making on the side for himself. It could be something he was doing for a valued client. It could even be something he was doing for the Bank itself. She pictured David's face very clearly – he was attractive. There was something kind about him. Something very charming and very real – much more down to earth, much more genuine than anyone she'd ever known. And the way he had touched her! She decided she was in love. It was only three months in Cardiff. It had better only be three months. She

9

scribbled over the words she had written, crumpled up the note and put it in the bin. At this office all the bins went for shredding.

Marcia came in with her long, immaculately manicured fingers wrapped around a cup of steaming coffee. 'You'll have to go down in a minute,' she pointed out as she took a bite from a biscuit. Lorna, who, on account of her erstwhile churning stomach had not yet negotiated any breakfast, decided to order a sticky bun for later. She realised that she had better tell Marcia that she was going away. After all, she supposed, it was Marcia who would have to keep things ticking over under David's watchful eye until she got back. Lorna eyed her secretary and decided that she felt not the least bit uneasy about leaving her to work closely with David. It would be fine. Poor Marcia, she wasn't a pretty woman – her lurid dress sense made her ridiculous and her typing speeds would always keep her on the lower rungs of the career ladder. On principle Lorna McLeish had never learnt to type properly. No, it would all still be here when she got back. It would be fine.

'I should tell you that I'm going to Cardiff next week. Just for a couple of months. They've asked me to give a course or something,' said Lorna as she scooped up the fluorescent files and sealed her fate.

One

Let me tell you first of all that this is a story about two girls who go in search of four men and I am one of the girls. My name is Libby Lucas. Liberty. I was named Liberty the year of Bloody Sunday. It was before Bloody Sunday, of course, when they named me. Mum and Dad were idealists. I suppose they had to be. A mixed marriage in Belfast is a difficult thing. The flickering tongues of suspicion are all around. You live in fear and you live in euphoria, for only true love could make you do it. Anyhow, this is the story of how my friend and I went in search of these four men. They weren't attractive and we didn't fall in love with any of them, but we did find them. Now let's begin the story.

It started that day at the Bank. Those drippy-nosed, sniffy bureaucrats had called me in about my loan. They had been quick enough to set me up with it when I had moved from Belfast to London. I had a good job to go to and I needed money to get myself started off. Not much – just a couple of thousand. Everything had been destroyed when the house went up so I needed to buy it all new. Now things were different – the office where I had worked was closed and I had taken a part-time job selling property, but it didn't pay a quarter of what I ought to be earning. The Bank picked up on it quickly – within two months. I'd never seen Lorna McLeish before – she wasn't the one I normally dealt with. She sat there behind a ferocious-looking desk reading the file as if I wasn't there and shuffling cards in her brain before she decided which one to play. She put down the closed cardboard file on the desk and looked up at me with the malicious green eyes of a Bank Animal. I wasn't going to let any safe-as-houses, pain-in-the-arse, Bank bitch torture me with her silences, and I knew I wouldn't be able to outsilence her about money – she was trained in it – so I figured it was best that I spoke first.

'I can't do anything about this money until I get another job. I'm only working part-time now – it's not even £80 a week. When I get another real job, in an architect's office, I'll be able to pay it all back. Quickly,' I explained.

She waited just long enough for the silence to become embarrassing before she spoke to me. 'Everyone has bad patches. But we can't leave a loan like this one outstanding for long. The interest piles up. I'm sorry, Miss Lucas. You'll have to give back the money.'

'I can't.'

'Then we may have to take action. I'm going to speak frankly to you. If you don't comply it will result in litigation. Can you borrow money from somewhere else? Have you anything that you can sell?'

I do, but she sure as Jesus wasn't getting it. It was the only thing that had come through the blast. My mother's ring. Diamonds don't burn. The gold was mangled, but I had the diamonds reset. The Government had paid for it. In the end it's the Government who underwrite all the insurance in Northern Ireland – they have to, because no insurance company would take the risk otherwise. They have to because if they didn't there'd be more pressure to stop the war. Yes, the British Government is hellish compassionate and they pay for most of the damage when your family gets

12

blown up – they rebuild the house although it is unsaleable and they send you to a shrink although no one alive can touch the gutteral sorrow inside of you. The only thing I really cared about were those diamonds. It was amazing that we found them, really. I think Ma must have wanted me to have them.

'Of course I don't have anything,' I said.

'I can give you another month, but we'll have to ask you to come in again at that stage and if there is no improvement I'm afraid we won't be able to do anything more. It's for the best, really. We find.'

She wasn't wasting any time about it.

'Fine,' I said and I just got up and left as slowly as I could. I wanted her to know I wasn't intimidated by her. Some guy even held the door for me as I left that creepy, old-fashioned building.

I owed everyone money. The rent hadn't been paid for three weeks and Petey was getting pushy about it. Ladbroke Grove was like that. I'd paid up front for months and now things were tight Petey got all smug on me. It was as if he revelled in other people's difficulties in a real I-knew-it kind of way. He was a slimy old man with thin lips and a well-clipped grey beard – the kind of man who listened at the door before he knocked, and called you dear all the time once you'd answered. Still, it was a nice enough bedsit – very big, painted plain white and the window had an iron balcony where you could sit in the summer and bake yourself.

It had been a golden summer the year before and I had lain in the sun a lot and meditated. The fortnight Petey had gone away we had opened the whole house for a party. Gabor from the flat upstairs had arrived with a keg of beer he got cheap from the night-club where he worked. Gabor was a bouncer. He was a muscly, dark-haired, pale-skinned guy who wore leather trousers and a big jacket. He said he was an actor. We were kind of friends that summer – he would make hot chocolate at midnight and pass it down from his black balcony to mine. We would sit out in the warm, dark night and listen to the scurrying of the birds, and talk while we sipped our cocoa. It was company for me through the sleepless nights – the blast had happened in the February and I moved to London in June. In December I had started sleeping again. Gabor was nice – the closest friend I had had in London, though I never told him or anybody about the blast. We used to sit there for hours, one night we even stayed up until the dapple of dawn hit the chill air. Gabor would play with his hamster, letting it run around under his shirt, and he would recite poetry – mostly Shakespeare – and I would talk about buildings and structure, because I am an architect by nature as well as by profession. 'Oh, the couple-coloured sky!' he had exclaimed after one all-nighter, when dawn came, all peachy and perfect, and I almost believed he was an actor after all.

Once, his hamster had fallen from his arm. It dropped through the grating and landed on my head and we had hoisted it back up in the empty cocoa mug. We weren't supposed to keep animals, but it was one thing that I'm certain Petey never knew about. Gabor kept the hamster in an old, empty box of Terry's 1767 Assorted Chocolates under his bed – we called it Sixty-seven.

Anyhow, Gabor had made friends with the minister from the church where the top of our street joined the main road. It was a small church with a leafy green garden around it. I don't think anyone ever went to the services much, but people used to use the garden in the good weather. The priest was called Des and he came to the party too. Half-way through, when we were getting drunk and mumblesome, Gabor somehow discovered that Sixty-seven had passed away and Des was enlisted to bury the poor thing, with full obsequies, in the garden around the church. I don't know how the Bishop found out, but Des was replaced the next week. Gabor said it was because he had officiated at a marriage on an ancient pagan site somewhere in Hammersmith, but I don't think that the burial of Sixty-seven helped. In the August of that summer Gabor went to Edinburgh to the Festival and he never came back. Petey cleared out his room after a month and sold the stuff to a junk shop to pay the back rent. There wasn't much there in any case.

I don't know if Petey ever found out about the party. He never said anything, but for the rest of the summer he came to the house every day. Petey would walk slowly up the path on those days, smiling a painted-on smile and walking like a mechanical toy, with his shoulders slightly too high and his legs a little bit stiff. I could swear he smirked as he passed under my dangling legs and pushed open the front door; the covetous old Puritan, for he was the kind who would denounce you if he could – tiny details were tucked away in his mind, for later. He'd remember if he saw you drunk, or if he saw you spending, he'd remember if you had had visitors or late-night phone calls and he would silently disapprove and note it for later, for a time when you might be vulnerable and he could relish it more.

When I got back from the Bank, Petey was waiting. He was in the main hallway fixing Do-Not notices to the wallpaper. Do Not Smoke. Do Not Leave the Lights On. Do Not Make Noise Late at Night. He had a prohibitive nature. 'Hello. Didn't expect to see you. Not working today?' he asked, as if casually.

'No.'

Petey smiled an ominous, too-nice smile. His brown eyes sparkled in anticipation. 'Look, dear, I know you've been having a little bit of trouble lately. Don't think it's gone unnoticed. We'll work something out. How much can you give me?'

I really couldn't bear it. He smiled a wet-lipped, wide grin and awkwardly moved too close to me. I think even if I had had the money I probably wouldn't have given it to him. I could see his fingers twitching, even though his hand was plunged into the pocket of his checked trousers, and he smelt of stale tea, just like the carpets did in that stinky hallway of his.

'I'll give you the lot, Petey,' I lied. 'I sorted everything out at the Bank today. I'll have the money by tomorrow. Come round at four.'

Petey's eyes betrayed his disappointment. He had wanted to patronise me, to cut a deal. He had wanted to tell me about the value of saving for the hard times and I surely wasn't up to that.

I tripped lightly up the stairs and into the sanctuary of my room, where I sat in the middle of the carpet and tried to decide what to take with me. All I really needed were my clothes. I started to pack them into a rucksack and when it was full, I stopped. What else do you take? Homeless people don't need alarm clocks or drawing pens. I stood in the middle of the room, fingering Ma's ring, which I wear around my neck on a piece of string. I surveyed the clothes that were left and decided Petey might get £20 for them down the market. It was unlikely he would give them to a charity shop. Then I just sat there and let myself be for a while. I knew exactly where I was going – I had the keys for Pagan McSwain's offices.

I had got the job at Pagan McSwain purely by chance. I had only just been laid off at Ramage Lloyd – the architect's office – which had gone into receivership, and Pagan McSwain was round the corner. It was January, which is a vicious month to look for a job, in any case. Pagan McSwain sold residential property all over the city and they needed someone to show prospective clients around prospective houses. It was casual labour – if they needed you, you worked, and if they didn't need you, you didn't. I made myself useful, offering to fill in on Saturday mornings in the office, and never refusing to show anyone round a house no matter how late at night they wanted to go. That was why I had the keys to the office – none of them wanted to wait till nine, when I often got back after the evening viewings. The office was on two floors – one at shop level where everyone worked, and a basement where there were toilets and a small kitchen and store-rooms. For some reason, they had even carpeted the downstairs area, so I figured that it wouldn't be too uncomfortable to sleep there and no one need ever know. The place was empty between seven at night, when the cleaner finished, and eight in the morning, when the staff started to arrive. I could hide my rucksack behind the boxes of stationery in storage. It couldn't be permanent, but it might do for a few weeks and I could use the computer there to type applications for architecture jobs as they came up. I suppose that was really my plan – to get another job in an architectural practice somewhere and settle down to normality again.

I don't know exactly when I had decided on architecture. The Troubles raged around us while I was growing up – the rubble of my childhood. People used to joke that Belfast was a city which hadn't been twinned with anywhere else, but instead had entered into a suicide pact with Beirut. Maybe it was that – the buildings disappearing around me in Belfast as I grew up. I always was practical that way – construction had become a growth industry and there was money to be made there. And then I sometimes used to think I had chosen architecture because we had visited Venice when I was twelve and I had been hit hard by the shabby splendour of it all. When they invented the transparent composite which you can't blow up and started building from it all over Belfast, I dreamt for months of the crystal palaces which would rise in magical splendour like the glass I had seen blown on Murano. Perhaps those vague memories were enough to inspire me. Lord knows, but architecture it was. I was quite good at it. Commended at Queen's and all. The Maze had won large prizes. The Maze. Never again.

That night I left the house delighting in the fact that Petey would be furious when he found out. I had gone round carefully lighting all the lights in the bedsit out of pure badness – to run the electricity meter down to the last unit. Then I walked to the office and let myself in, checking that no one on the street took any notice of me. I didn't need to switch the lights on. The whole place was bathed in the snowy reflection from the lit window display, tinged with the blue of Pagan McSwain's corporate identity – everything, from the carpet to the white boards, was imprinted with it. I expect they got a job lot. It was a big company (there were offices all over the world) and it was incredibly regimented – there were procedures for everything. Anyhow, I sneaked downstairs and switched on the light in the bathroom. With the door open it gave me enough to see by down there. It was warmer in the office than it had been at the house and it was free too. I walked around, opening all the cupboard doors, deciding where I was going to stash my rucksack. I finally settled on the very farthest corner of the store-room – it was where the 'For Sale' signs were stacked and there were enough of them there to make it unlikely that they would ever get to the bottom of the pile in one day. If the supply got low I would worry about it. I made myself a cup of tea, lay down flat on the floor and congratulated myself. I would get up at seven and go out for a swim at the pool. I could get clean there – then I would be back by nine o'clock to work for a few hours. Things were going to be fine.

Trish was the Senior Negotiator and she liked me. I was the smartest viewings lady that she had ever had. I could work the computer with ease and type faster than the typist who came in and plodded part time at fifty words a minute. I could also chat up all the customers – the poor ones who were buying crummy little repossessed flats which would probably be repossessed again in a few years and the posh ones who were trying to make an investment as well as a home. It didn't matter to me which ones I sold – there was a flat-rate commission for salespeople like me. I got £6 on top of the stingy hourly rate for every house I sold, no matter how long it took to sell it, or how large or small it was. I think Trish was on a percentage. Anyhow, she liked me and I also liked her. She was plump and pleasing and bought packets of Smarties for the people who sold things. 'Well done,' she would say with feeling, when you had gone beyond the call of duty and into the realms of creative estate agency practice, and then she would waltz round the office singing 'I'd feel blue without you' and we would all laugh. I had to write short reports on standard, blue-edged forms, after viewing the houses: Mrs Smith doesn't like the conservatory – she feels it is placed poorly to catch the evening light. Mr Jones says he wouldn't live in a shithole like this if we paid him. That sort of thing. I wrote up a storm of irreverent, syntactic magic to keep them amused in the office. Trish had sent some of my reports up to Head Office – she thought they would make amusing reading in Pagan McSwain's staff magazine, which came out quarterly. Two weeks later a lady had arrived to meet me. She was tight as a coiled spring could be – with bright-red lipstick and a size 12 suit. I think she was a 14, really, you know. Anyhow, she bulged at me for half an hour, talking about how interesting and refreshing the reports were and then, before she left, she told Trish in private that I shouldn't wear my skirts as long as I did. Trish was mortified. She took me into the back office and asked me to wear a proper suit as much as I could and I said I would try to find a suit which was one size too small for me, since that was obviously the way executives did it. We went out for a drink that evening and Trish confided in me her heartfelt desire to get out of property and into human resources. I haven't a clue if she ever did move on eventually. Anyhow, I don't think she copped on that I was living at the office, but I suspect that even if she had, she wouldn't have wanted to lose me over it, for I was a delight.

I had reckoned it would take a couple of months to get out of the office and into a new flat; but actually it took less than a week. It wasn't a bad week – I swam every day first thing in the morning, had a shower, then I went to the covered Mall nearby and had breakfast by the fountain. At about half past nine I called in to the office to see if they needed me. If they did I worked, and if they didn't I went to the library and scanned the morning papers for a sniff of more gainful employment. Behind the Old Bailey there was a little coffee shop where they did a mug of cocoa for 60p and they had low, comfortable, cushioned armchairs. I would sit there for hours over a cup and listen to the barristers talking to each other. Once or twice I was eyed suspiciously and all conversation about the case suddenly ceased, but in the main I suppose they didn't notice me. It's not as if I stand out – mousy brown eyes and mousy brown hair are hardly eye-catching. It's not so much that I blend in – it's just that I don't stand out. After cocoa I would walk around the City looking at the buildings, especially the spires. I loved the skyline. They can tamper with the stuff on the ground – paint and restore and polish it all – but the skyline is the skyline and with the stringent planning requirements which prevent building higher than has already been built, well, there isn't a lot they can do to it.

One evening that week I had gone to a night-club called Violets and I had lost myself in the music the way I often lost myself in the City. I think the other people there were dedicated partygoers – high on speed and E, which they ate routinely, like the disco biscuits they are. They danced frenetically, with total commitment, their skin shining with sweat and their eyes like fireworks. I hadn't taken anything – it was just as if I had fallen under a spell. I danced until three in the morning and walked back to the deserted office in a trance. I must have looked as if I had got laid. I was careless the whole of the next day. Anyway, at night I slept on the carpet in the office, which I didn't mind at all – it reminded me of camping in Donegal when I was a kid: it was like sleeping in a cave. Up the stairway I could see the lights of moving cars on the road as they swooped by. It was an OK week and then the chance came to move on.

Pagan McSwain didn't just sell houses – it also had a factoring service. This was usually for corporate clients who had repossessed properties and didn't yet want to put them on the market, but wanted someone to keep an eye on them. I had considered moving into one of those, but repossessions were risky – sometimes the previous owner came back and was difficult and, of course, there would be neighbours, and neighbours at repossessed properties are, in the main, nosy people. On the Friday of that week the keys were deposited for a property which was not repossessed – it was a private job for someone at First Caledonian. It was Lorna McLeish's flat: 59/8 Huntington Villas. I couldn't believe it when I read the file. Three months in Cardiff. In another circumstance I might not have jumped at the chance, but hell, it was so fitting. I decided to swing over there and take a look.

The flat was just like Lorna McLeish. It was kind of beautiful and basically well put together, but a bit tight-arsed. Huntington Villas was a converted factory in Battersea about five minutes from Albert Bridge. It was a nice conversion, spacious and practical. The buildings were brick and most of the complex was four storeys high. I don't know what they had made at the factory, but the whole space must have been open to start with – just floors and floors of big, empty spaces with well-laid, tongued-and-grooved wooden floors. It was a dream. The idea had been to make up-market luxury flats, so there was plenty of parking and a bit of extra space in each of the rooms. A lot of the original details had been renovated – the old beams, the oak floors, the lot. Lorna McLeish's flat was on the top floor and occupied the end site. That made it one of the best in the building. There were three bedrooms, all kitted out in Habitat gear – one cold grey, one denim blue and one dusty pink. The kitchen was a small galley affair in chrome and white and the bathroom, for some reason, was hot yellow. She must have painted it herself. In fact, you could tell what she'd added. Anything that didn't quite fit. Her things sat strangely in the place – it was almost like she was on a quest for quality and everything she bought was to prove it. But the living space was wonderful – they had incorporated an original cupola and it lit the whole space with the sky's own light. Lorna McLeish had bought brown sofas for what was the most magical part of the flat. It was like shitting just at the wainscot under a Hockney. She had left the place immaculate, though, just like you'd want it to come back to. I looked through all the cupboards – tea and coffee, suits and dresses, Wash 'n' Go shampoo and Marks & Spencer soap – and decided to weigh up the odds. This was a large complex – it didn't seem all that friendly. There were four other flats all on the same corridor, but Lorna McLeish didn't strike me as the type to have the neighbours in. I hadn't seen any Residents Association notices on the board downstairs. I would be discreet and I always had the cover – only to be used in desperate need – if anyone asked, of working for Pagan McSwain and saying that I was just checking on the property. I figured that the bitch could help me along to the paying back of that bank loan. She had been concerned, after all, that the Bank should be restored its money in good time. I had a set of keys cut and that evening I removed my rucksack from the store-room and made my way to Huntington Villas where I lay on the floor beneath the cupola watching the sky until at last I slept, dreaming, I'll wager, the sweetest of dreams dreamt by a squatter in London that night.

In the morning I sat at the window and watched the single people going to work. Some of them lived together, but they still seemed to be single. I figured it was a place of dinner parties and ironed night-shirts. At ten o'clock the cleaning ladies arrived *en masse* – in the file at Pagan McSwain it was noted that we should organise cleaning once a fortnight. I wondered if that might be for the benefit of the neighbours. I would have to find out when Trish had set it for. I had three months here – three free months of home and shelter – to pay off my debts, find a decent job and make a fresh start in London. I fixed myself a cup of tea and settled down at the window again to feel the rhythm of the place, when the phone started to ring. The answerphone took it and a man's voice, flustered, said, 'It's me. It's David. I don't know why you aren't in work today, Lorna, and I am sorry about the argument, but please, please ring me. I can cover for a couple of days for your absence, if it's time you need. Please call me back.'

Poor David obviously hadn't been told about Cardiff,

I thought, and took my tea through to the bedroom where I more thoroughly investigated the clothes which Lorna McLeish had abandoned in London for three months. She was a good two sizes larger than I was.

Two

So many people have lost people because of the war in
the North that the sorrow pulses like a buried drum-
beat in the psyche of the nation. It crosses all boundaries – an uncle, a grandfather, a great-grandmother, a
cousin – and it goes back to the Famine and beyond.
Everyone in the Six Counties has it in them somewhere, that little aubade to the rising dawn of the
sorrows hammering away, and they march into the
future to the rhythm of the past. I always thought the
Brits should pull out. If anyone asked me where I came
from I always said that I was Irish. I've never felt
British. The Treaty which split the island wasn't fair.
You should read it. But all that became beside the
point. The whole thing got so vicious there was no
going back and it was like you couldn't go forward
without going back first. Every generation carried the
wrongs of the past with them and it felt like there was
no way out towards peace. I read, once, in the kind of
hippy book of which, for a short while, I was fond, that
some mystics believe there is an eighth chakra opening
up. Evolving. The chakras are like paths of coloured
light which run through your body. Your own private
rainbow. You are supposed to meditate on the different
colours to bring yourself enlightenment. Each colour
means something. Anyhow, they reckon there is an
eighth chakra evolving. It's pink – the colour of peace.

We are just starting the age of Aquarius now, you know, and they reckon that the eighth chakra will be opened by the end of the age. That's over a thousand years away. I don't think real peace will come to Ireland any quicker than that. I don't see how it can.

The fighting in the North was peculiar in that very few people experienced it as open war. It was more of a strain. A subtle kind of torture. Everything was hidden. People used their religion as a marker, as a mask and as a cover. You became the sum total of where you lived, where you shopped, which church you went to, how many kids you had and which taxi company you used, and you only associated with people who had the same responses on their list. I knew someone once who moved into an area in the country and the neighbours wouldn't let him run cabling across their land to make temporary repairs to his house; they wouldn't let him run water pipes under the common land in front of their houses so he could install proper plumbing. They thought he was Catholic. They didn't think there was anything strange about doing that to a neighbour. They didn't think that they were bigoted in any way. That kind of ignorant behaviour became normal for people, and worst of all, you knew why they had done it and you knew that in the same situation you might have done it too. You couldn't really trust anyone – not the security forces, not the people you lived near, not anyone. You had to protect yourself and the safest way to go about it was only to speak to, only get involved with, only allow yourself to contact, people who were living the same life as you were. You stuck to your own. It wasn't completely safe but it was safer than anything else.

That's why there was no way that peace could work – the best that anyone could hope for was a stand-off. The differences had gone on for generations and well, if we could allow a few more generations to pass, perhaps there would be people who could think about making peace. You can't make people forget their dead, you can't regret years and years of the most vicious kind of hatred and violence and turn over a new leaf. You can't change a psychopathic killer. No matter what they think they are motivated by. No, if peace came it would have to do so when there had been time to allow the hatred to grow out of people's thinking: if peace ever came it would take a long time in the coming. They could sign treaties as much as they liked, the real war resided in the hearts of the people and if there was to be a real peace then it was in the hearts of the people that it would have to grow. That's what was all around me as I was growing up in a house which was an advertisement for non-sectarian living.

In my first year at college there was a huge gig at Stephen's Green in Dublin. It was called Rock for Peace and it was on St Patrick's Day. There were fifteen bands all set to play on a temporary stage. Some of them were big names – the Stallions of the Soul, who were touted to be the next U2, and the Little Monkeys, who had hit number one in the Indie Chart the week before. Everything was donated – all the equipment and everyone's time. They wanted volunteers so a lot of us from Queen's went down to help with the lighting rig and the security and stuff. I was really excited. We travelled down from Belfast on a big yellow bus – it was covered in daffodils – and they had set aside rooms for us at Trinity Hall. We had a great weekend hanging out in Dublin as usual, with everyone on the streets wearing yellow T-shirts with 'Peace' printed in pink on the front when the weather held. Then, when it rained, the whole city seemed to don a plethora of woolly jumpers in all the hues of the heathery hills. Style-conscious Republicans wore a lot of tweed and woolly jumpers. Or so it seemed. The first Aran jumpers, you know, were knitted with good-luck charms encrypted in the pattern. The symbols were there to protect the wearer. Originally, they were worn by fishermen and the women of the family knitted these charmed woollies to protect their men from the wild, wild sea. Families wore the same symbols. That way, if there was a shipwreck and a body got washed up, they could tell which family the sea-rotted carcass came from. They knew who was responsible for burying the dead.

It was a great weekend, that weekend, the mildest St Patrick's Day for a long time, so that the magical jumpers were barely evidenced at all. Because we were there to help with the gig we had got our yellow T-shirts for free and wore our security passes with as much pride as if they were medals for outstanding coolness awarded by some icon of our times. There was a tremendous cachet around being from the North and having lived on the cutting edge of the Troubles. It was often like that when I visited the South, but that weekend, because of the concert, it was as if everyone wanted to talk to you about the Troubles. It was a different world down there, though. People who haven't lived in a war zone can't really understand it. I remember standing at the sound check and some guy, who insisted on his name being said in Irish (and I think his name was Patrick, or rather Padraig) was giving it laldy. He swooped all over the show, dancing up a storm, with his eyes shining, and when the music lapsed into silence he turned to me and said, with all the passion of his fresh-faced, dancing Irish spirit, 'Yes. Oh, this'll show them!' as if the Little Monkeys and the Stallions of the Soul were going to bring peace where all major world leaders with soldiers at their disposal had failed.

It was a long, wild weekend. The pubs in town were all packed to the gunwales every evening so that everyone ended up outside in South Anne Street dancing on the brick pavements and darting in and out of the Coffee Inn for plates of chips and pots of tea. Some of the Little Monkeys donated a free acoustic set as they sat on the pavement. It was a million miles from anything militant. It was preaching peace to Southern kids who had not really known the war, though it was tremendous fun. I met a girl called Annie who was kind of plump and kind of stupid. She smiled the fixed smile of a doll. Well, we got talking and she said she figured that it was important to show how many people wanted peace. Actually, I think someone had told her that it was important to show how many people wanted peace. Anyhow, I disagreed. I carried the grey shadow of the North with me and I knew that both sides were counting on the majority to push for an end to the Troubles. You couldn't win. You were part of their strategy no matter what you did. The Provos figured if they made normal life impossible in the North, the Brits would be under more pressure to come to terms. The Unionists reckoned that if the tide of public opinion was for peace, then it was also against the Provos whom they, of course, considered to be the main aggressors. The worse the Troubles got, the more money was poured in on both sides, so in the end the militants, particularly the people at the top, had a vested financial interest in perpetuating the war in any case. That was the torture of it. Annie's dull brown eyes glazed over. She'd rather have been necking one of the roadies in the corner. In the end that was exactly what she did. I ended up at a gallery opening on Dawson Street, nibbling little sandwiches and staring, rapt, at the Art. It was a special exhibition to tie in with the concert – paintings of doves and reconciliation and lithographed photos of the peace marches and the riots which had gone on in the Seventies. I got chatted up by a horrible little man who turned out to be the *Irish Times*'s most virulent and ferocious art critic.

I didn't try anything else on the peace theme until I built the Maze. They let you take fifteen per cent of your final result on a practical project like the Maze. Most people couldn't be arsed. The percentage wasn't high enough to tempt them off paper. But I was desperate to get building. And it was a great idea. The Maze was academically perfect – it was both art and architecture. Damn it. Too academic by far. There was no fear in it. They didn't like that. When Ma and Dad were blown up I was inundated by letters of condolence and I was visited by other people who had lost their parents and who sat with me, and nodded in agreement with anything I said. For a whole month everything was vague and everything I did was reinforced by the logic of other people agreeing with me. It was cold, non-sectarian comfort, though. People would talk about forgiveness and I knew that I would never be able to forgive for this. It would beat my own drum for ever more. I was staying in a hotel, then, because the house was uninhabitable. They had a dreadful time the first few days trying to figure out what kind of a priest they should send me and how to lay Ma and Dad in the ground. In the end I asked for a Church of Ireland service so they were buried in Donegal. I wanted the bombers to feel bad about it, because, like everyone else, I thought at the time it was bombers. I suppose I'd still have chosen Donegal, even if I had known it was just some poxy Provo arsonist's way of making a point.

The funeral was huge. People came from everywhere. The Prime Minister of Britain and the President of Ireland sent messages of condolence. I remember pushing the papers into the pocket of my new black coat. I left that coat in Belfast. I wonder if anyone kept it. The papers are probably still inside. They had sent me a psychiatrist straight away. He had come from London because the usual guy who worked in Belfast had gone on holiday. His name was Lloyd Baker and he specialised in grief. He was OK. I think I was supposed to talk to him, but I didn't. There was no use in trying to feel better. I knew that no one could do that for me and I didn't want it for myself. I threw a white flower into each of the graves and the shrink asked me about the rest of the family, but I only shrugged him off. We didn't have any relations any more; from what I know, the family had been badly split when Ma and Dad had run off and married. I got cards from some people who were family, but I had never met them and I decided that I would rather stay on my own some-where, although in the end I wasn't left alone at all because I had an RUC guard all the time and the Press went crazy about the story. It would have been less dramatic if they had known we were burnt out, but at first they thought we were bombed, which was unusual for a private house. We hadn't been. The house just blew up because of some fault in the gas piping. The fire started when they pushed petrol-drenched rags through the letter-box, swiftly followed by a box of lighted matches. When the fire started the gas ignited and it had the same effect as a bomb in any case, and the Press took it as a sign that the Troubles were about to escalate. They wouldn't leave me alone. Now, I hardly blame them, but at the time I was hellish bitter. Lloyd the shrink stayed for a week. He was devilish handsome in the way that thirty-year-old professional men seldom are. Usually to be motivated enough to make it by the time you are thirty you have to be a kind of strange person. Lloyd was quite normal, and relent-lessly low key. He never wore a suit, for which I was quietly grateful. The presence of so many uniforms made me jumpy in my grief. Every day he would come and sit with me for an hour. 'You don't have to say anything,' he would assure me. So I didn't. We ended up watching TV together. The rest of the time he left me well alone. The other people who came were kind enough and decent, but when Nicola arrived things changed. I sent them all away.

Nicola came in the fourth week, brought by a lady from Newry whose husband had been executed by the paramilitaries. He had refused to hand over the keys of his car. Nicola was a spiritualist, she spoke to the dead – or rather, she was a medium because they spoke to her. In a place where often death does not fall gently as the snow it is a tough job to be a medium – I expect that in the North you become an industry. She was about fifty and she had a dreadful cough so she croaked as she spoke and whooped now and again like a banshee when she tried to catch her breath. She called me darling all the time as if she meant it. Somehow I felt that I had known Nicola many times before I met her – she looked very ordinary, very poor, really, with her black leggings and her acrylic jumper. She wasn't beautiful – her skin was uneven and her hair was dyed somewhere between blonde and brown – but I just felt that there was love in her. There was a bigness there and I suppose that is why she was the first one I cried in front of. I was so sure the Press were all over the place that I had sat tight-throated and solemn, holding myself back from the tears. I was determined that they weren't going to get another front page out of me.

Anyhow, they asked me if I wanted Nicola to sit for me and the lady from Newry assured me that it was quite all right because she had had a priest with her when Nicola had gone to the other side to speak to her husband. I agreed to do it. I have no idea why. It's not something which comes naturally to me. Anyway, I agreed. We were left alone and Nicola spoke for a bit about my parents – nothing she couldn't have got out of the papers, just snippets about their names and that she couldn't see them but she saw a hard hat (which was Dad's). The dead don't speak coherently.

'Darling,' she said, 'this may sound strange but I am

getting three candles – there aren't three candles there any more. No more than that, just three candles, does this make sense?'

I nodded, horrified. She couldn't have known that. No one did. It was a private message from the grave. Ma used to light three candles in the kitchen window each evening, a happy thought for each of us to burn as brightly as the truth in our hearts. I cried the great heaving sobs I usually bottled up until bedtime.

'Are they all right?' I asked.

'Yes. Yes,' said Nicola. 'They are in a safe place. Do you want me to go on, darling?'

I shook my head. I couldn't bear it. It was all my fault. I had as good as murdered them. I should never have built the Maze.

Three

So that is how it happened that I left home, friendless, at twenty-one. I had started out with a veritable partyful of friends from Queen's but it was all a bit heavy for kids at college. They didn't know what to say and neither did I. In the main they were from England, so it wasn't inbred in them in any case. It's a lot to come to terms with at a tender age and twenty-one is tender, no matter what the magazines say. It's just you don't realise it at the time.

Up until then things had been relatively easy. School was inevitably a bit tough. Ma and Dad had chosen, after lots of deliberation, a progressive Catholic school just outside the city. I never figured out what was progressive about the place, except that the teachers weren't nuns. Schools are ferociously important in the North. It's one of the first questions a stranger will ask you – which school you went to – and it doesn't matter what your age is. They ask old people too. It indicates which side you are on. I don't remember too much about school, except I didn't really make any friends because my parents' marriage was mixed. How anyone knew, I'll never figure out. Kids of five years of age in the North know what they are looking for.

Academically I did well, though, and it wasn't a nightmare or anything – I played hockey and read a lot. I was accepted to Queen's after my A levels and things changed a bit. I had rocking good fun at college. Since the Troubles it was hard to have a good time in the North. Belfast was closed by eleven and the clubs, such as they were, were for businessmen. The Students Union was open, but we wouldn't have wiped our arses with it. We travelled South to where the juice rode rich. We would drive over the border – it was two and a half hours to Dublin – and relish the Catholicism. The road where I was brought up was Catholic, but it was well-to-do Catholic, next to a well-to-do Protestant street. There had never been a killing there before. I really believe the neighbours hated me for bringing it to them. Anyhow, Dublin was a city of seedy night-clubs and back-street bars. There is nowhere like it on the planet. We would stay up all night dancing and drinking after hours and, at breakfast time, we'd end up in Bewley's clutching frothy mocha coffees in silence. You see, we had taken so much cocaine we couldn't speak. We usually regained our vocal capacity early in the afternoon. Then we'd drive over to Mrs Curran's in Drumcondra.

The boarding-house was painted magnolia. Even the outside was painted magnolia. I pitied whoever had had to do it. Magnolia is one of my pet hates. People think it's a neutral colour, but it's not. Magnolia is tinged with pink. It's a shocker, isn't it? Anyhow, I figure people choose it because they don't have enough balls to paint with white, and are too snobby to paint with cream. That just about sums up Mrs Curran. She was great, though. We would arrive about four in the afternoon and she would have baked fresh currant scones and apple pie and she would pour out these great big mugs of steaming, strong tea. Mrs C always had empty beds – she had five sons, but they never seemed to be there much. I met two of them – Conor and Liam. They were big, strong lads, just like she always said. The family spoke Gaelic in the house.

Once a gard had called in for Liam while we were there. Mrs C had closed the inside door and had clattered round the kitchen, hoping that we wouldn't hear what was going on. Liam stood fearless and spoke fluent, swift Gaelic and nothing else, no matter what the gard said. I think the poor guy had some of the language, but not enough to keep up with Liam. Eventually the gard gave up and went away. I suppose they must have sent a linguist back later. Another day, Conor had sat in the garden with us, when we were down once in the summer. 'This is the life.' He had smiled, basking in the sun with his thin eyes closed. I could feel them darting behind his eyelids, though. I don't think his eyes would ever have stopped. He talked about the country – the boys spent a lot of time in Connemara at the Gaeltacht. 'Living off the land,' said Conor. 'That's the real freedom. The land is so rich. I only wish me ma would come.' Mrs C had smiled fondly at him. Somehow I couldn't see her skinning rabbits and gutting geese. She had set up the ironing board at the back door and was smoothing endless linen things with her rough brown hands before ironing them. I think she did all the laundry for the church. The rest of her sons were only pictures on the wall.

After the tea, usually we would sit in front of the telly for a couple of hours, have showers and go to bed at seven. The telly used to shock me. The news in the South was more detailed about the Troubles. It made me realise how much people didn't know about what was going on – how much wasn't reported in the British papers or on national TV and so wasn't available to people; even people living in the North wouldn't necessarily know what was going on. After all, if you are living in Derry and there's a shooting in Ballymena you don't automatically know about it. The local TV covered the Troubles in more detail, I suppose. People were hurt every day. The soldiers were always there. If it had been Liverpool or Manchester or Glasgow, it would have been on the front page until it stopped, but I realised it was possible, on the mainland, to ignore the war for most of the time because the day-to-day hatred was censored. There was some guy, with a Gaelic name, who was a video artist and he got a lot of money from an American Foundation to video himself saying horrible things about the Brits and then to tape the nine o'clock news over himself. That was how they saw it in the South – most people were Republican but not militant. The North was like Britain's secret colony. No one really knew what was going on there. There was an enormous amount of disinformation – some of it was just patently stupid. I remember MI5 at one stage had gone on TV and had headed up serious discussions about how static from ladies' nylon underwear could set off explosives. I think that they were trying to stop women from transporting bombs on their persons. We rolled around the floor in Mrs C's living-room, convulsed with laughter, as we listened to the debate and we joked about the sudden run there would be in Clery's on hundred per cent cotton underwear. Also around that time, Amnesty International got involved in monitoring what was going on in the North. The Loyalist paramilitaries were overtaking the IRA in the killing league. That stuff got coverage in the South which it couldn't have hoped for in the British media. We listened in silence. Mrs Curran didn't get involved with it, though. When something came up on the news and we were talking about it, she would dive into the cupboards in the kitchen and crash around until we stopped. Bed was at seven – we always told her we needed an early start and so by two in the morning we'd be back in the city at a night-club or in a bar, and she would think we were on our way back to the North.

She would leave us sandwiches on the kitchen counter for the journey. She was a pet, really. Afternoon tea, a bed, a shower and a picnic and it only cost £10 each.

What with living at home and staying at Mrs Curran's, I managed to be a late virgin. I wanted to have sex but I was scared of giving in to the strange desires within me. When I was nineteen I had started to imagine what it would be like to be fucked by one of the soldiers. I had better get this absolutely straight. I don't mean the RUC or a Brit officer or anyone like that – I mean one of the big, muscly, scared soldiers who walked up and down the road carrying machine-guns and covering each other in case of danger. The kind of soldier who operated the road-blocks and checked your passport. They were young, like me. They were usually English and they hated being in Belfast and everyone hated them being there too. At least, that's what it felt like. Even the Protestants didn't want the army there and in the end it was the Protestants who they were there for. You see, in the beginning the troops had been deployed to protect the Catholics and they were greeted with open arms – it had felt as if the things that had been going on were gruesome enough to shock the British government into action and at least they were prepared to do something. That lasted a few weeks. Then people realised that the troops were going to escalate the problem and, what's more, that they were there for good. You couldn't see the soldiers as people. They were icons. That is why, I suppose, I focused on them. It wasn't that I wanted to go out with one of them. It wasn't that I even wanted to know anything about them. I just wanted one of them to ram me up against a wall, in the darkness of a winter night, and do me. I never quite worked out whether it was something very deep in me and I wanted the Brits to fuck me like they had fucked the country, or whether it was because I wanted to look into his eyes and see a small piece of something human. This, I suppose, was the sort of thing which might have kept Lloyd Baker interested for an afternoon. No matter.

In the end I lost it to Matthew. We met up a lot in night-clubs in Dublin. He was in a band, the way that most boys in Dublin were. I never saw him play. I don't know if he ever did play at all, but he went to all the best night-clubs. For a while, there was a bash called Olive in the Basement Bar. Olive was very funky. There were balloons and sweets and lots of drugs and everyone dressed up and danced and danced. After the club had wound down we would go to the Living-Room. The Living Room was a pub which opened again at half past midnight, an hour after it had closed. It was down an alleyway past Temple Bar. I don't think it was a very popular bar during legitimate hours, but during the late shift it was packed. Anyone who didn't feel like going to a regular night-club flocked to it after the pub, and people who had been dancing rolled up even later so that they could wind down a bit. There was an open fire and big, squashy, bashed-up old armchairs. They played background music so you could talk, although in one part of the pub there was dancing, and they only served Guinness or whiskey. At least that was all they served after hours. I drank whiskey. One evening I was curled up in an armchair and Matthew arrived and he was upset about something or other, so I comforted him and I ended up on his knee and I could feel him getting hard for me. He took me to a house in Rathmines, which he said he was looking after while his sister was on holiday. We went to bed and I just remember how surprised I was because you aren't supposed to enjoy it your first time, but I did, I really did. All the same, I knew I had enjoyed *it*, and not necessarily *him*, and in the morning I crept away before he woke up. We never spoke again, though a couple of times I saw him in clubs, wheeling around the dance floor like the good-time talent that he was, with his long hair like a halo round his face.

Looking back on it, I don't think we only went to Dublin for the good time, though. I didn't, anyway. I went for the freedom of speech. It was a great feeling to be in the majority for a change. There was added confidence in it because everything was so serious up North; and after all, most people there were for the Brits. But in the South there was a healthy irreverence for the Troubles. You could hear them in the coffee shops, in the pubs, on the Dart, reading the paper and sighing 'Looks like the lads have been at it again' at the news of another atrocity. Just the freedom of sitting in Mrs C's back garden, gossiping about people we knew who were doing a line with RUC officers. Joking about the Catholic girls who would never get to heaven because they had committed the sin of shagging a Protestant policeman. It was a mortal sin, too, sleeping with the RUC. We laughed at their audacity with the flippant cruelty you'd never allow yourself at home. Catholic girls who dated RUC men ran the risk of having their faces scarred and their hair cut to the bone. Though that summer it happened to someone I knew. She was a girl I had been to school with. And once you knew someone like that yourself, you never discussed it again, no matter where you were. But just even the general, crazy war thing – no one talked about it in public up North. People were too scared. Even Dad was scared. He was a foreman at a yard where they took on Government contracts and where they employed anyone, Catholic or Protestant, who could do the job. People got kneecapped regularly. The first sign of trouble was the attendance. If none of the Catholics clocked in in the morning you knew the IRA were planning something. If none of the Protestants clocked in, you knew the UVF was on its way. Dad had to be a prudent man for the middle way was a veritable tightrope. Neither side wanted co-operation, so the Unionist paramilitaries had a go at the company for employing Catholics, and the Republican paramilitaries had a go at the company because they did work for the army from time to time. That was the way it worked all over the province. The idea was to bring the country to a standstill. The terrorists were mad and everybody knew it, but no matter what your own view was and even if you stood up for it, there were extremists out there killing in your name, and you didn't want to be associated with them. There were so many wrongs piling up on both sides, so much of the past being dragged into the present, that living there was like carving the story of your life on to a sepulchral monument.

People ignored it. I remember someone saying that they didn't notice the soldiers much and that you got used to it. Well, I suppose you didn't notice it in that it didn't occupy your every waking thought, but you still wouldn't hail a cab on the street and no cab would stop for you if you did. That's the way it was – you didn't trust anyone unless you knew where they were coming from. You didn't even trust the army – I mean, no matter which side you supported, though especially if you were Catholic. More than one in ten of the killings in the Province during the Troubles were the responsibility of the security forces. Of all the people they shot almost all were Catholics and over half were unarmed. You couldn't trust the forces. Not the army. Not the RUC. Especially not the RUC. The UVF death squads were manned by off-duty policemen, you see. That's what everyone said. Some of them got over-enthusiastic on duty, and that was acceptable – the forces didn't seem to mind that too much. One time there was a soldier who had shot this guy. I can't remember the circumstances exactly, but anyhow, the soldier was charged with murder and he was tried and sentenced to life imprisonment. In the end he served less than three years of the sentence and then he just went back into the army. They took him back – no problems. There were stories of people who were shot and captured and questioned, then just executed on the spot by the security forces. Stories of guys who were hounded and intimidated over a period of months and eventually ended up dead, with the forces telling one story about the final murder and bystanders another. They were mad as hell that they couldn't get the military advantage. They were furious because the terrorists were winning the war. They were a peace-keeping force with the venom of an opposing army and that is a chilling thought, no matter what side you are on. The fear hung like a frozen spider's web over the city and meant that you didn't drive down some streets, but you drove down others. You left with your family if there was a march by either party. You didn't talk about it, but you were always watching.

It was the web of the city, of course, which had given me the idea for the Maze and it was Queen's who had funded it. I had applied to the Martin Burnside Memorial Fund to provide money for materials and they had granted £5,000. The Arts Council had matched the money and the City Council had let us use a small plot of land in Ormeau Park. In the name of Art.

Four

It didn't take me long to get bored in Lorna McLeish's flat. After two days I had nosed around enough so I knew where everything was and I had got over the luxury of it all. Lorna's friend, David, had given up calling. I was ready for some progress.

It came when I was having lunch at the fountain in the Mall and my heart went out to Becka. She was at the fountain too, with her head bowed, and she was looking at the bubbles with eyes the same colour as the water, and she was still like an animal is still when it is tired. I had a hunch that she wanted to get in there and splash around for a bit.

'Are you OK?' I asked.

'Yeah. Fine,' she replied.

She was about my own age, unkempt and badly dressed. She was wearing the kind of clothes they import into the country from Asia and sell in shops called RAA and Flowers in Your Hair. There were small holes in the trousers. She tossed back her mousy brown locks. We could have been sisters.

'I'm trying to figure out where to go,' she said. 'I don't know whether it's better to stay in London, where it's warmer than most of the country, and there is lots of help, or whether to go to Scotland.'

'What's in Scotland?' I asked.

'I don't know,' she replied.

I laughed. 'That's not necessarily a good reason. But it's not necessarily a bad reason either.'

'Becka,' she told me. 'I'm Becka.'

'Libby,' I said and we shook hands. It turned out that she came from Glasgow, and she had left four years ago and had never gone back. But she'd fallen in love and it hadn't worked out and that's why she was thinking about it now. Family. Going home. I was jealous.

I knew immediately that we would be friends. It was an instinctive thing. A genuine rapport. I took her back to the flat, of course, and told her the story about the Bank and having three months to sort out a new job.

'Wow,' she said when she opened the cupboards and saw the array of different kinds of tea and coffee with which Lorna McLeish adorned her food shelves. 'I was thinking of getting a job. A temp job. I can type.'

'You can stay here,' I said, 'for the three months if you like. If you're going to Scotland you might as well do it with some money stashed away.'

She looked at me with a sharpness in her eyes which faded quickly into the open gaze of mellow complicity that comes from knowing that something will turn up, and indeed, probably already has.

'We'll see,' she said in reply. 'We'll see.'

But she did stay and we had a lot of fun. Becka turned out to be handy with a needle and she took in most of Lorna McLeish's abandoned clothes so that they fitted us. We got drunk and paraded them around the bedroom, laughing at the crash diet which Lorna would go on when she tried to fit into them on her return. One cooked breakfast too many in Cardiff. We tried to clean the flat, but the hoover was blocked. The cleaning company would bring their own anyway, and we didn't have to make much mess. We settled in like a couple of pros. Becka had squatted before, of course, but nowhere that had running water and a working toilet. It was a life of luxury.

Becka is my only friend. There are other people I'm fond of now, of course, but she's the only person, outside Ma and Dad, that I have ever really felt for. I would kill for her. Even now. I don't care about the money. There isn't much I do care for. I'm a loner. I always was. Even since my school days. Even in college. I never trusted anyone. Becka is my only friend. My soul is naked before her. She'll be with me for ever. I could never betray her no matter what she does.

We tried not to put the lights on after it got dark. We tiptoed around in the evening. We checked the hall-ways before we left. No one spotted us. It was a time to get over the ills the world had thrust upon us. It was also busy season for the builders and subsequently there were a couple of openings in good practices in the City. I preened my CV and considered making a pop-up version out of modelling card. I picked out one of Lorna McLeish's suits to wear to the interviews for luck. They wanted people at Greyfriars Clarke and they wanted people at Charlie Campbell's. I applied for both. Becka got a temp job straight away. Once she was dressed in Lorna McLeish's clothes and we had cut her hair, she looked very respectable. We had spent a whole evening in Lorna's cosmetics box, painting our nails in chic Chanel, and rubbing seaweed cream into our city-fatigued skin. We looked very well on it.

Becka scrubbed up OK. She came to pick me up at Pagan McSwain one afternoon and she looked just like any of the other office girls. Maybe a bit better. Lorna's abandoned suits were immaculately cut. You can blend in anywhere. Isn't it strange? She went to an agency and they tested her typing, and we made up some places that she had worked and hey presto, they got her a couple of interviews. The first one was a big lawyer's office, and she couldn't blag her way through the jargon, but we think it was the fact that she came from Glasgow that helped with the second. She got a job for a month at First Caledonian. It was secretarial work, in one of the bigwigs' offices. It paid £190 a week. After tax. We got a taxi home. Well, prudent as ever, we got a taxi as far as Albert Bridge and we walked the block back to Huntington Villas.

'You should have gone for a temp job all along,' said Becka. She was right, but I had a good feeling about the real jobs I had applied for. I resolved that if I didn't get one of them in a week, I would reconsider.

The night that Becka got the job Lorna's friend David started ringing again. We were celebrating in the living-room under the cupola. There was a full moon that night and we had cracked open a bottle of Lorna McLeish's best white wine. Becka had made cheesy beanos, which were toasted cheese with beans on top. You can make them with hot chilli in the beans if you want to get spicy about things. We didn't. It was a great picnic just as it was – cheesy beanos being one of the greatest things you can make at short notice. We set the food out in the clear light cast on the carpet beneath the cupola. We were very easy together, Becka and I. She had moved around the country so much I expect she would have settled in easily anywhere. She was used to it. She had travelled a lot as a kid too. Her father was some kind of scientist and he'd gone from lab to lab, I suppose. She was born in America, but they had come back to Britain when she was quite small. She'd lived in Brussels too – he had taken work at the EEC – and when she was twelve they had ended up in Glasgow where they had stayed until she left home.

'The longest I've stayed anywhere,' she said. 'I'm so happy about getting this job. It was the right thing to do.' Becka went back into her room and returned with a small wooden box. It was an old, beaten-up thing. She said she had found it in an abandoned shoe factory

46

where she had slept for a while. 'I keep all my best secrets in it,' she joked as she opened it. Inside there were pouches and phials and little tins. She drew out a suede pouch and emptied the contents on to her palm. 'These,' she said proudly, 'are magic mushrooms. I got them in the Dales last autumn. I dried them. They are really good.'

We'd finished the beanos, so I put the plates into the kitchen sink and returned to the picnic with a bowl of hot water. We soaked the mushrooms up and fried them in a little garlic paste and butter. Lloyd Grossman would have been proud. They were delicious.

'What else have you got in there?' I asked.

'Everything,' she said. 'Potions and pills.'

'Were you dealing?'

'No. I was healing.' At the bottom of the box there were thin, three-inch candles of all colours. Becka took out a pink candle and a green one. She set them up on her empty plate and lit them. 'We are going to be happy. We are going to find true happiness, content-ment and repose,' she said very definitely.

That's when the phone rang. It was him again. We listened to the machine. Lorna's voice, clear and to the point: 'Not here just now. Please leave a message after the tone.' He sounded panicky and upset. 'It's me again, Lorna. It's me. I've spoken to Personnel – they will write to you at the end of the week. Hell, you've even had me checking hospitals, for Christ's sake. But I suppose this is it. You don't want to see me again. Well fine. I'll miss you. I do love you, but I can't go on speaking to a machine. Think about it. Ring me. Even in a week. Even a month. I'll wait for ever. I love you. I really do.'

'Wow,' said Becka. 'True love and she turns him down to go to Cardiff. Some girls.'

'There is a difference between waiting for ever, and waiting for a month,' I pointed out.

We ran the tape back to make sure that was what he had said. There were six messages on the machine, all from David.

'God love him,' I said. 'I believe him. She was a total bitch to me. Bet you she was no fun to go out with.'

And we went back to the wine with renewed gusto and as the candles burned Becka told tales of the hearts she'd broken personally, on her adventures around the British Isles. She had been living in a squat in Kilburn with a boy called Johnny who made jewellery and sold it on the streets. Becka said it was the most amazing love affair she had ever had. She said the strangest thing. She said, 'I fell in love and I couldn't bear it.' I would have asked her more about it then, only I got the feeling it was something bad, and when you are taking mushrooms and you get emotional and start to think about bad things there is a point when you can go either way – you can turn into a screaming, angst-ridden lunatic or you can just not think about whatever it is any more. Becka decided to drop the subject and I didn't pursue it. I told her, for some reason, about wanting to do it with a soldier. The mushrooms were great – they heightened everything into a terrific, love-dazed, heavenly dream. And all night we gazed, with wide cat's eyes, at the clouds moving over the inky sky and the full, bright moon behind them.

Five

It turned out that Becka was working in what had been Lorna McLeish's office. They had obviously decided to take on an extra pair of low-profile hands, to cover for Lorna in her absence. There was already one person there, called Marcia. Becka reckoned Marcia was the laziest person she had ever met. I never thought that a big bank like First Caledonian would tolerate that sort of thing considering how tough they had been on me, but there you are. The befreckled Marcia ate two big packets of chocolate ginger-nut biscuits every day and drank interminable coffees. She chatted to her boyfriend on the phone, read the *Sun* and gazed out of the office window for too long at a time. Becka reckoned, though, that she was the fastest copy typist in the country. When work did come in, Marcia would sit poised at her machine with her perfect deportment showing off her jade woollen suit and she would rattle away at over a hundred words per minute. It was, apparently, the only exercise she ever got. She had extremely supple, thin fingers and a big, fat arse. Luck of the draw, isn't it? Marcia and Becka were working for Lorna's erstwhile boss, the star of the answerphone messages, Mr David Curran.

Becka recognised his voice as soon as she met him. He didn't have any accent in particular, just a warm way of speaking to you. Even when he had got cross on the answerphone, he had still sounded friendly. He was an extremely good-looking man. Lorna had good taste, anyway, we figured. He was about thirty-five years of age and had those preppy good looks that the magazines always go on about. He could have played James Bond if they had glossed him up – a bit of Brylcreem would have done wonders. Marcia was in awe of him. He was rumoured to command a salary in six figures and he drove a racing-green Jaguar, under-written by the bank. Some days he had a chauffeur.

Marcia waxed as lyrical as she could to Becka. 'He's gorgeous, isn't he?' she cooed, all girls together. 'Oh I'd get rid of my Benji in a moment, just give me half a chance. He's just wonderful. Green eyes. Oooh. I wonder who gave him that friendship bracelet. He isn't married, you know,' she said.

Becka encouraged her like nobody's business. 'A guy like that,' she said sagely, 'must have so many wom-en . . .'

Marcia jumped to Mr Curran's defence. 'No one ever calls here. I've never seen him even as much as have lunch with a woman if it wasn't for business.'

'Maybe he's gay,' mused Becka.

'A guy like that!' exclaimed Marcia in disbelief.

And Becka let it be. But he was wonderful. Everyone said so. It was as if he had cast a spell over the whole staff. Even the doorman liked him. Becka said it was amazing.

It was a busy time for us. I did get called to interview for Charlie Campbell, but not for Greyfriars Clarke. Becka helped me rehearse. We chose a very plain plum-coloured suit and a utilitarian, white, starched shirt and we went through everything I had put on my CV. Their letter said that they had already contacted Mr Ramage, who was my old boss, and I knew that he had liked me. He must have given them a good reference anyway, because they wanted to go ahead and meet up. I was really excited.

It was at the end of the first week that Becka found the paper. She had been delivering files from Lorna's office to David's, and she had noticed it in the bin. She said it was as if her eyes had been drawn to it. It was lying on top and the bin was nearly full. 'I'll empty this for you,' she said. Smart girl, our Becka. That evening she came home with a dilemma. On the paper were written, word for word, the messages he had left on the answerphone with the dates and times he had left them. He had ticked them off after each call. The ticks were in different colours of ink. We held a meeting in Lorna's kitchen, sitting on the floor, wedged between the galley units.

I must say, in the beginning I was for leaving the whole thing alone. I mean if anything fishy was going on and Lorna McLeish was involved, I really didn't care. Becka was more interested, though, because she worked at the Bank and wanted to nose around to spice up her working day. I agreed to get the contact number for Lorna McLeish from the file at Pagan McSwain and the next day Becka rang the number and asked to speak to her. She was going to ask some stupid question about something at the office if she got through. She didn't, though. They had never heard of Lorna McLeish at First Caledonian's offices in Cardiff. She wasn't there. She had never arrived. And they weren't expecting her. So Becka, with her keen investigative mind, looked up Lorna McLeish's bank accounts on the office computer and discovered that there had been no withdrawals other than direct debits since Lorna McLeish had left her keys at Pagan McSwain ten days before. Nothing had so much as gone on a visa card. We swithered a bit. Wherever she was, she wasn't spending any money – apparently she was living on thin air or someone else's ample resources. Two days later, just when we were getting tired of the puzzle and giving up on caring about it, Becka noticed that salary money had gone into Lorna McLeish's bank account. The entry was marked 'final payment'. Lorna McLeish was living on no money, which was just as well, because she didn't have a job any more.

Six

First Caledonian had an occasional End of Financial Year party in the first week of April. It was an accountant's joke. Someone at the office said that if there was any money left aside in the entertainments budget in the last week of the year they threw this party, so that they ended dead on budget exactly at the end of every year. Everyone at the office was invited and sometimes they had girls who weren't from the office, because the London branch had too many men in it, and not enough girls to chat up. Those accountants are devils. Becka got me an invite. The party was on the evening after the Charlie Campbell interview. It had sounded like a good idea a few days before, but I wasn't in the mood when I actually got there.

The interview had been tough going. It had taken me ages to get to Pimlico, as if London had been switched to slow motion for the morning, or maybe I was operating in fast forward. Anyhow, I wasn't comfortable. All the way over there on the tube I got more and more uptight. In the end, I got off the train and walked the last two stops. That definitely cleared my head. Charlie Campbell's offices were in one of the beautiful Georgian buildings on the crescents near the Tate Gallery. Inside, the whole place was restored to perfection, the light played around the hallway, as if the whole house had been built just to trap it. It was a beautiful place. The firm was very famous. I remembered a rumour I had heard when I first arrived in London that they were considering moving to the Docklands and purpose-built offices there to allow them to expand. I heard quite a few people saying that if jobs ever came up in Charlie Campbell's they would be going for them.

Charlie Campbell himself was a piece of architectural folklore. He had gone to art college and dropped out and travelled the world and when he came back he trained in Milan. Christ knows how he arranged to get taken in there. He must have had one hell of a portfolio. He graduated at twenty-nine and by the time he was thirty-five he had set up his own offices in London and had netted some of the most lucrative contracts in Europe. Rumours abounded about Charlie Campbell – he must have had sticky fingers if he really had them in as many pies as they said. He certainly owned a lot of property anyway. I had seen him once as he passed me on his bicycle. He, rather famously, eschewed the company car. No one at Charlie Campbell's had company cars. No one wore suits. This was all information which had been the subject of discussion in architecture magazines – responsible journals of serious debate. We used to get all the periodicals in the office. I had devoured them – read them cover to cover the same day as they came in. Anyhow, because of the suits thing, my outfit for the interview had taken several days to decide upon, but in the end I figured that although you might not wear a suit once you got there, you probably ought to do so for the interview. Out of respect.

When I arrived there was a team of three to interview me. There was one woman and two men, one of whom was Charlie Campbell himself. He was quite encouraging – still young to be in charge of a firm like this, and kind-looking. He had muddy brown hair and watery blue eyes, but you hardly noticed all that because he was wearing the most extraordinary checked trousers I have ever seen. They were kind of baggy, with purple and blue squares. He looked like he might break into a juggling act at any minute. The woman sat to his left – she was vicious, though. I don't know if I just rubbed her up the wrong way or if she was like that with everyone. She had a blonde bob and questioned everything you said. The other guy didn't say much – he was balding, with a white beard. He was kind of lanky and dour, but you knew he was smart. He looked up at you in all the right places with a wry smile playing on his lips. Charlie did most of the talking.

'Please come in,' he had started. 'We've been looking forward to seeing you.'

I nodded my hellos and he introduced the panel. The woman was called Kit Cameron. She shook my hand loosely, just like it says that you shouldn't shake someone's hand if you want to impress them. The guy was called Jack Wright. I noticed, as I clasped his fingers, that he bit his nails.

I turned down the offer of coffee or tea and settled down round the table with them. We talked for a bit about training at Queen's and where my interest lay and that kind of thing and then Charlie did the inevitable. He asked me about the Maze. He said he had read about it at the time. He asked if it was still there. I didn't know. I had resolved to talk about this. I was prepared. It was, after all, the most interesting thing on my résumé. I had a speech planned for it.

'Well, I got the idea from the city,' I started. 'The streets in Belfast aren't just streets – they tell you a lot. There are some streets you only go down if you are Catholic and some you only go down if you are Protestant. People relate to the cityscape in certain ways according to their culture. If you come from the outside it is a maze all right. So I had this idea to build a maze – a rotating maze. One that you would only be able to find your way through safely if you knew the rhythm of it. It was just after rotating advertising boards came out – you know the Adshel ones which can display three adverts at once. All the walls of the maze could rotate to be either the colours of the Irish flag, the colours of the British flag, or blood red. You had to find your way through on the colours of your choice. You could get through on any of them, but the rotation wasn't even. Sometimes it would turn to one colour and unless you had sprinted along to the next part of the puzzle you would be caught in the opposing colour. The idea was to make people strangers in their own city – to be able to look at it from the outside again. You could rehearse it – not like in real life. You could try things that in real life were forbidden. You could walk straight down no matter what colour was on the walls if you wanted to.'

I was doing OK. Jack Wright was nodding sagely and smiling a lot. Kit Cameron sat with her lips pursed. Charlie Campbell was rapt.

'We built the installation on a site at Ormeau Park near the centre of Belfast. It wasn't a big site. About quarter of an acre. The Arts Council co-funded the project with a private trust fund. There was a lot of press interest of course.'

'Wonderful,' murmured Charlie. 'I do remember you being on the news one evening.'

'Yes,' I said. 'It caused a lot of trouble. I wouldn't go back to Ireland again.'

'Must be the only place in the world, outside of communist states, where architecture is political.' Charlie smiled. 'Well we don't get such exciting projects here, Miss Lucas.'

I was absolutely sure that wasn't true. Although exciting might not be just the right word for the Maze.

'My last job was just quiet enough for me,' I replied.

'Yes,' Kit Cameron said, lifting up a paper in front of her. 'They went into receivership.'

'I think it was bad debts,' I said. 'One of their big clients went bankrupt and that was it. I liked working there. There were lots of different projects – I did three months on designs for the new Tasty Boy motorway cafés and then I did a week or two on the renovation of the Cosby Arcade. There was quite a bit of planning work too.'

Charlie Campbell came to the rescue. 'I know Martin Ramage, actually,' he said. 'It was a good practice. He'll probably start up again soon enough. He speaks very highly of you.'

I blushed.

'Tell me about this Pagan McSwain job you have been doing,' he said.

'Oh, it's just residential property,' I replied. 'I sell houses for them and do a bit of administrative work. It's been good, though, because it has taken me all round London. I'm quite familiar with the city now.'

'Favourite building?' said Jack Wright.

I decided to joke. 'Home is always my favourite building, Mr Wright.'

They laughed. Silence. I realised that I had better think of something quick.

'I like pictures of old buildings. You know when you see renovations and the lawn is perfect and the whole place is sanitised. I like it when you see Victorian pictures of how the old buildings really were, with crooked chimneypots and mud all over the place. I like MI5's new premises, though,' I added so as not to seem too retrospective and just in case the Docklands move was still on the cards.

'I visited Venice when I was in my teens. I don't have a favourite building there, but it is definitely my favourite city.' I talked for a bit about the Doge's Palace and St Mark's Square and about bridges. I had loved the bridges in Venice. It made you think differently about roads and overpasses – about the way one building blends into another and the relationship between the structures. It had really been a magical trip.

Charlie Campbell grinned at me. 'Thank you so much for coming in,' he said.

I arranged to ring in and find out their decision. I told them I was moving house and that it would be easier, since I wasn't sure exactly which day we would be going and when the new telephone would be connected. As I left the building I passed scurrying flocks of architects in T-shirts who were walking *en masse* down the corridor. If I got the job, I made a mental note, I would have to go out and buy some extraordinary T-shirts.

After I left the building I walked over to the Tate and it was as if I floated around the rooms. I was kicking myself, though. I knew there was more I could have said. There was certainly more I should have said. The only place in the world, outside a communist state, where architecture is political. Goddamn it. The only place in the world where there are large amounts of people opposed to peace – where there are political parties actively opposed to the notion of it and where there are enough people to elect the leaders of those parties into power. The only place in the world where people are so desperate for some small peace of mind, even if it is only temporary, only fleeting, that they equate the word 'ceasefire' with the word 'peace', because they know it is the best that they can hope for. I sat in front of a large blue canvas and I cried quietly to myself.

I hardly noticed Charlie Campbell when he sat down next to me. I must have been the only person in London who wouldn't have noticed him. His trousers announced him. He handed me a bright-pink handker-chief. 'What's up?' he asked.

I was startled. 'The Maze,' I said inexplicably.

'Well, you can cheer up. You have got the job. Can I buy you some lunch?'

'Thanks,' I said, and I even managed a grin.

It would have seemed rude to turn him down, although I truly didn't feel one bit like eating. We went to the Gallery café and I toyed wastefully with a large plate of salad and a baked potato. He wanted me to start work in three weeks. Three weeks. This was heaven. And I was going to be paid on a higher salary point than I had got at Ramage Lloyd. It would be nearly £500 a week after tax.

'You shouldn't cry about the Maze,' Charlie Campbell observed. 'It's what got you the job.'

I didn't explain to him. After lunch I went to Pagan McSwain and handed in my notice.

Trish was devastated when I told her I was leaving and amazed when I told her about the money. 'My God,' she said, 'we were lucky to have you for as long as we did.'

It was only then I realised that when I left Pagan McSwain I would have to move out of Huntington Villas and leave the ghost of Lorna McLeish behind for ever. It was strange how she had become part of whatever we did – the clothes, the flat, the messages on the answerphone. It was all intriguing.

After celebratory coffee and Smarties at Pagan McSwain, I secured the rest of the afternoon off and walked over to First Caledonian to bear the glad tidings to Becka. Marcia made us coffee and biscuits. 'Here you are,' she cooed, today clad in a shocking-pink woollen suit, with matching nails. 'This is to celebrate. And good luck to you.' I was beginning to feel as if I would explode if I ate anything else. We toasted my success, then some typing came in on an audio tape and Marcia decided to get on with it. She sat in the corner, rattling away on a huge computer, with the earplugs of the audio machine firmly lodged in the waxy crevices above her lobes.

'So what's up?' asked Becka. 'It's what you wanted, isn't it?'

'I just got upset. About this project I did when I was at college. It was silly of me,' I replied. I really didn't want to go into it. All I could think about was me on the telly getting carried away. They all picked up the quote. Every station. 'We have to be prepared to put everything we have on the line for peace. We have to want it more than anything.' Oh God. And they took me at my word. Bastards. Ma and Dad died the next day. And all I could see was me on the news. I hadn't gone home till late, but I'd rung them and they'd watched it. They were even proud. My eyes filled up. Becka put her hand on my arm. But I held it in.

'Never mind. It's nothing. Becka, when I leave Pagan McSwain we'll have to move house. Will you come with me?'

Becka thought for a moment and then slowly shook her head. 'No. I couldn't. This is just a jape for me. A bit of a joke. Some extra money for a few weeks. I don't want this for more than a little holiday. I'll go to Glasgow for a while, like I planned. I'll miss you, though. If I come back to London, I'll visit you.'

It was all too much. I cried, this time, my head bowed low into the mug of coffee.

She reached out and held me tight for a minute. 'Hey, hey, what's all this?'

'Nothing. Nothing. Hey, I'll miss you too,' I said, though I wanted to tell her she was the only person I had got. I wanted to beg her to stay. If she went I would never be able to tell her about what happened and I wanted to tell her about it more than anything.

Seven

One thing I'll say about First Caledonian – they surely know how to throw a party. I had always thought that the building where the bank was housed was incredibly dark. The hallway certainly was – there were no windows that I could see – and the concourse where you had to go to get your money was dim on account of the trees running all the way around the back of the building. The party, though, was upstairs in a gold-leafed reception room which faced south. First Caledonian must have had a lean year entertaining their clients, because no expense was spared for the mop-up party. There were waitresses in natty black outfits with white, frilly aprons, who handed round trays bedecked with long glasses of champagne or short tumblers of whisky. Other waitresses handed around trays of smoked salmon, delicately coiled around generous curls of cream cheese. 'More celebration,' said Becka and downed her whisky so quickly that she managed to take another tumbler from the same tray before the waitress moved on. I opted for champagne – I didn't want the whisky to make me even more maudlin.

Becka introduced me to some guy who looked like a barman but who turned out to be Head of Security. I wouldn't have trusted him with my secrets – in less than five minutes he had told me that although he was still married, he slept on the sofa at home. After about half an hour the music started. An older man in a black suit stood at the end of the room next to a big grey compact disc player. Do you know, they play classical music for parties at the Bank. Civilised to the end. Actually it was kind of groovy. I longed to dance, but it didn't seem to be *de rigueur*, so I chatted my way in a clockwise direction around interminable men in suits, and Becka worked anti-clockwise. It was amazing. There were almost no women at all – only a few secretaries in those gaudy woollen suits and a very public-school, happy-in-a-hockeysticks-kind-of-way lady who had probably been head girl at Bedales in her day. Marcia set the standard on the gaudy-woollen-suit front. I think she would have glowed in the dark. It gave me new respect for Lorna McLeish – she had been quite high up here by the sound of things. Maybe it had all got to her and she had run off, faking Cardiff, to escape from the relentless pressure.

It took me a second or two to realise why Becka was gesticulating at me and rolling her eyes, but the minute I saw him, I knew who he was. David Curran certainly was an astonishingly good-looking man. Not a Greek god, mind you, more touchable than that. He was seduction itself. The interest around him as he entered the room was palpable. This was a man who got served easily wherever he went, and who never had to wait for a taxi or search for a parking space. He was truly blessed among bankers.

I edged closer towards where he was standing, making small talk. Becka was closer still. He smiled at her and they clicked their glasses and made a toast.

'Long life,' said Becka.

'Good life,' he retorted. 'Quality over quantity every time.'

Becka giggled as she sipped from her glass. He certainly had a charming way about him. When I turned back he had moved on from Becka and was telling a blonde and rather eager girl about something called the Gobsmacked Club. It was a crowd of his old friends, all of whom were gobsmacked by their own success.

'We go to the football together and for chips after.' He smiled.

Seeming humble too, I thought to myself. But too smooth. I had met men before who made out that way – who put up that front. Something about him interested me, though. I suppose I thought of Lorna McLeish and I wondered how he, as he seemed to be, could choose for himself a woman like her. Someone devoid of humour and of passion too. Perhaps I presumed too much, but the flat, her clothes, the way she was – well, a man who was really the way David Curran appeared to be would choose someone more joyful, surely.

Becka had moved towards him again. She was smiling and I heard her say 'my friend from Ireland' and across David Curran's face there flickered the merest suggestion of awkwardness, so I knew that he was Irish too. From somewhere he had long buried. He was a chameleon. He had rid himself of his accent all right, but kept the winning ways, the charm that Irish people have routinely. They did tests a while back on Irish people and they found that the Irish vocabulary is the widest in the world. It's something all Irish people have – and it is charming, as expression usually is. David Curran had cut his accent and kept the charm. He had moulded himself into something that he was not. Looking back, I suppose then, that was exactly what I wanted to do – it would have let me leave the past behind and God knows I longed for that more than anything else.

I decided I wanted to meet him, so I smoothed my hair, pursed my lips and just walked over to him and said, 'Hello. How's about ye?' That jarred against him. In fact, given his smooth persona, I expect he had never looked so appalled in all his life. You would think that I had said, 'Hello. I am going to kill your dog.' You would think that I had said, 'Hello. I am a Martian and I am going to take all my clothes off and mutate now.' Well, *I* didn't know the guy was being threatened. Anything west of Britain and east of the States was going to make him jumpy. But at the time I was blissfully unaware of how much I was putting the wind up him. And, well, he was fierce good-looking and there was that extra quality, that mystery element of not quite understanding him, of feeling he'd hidden something – that Lorna McLeish factor – which made him dangerous to boot. I decided to try to pick him up. It's not that I usually flirt, but I'd had a few glasses of bubbly by that stage and I was in the mood. It was just as well that I was. If I hadn't been so flirtatious none of the rest of it would have happened and Lord knows where I'd be now.

'I'm Becka's friend,' I added, glad I seemed to have caught him off guard.

He stammered (and he definitely didn't normally stammer), 'You . . . you're from the North.'

Poor bastard.

I smiled. My accent always heightened when I had had a few jars. 'Belfast,' I said. 'I'm from Belfast. My name is Liberty.' Come to think of it, I couldn't have made it up better.

He splashed his drink all over his tie. 'Liberty,' he said, absolutely incredulous.

'Yes,' I replied. 'As in freedom. Most people call me Libby, though. And you are . . .?'

'David,' he said too quickly. 'David Curran.'

'Isn't this a great party? Great crack. It's nice to know that accountants have a sense of humour, don't you think?' I was quite enjoying myself.

'Sense of humour,' he repeated, with panicky, wide eyes. I really seemed to have wound him up all right.

I carried on regardless, 'I am here under false pretences, though. I don't work at First Caledonian. Actually I owe the Bank a bit of money. So you could say that I am a valued customer,' I added, and I gave him what I thought of as a jaunty wink, and then lost him as he was rescued by the older man who had been in charge of the compact disc player. They wandered off together, but I did notice that David kept looking at me. All the time. Perhaps he missed home, I thought to myself. Perhaps he just downright fancied me. One way or another, I figured my luck was in. I caught him glancing at me once or twice and so I winked at him again. I reasoned with myself that he might be a bit old to be my type, and he obviously wasn't going to be over Lorna McLeish yet, but maybe, since I was leaving the flat anyway, I might adopt him for a bit. A one-night stand. Or maybe a few nights. At least some snogging might cheer me up.

As the party was winding down, he sidled back over to me, by which time I was chatting to Becka. 'Could I have five?' he asked. He seemed to have recovered his composure.

I stared at him in incomprehension. 'Sorry?'

'Minutes. Do you have a moment to have a word?'

'Oh. Yes. Sure.'

He pulled me out of the golden room and into the corridor. I expect he thought he should confront me. He was trying to be brave. 'I don't know why they sent you, but I want you to tell them that it's scaring the shit out of me and that they can stop now.'

'What?'

'Don't start that.'

'What?'

'Just tell them,' he said. Coincidences like me just did not exist in the world David Curran inhabited. If there was an Irish girl called Liberty chatting him up, then she was there for other than social reasons. 'Tell them,' he repeated.

I must have a nose for trouble. In fact, I definitely do. No contest about that. I was intrigued and I didn't realise how reckless I was being – there wasn't time for that.

'OK. Sure.' I played along. I needn't have done that, but I had had a few jars to drink and this was weird but kind of interesting and I was playing a game without really thinking. I winged it on inspiration. 'About Lorna,' I started, prospecting for further information.

'OK. OK,' he interrupted. 'Not here. And not you. I'd rather deal with the lads.'

I wanted to know what was going on. More than anything. But he wasn't giving me any more.

'Fine,' I replied and we went back in to the party.

Becka was dancing with the Head of Security. I don't think he had much of a background in formal dancing – it looked more like they were going for a short stroll around the room together. I decided to reef her out of his arms and to get her to come with me. I had decided that we should follow David home. I wanted to know where he lived. I wanted to find things out just for badness. Something was afoot.

'My God,' I said as Becka and her man waltzed past, 'we are going to be late. Becka, it's after eight. We have to go. We had better go now.'

Becka relinquished the vicelike grip of her partner and we made our exit.

'Something is going on. Something is going on about Lorna McLeish,' I told her. 'And I want to follow David Curran home.'

'Why?' she asked. 'I have his address on the office rolodex, if that's what you're after.'

'Yes,' I said. 'Go and get it.'

Eight

It probably seems unladylike to break and enter in the way that we did, but we figured that he was going to be tied up at the party for a while and we might as well take our chances. Marcia had told Becka that the Big Boys had a light supper, brandy and cigars after most people had left. That sounded like it would go on until ten or eleven at night at least. It's not really that we cared at all about Lorna McLeish, you understand, it's just that I like to know what's going on. I like to know why things are the way they are. Something was surely going on. There was no question of that. And I wanted to know what it was. I might have been drunk. I might have had a tough enough old day. But if there was an explanation out there, I still had the energy to go in search of it.

We got a cab to Chelsea Harbour and walked from there. It wasn't far. We hadn't a clue what was happening. All we knew was that David, good-looking as he was, charming as he could be, was covering his tracks for some reason. Some Irish reason. The idea of stumbling on anything really important was out of the box. Crazy stuff. So we were looking for a rational, low-key explanation – a nervous breakdown or another mistress or something of that order.

David lived in a nice place. The cars parked on the street were worth as much as houses cost for normal, average people. It was the first time I had broken and entered without having a key. Becka, though, had done this before. We stared in awe at the alarm box outside the front door of the up-market mews. Then we cased the joint – walked around so we could see both sides. At least he didn't seem to have a dog. We got ready to run if we had to – after all, if we ran up the street a little way and then walked as normal, we'd just be two nice, well-dressed, middle-class girls out for a walk. We would probably get away with it. Emboldened by this, Becka forced a small window at the back of the building. No alarm bells struck out. Actually, I think the thing must have been turned off, because in the end we went all over the show and there wasn't a peep out of it at all. We couldn't switch on any lights, of course, but we were used to that by now, and the orange street lights from the cobbled walkway outside cast the kind of light that you could almost read by. We established pretty quickly that Lorna McLeish wasn't there. In fact, there was no evidence of any woman – no ladies' clothes, no perfume or make-up in the bathroom. Nothing.

Becka took a fit of the giggles. 'My God. What are we doing?' she laughed.

'Something's up,' I said, 'and I thought it might be up here.'

It didn't look like it. We sat like rag dolls on the plush carpet in David Curran's living-room. I couldn't tell what colour that flat was – the whole place just looked like shades of brown and orange and it smelt like bubble gum. It was a bachelor's pad all right. Almost certainly. Nicely kept and everything, but still, the haunt of a man who lived alone.

'Maybe we should go now,' said Becka. 'Unless of course you fancy swapping our squat. He'd probably hardly notice us.'

I got up, walked over to the bookcase and casually

picked out a leather-bound volume. It was an album of photographs. I flicked half-heartedly through the pages. 'There's Lorna McLeish,' I said.

'Yeah, yeah. We know. He knew Lorna McLeish. We know that.'

I was losing concentration. And I was still drunk. I should have paid more attention, but Becka was putting me off and I loosened my grip and dropped the album. If I hadn't done that I probably never would have looked at the first few pages. But there it was. Curiouser and curiouser. A young, oh, very young David Curran in a family portrait. I knew who he was. I knew that lovely smile. The photo had been taken one sunny day in the back garden of the boarding house in Drumcondra. David Curran was Mrs C's son – and there he was with his four elder brothers. They were posing like a football team around their mother, who positively glowed with the excitement of having her strapping progeny around her. David couldn't have been more than fourteen or fifteen, but Conor looked at least twenty-five. I had always assumed Conor was the youngest, but that patently wasn't true. David was the baby. The one who got away.

'Wow,' was really all I could manage by way of reaction to this. I pulled the photograph out of its cellophane binding. On the back, in the scrawly old hand of someone who learned to write when schools were strict about it, was written 'May 1979' and the names in Irish from left to right in the photograph, 'Conor, Padraig, Daithi, Liam and Donal'. Poor Mrs C – she hadn't even rated herself in there.

'What is it?' said Becka, who came over to have a look. 'Is that him, do you think?' she asked.

I nodded. 'It's him and his brothers,' I said. 'He has four of them.'

'Obviously,' said Becka.

'No, you don't understand. I know them, I used to

stay at this house. It's in Oak Avenue in Drumcondra. His mother is nice enough. A bit of a loony. I've met two of his brothers.'

'Well,' said Becka, 'that will give you something to talk about the next time you meet him.'

'Something is really wrong here,' I said, and then we heard the key turning in the lock.

There isn't a lot of storage in mews flats – most originally had a big hayloft, but David Curran's, like most of the mews flats in London, had been converted. If we hadn't panicked we would probably have made it out of the back window again, but, well to be frank, we did panic. Before David made it up the stairs, though, I had thrust the photo album back into the vacant space on the shelf and we had both dived across the hallway and into the wardrobe in the bedroom. This was not an ideal place to be located. It being late at night, he was almost certainly sure to come into the bedroom fairly soon. He was pretty sure to want to take off his clothes and hang them up. The wardrobe was fairly large, but also fairly full and didn't readily accommodate two normal-sized girls. If he turned on the light and opened the door, he'd probably see us. I can't honestly say that I was scared, but I didn't really want to get caught in the guy's wardrobe with my friend.

'One of us should go under the bed,' I whispered.

'You,' mouthed Becka.

Some wild adventurer. I could hear David in the living-room, so I gingerly pushed open the wardrobe door, sneaked across the carpet and rolled under the bed. There wasn't a lot of room – it was a low sort of a bed. Luckily it was a double, so if he lay down, as long as I stayed wherever he wasn't, I would still be able to breathe. I figured that once he was asleep we could sneak out. These are the sort of things that I was thinking about, when he did come into the bedroom. My heart was hammering. You can't imagine how annoyed I felt when he took off his tie and threw it on the floor. Perhaps the wardrobe would have been safe after all. No. No. He opened the wardrobe door and took out a coat hanger for his jacket. Quite right. It was a very expensive jacket. Then there was a little unexplained pause. The kind of pause which shouldn't really have been there.

'What the hell?' he said, and extricated Becka from between his perfectly laundered shirts.

'Oh my God,' said Becka. 'I can't explain this. I can't even think of anything to explain this.'

There was no point in lying when you could tell the truth. The closer it was to the truth the less there was to get caught out on. I willed plausible replies in her direction to little avail. There was a silence.

Then he took the initiative. 'Why?' he asked.

'I wanted to see you.'

'What?'

'Well, we had danced together. You got me a drink.' Becka was struggling for the moral high ground. It wasn't going to work.

'Jesus,' was all David could say.

'I wanted to see you. You know,' Becka continued, 'I'm drunk from the party.'

'Fuck,' he said.

'And I panicked and I hid in the cupboard.'

'Oh no. No way. What's going on here?'

'I'm sorry. Maybe I had better go. I'm drunk. I never should have. It was a silly thing to do. You'd better get someone else to work, I mean, this is ridiculous. Excuse me. Please excuse me.'

Social death in a banker's bedroom. I just closed my eyes and offered a silent prayer. I think he was just so shocked that he let her go. I heard her footsteps hammering down the stairs and the bang at the front door. Then there was this silence and he came and sat on the edge of the bed, picked up the phone and dialled a number.

'Conor,' he said, 'what the fuck is going on?'

There was a short silence, then David seemed to cut in. 'Don't start that Gaelic crap. You know I'm better in English.' Pause. 'No, I won't. First there is this noxious Northern girl at the bank, and she freaked the shit out of me and don't tell me that you didn't know, because if you didn't know you better start worrying, because she knew things. You don't have to push the point, you know. I know fine well you can get to me. You don't have to freak me out, planting people at work. And then I get home and there is this other girl, who is a temp at the office, and she is in my wardrobe, for fuck's sake.'

There was a little pause, but I could imagine what Conor was saying. I could imagine the frantic darting of his shifty eyes.

David seemed to cut in on him. 'Don't piss me around, Con. Look, you do whatever you like with Lorna. You are going to do it anyway. You do whatever you have to do. I'm covered, anyway, should anyone ask any questions. I left the messages, just as we arranged. I hope we don't need to use them. Is she there?' There was silence. 'Don't threaten me with her, Con. If you can let her go some time that would be great. But if you can't let her go then you can't and that's that. I wish she'd never stumbled on the whole thing. She doesn't deserve it. I'll transfer the money just as we discussed. But that's it. No more. Next time you can shoot me. Next time you can fucking shoot me if you want to. And you can explain that one to Ma. *Slán,*' he said and then put down the phone and lay out on the bed.

I was terrified. I have never been so terrified. It was a fear bred of generations.

David stayed on the bed. I heard him toss and tussle

with the pillows and settle himself until he was comfortable. It sounded as if he was wrestling with himself – well, I suppose he was. After a few minutes he picked up the phone again and dialled a long number.

'Ma,' he said softly, and then he spoke Gaelic.

I didn't pick up too much of it, to be honest. He called her 'cara' all the time. He called her dear. He didn't mention his brothers. When he put the phone down I heard him sobbing and he moved around the bed some more. I waited for nearly two hours before I so much as contemplated moving. Even then I was too scared. I just lay there while he slept, thinking of what a coward he was beneath his glib veneer. He had handed over his girlfriend. He was giving money to his brothers and they'd use it to kill people. I was terrified of him and I just lay there, hidden. He went to work at eight. I listened to him wash and dress and get himself ready for his day at the Bank. He was getting wary, though. He set the alarm this time. I could hear him at the bottom of the stairs, punching in the numbers and getting the high-pitched tone that gives you thirty seconds to get out. I made for the window at the back, but as soon as I opened the latch the bells started. I ran as fast as I could and hailed a cab on the main street. I don't think he saw me. He probably thought he had left that window open all night.

When I got back to the flat Becka was still wearing her party clothes. She was asleep on the floor. I burst into tears. 'Oh, Christ,' I sobbed. 'Oh Christ, it's come back to me.'

Becka woke up. She had a hangover because she'd slept. I was too upset to have one. She disappeared into the bathroom in search of Resolve powders and emerged triumphant with a fizzing glass of murky liquid. By this time I was almost hysterical. Becka just held on to me. It took a while before I calmed down, then we went into the kitchen and made a pot of tea and some toast and butter.

Becka really wasn't with it yet. 'Were you there all night?' she asked. 'What happened?'

I explained in some detail. But hell, it sounded so crazy. 'It has to be IRA,' I concluded. 'It has to be. They are from the South.'

'Well,' said Becka, 'we should call the police.'

But I knew the police wouldn't be able to protect us. I knew that with a stone-cold certainty about me. Becka, you see, had been brought up, for the bit that counts, in Scotland, and in Scotland you can probably trust the police to protect you. I knew better.

'They are terrorists,' I said. 'They are terrorists. They would shoot their own brother. They'll probably murder Lorna McLeish, you know. He gave them the OK last night. That, of course, is assuming they haven't done it already.'

'If they haven't killed her, it's more likely the police will be able to stop them than we will.'

I was doubtful. 'The police couldn't stop your granny going to the bathroom, if she wanted to. It's a different world. They get you back. They would get us back.'

I took a deep breath. 'I left Belfast because my parents were killed. It was my fault. Everyone said it was because of Dad's job. They meant to burn us out, but it went wrong. The whole house blew up. He'd worked in that job for years. It was me.'

Becka didn't know what to say. That's the trouble. The people who know what to say are a pain in the arse, and the people who don't know what to say are the ones you like most of all. There was a bit of the Scottish nanny in her, though. She put the dishes into the sink, turned round and said, 'Right. Showers first. Then we sit down and we talk about this properly. I can't think straight.'

It was a relief to get out of Lorna McLeish's suit. Once I knew what had happened to her, it wasn't so cool to wear her clothes. It occurred to me, in the shower, that it was dangerous for us to be in the flat. Not that the Currans might get to us here, but if anyone found Lorna McLeish's body, once they had identified her the police would go straight to her home address. The IRA wouldn't claim the killing. She was an undercover victim. She might lead them to David and they probably didn't want that – any connection made it one step closer to them. The police would want to find a guilty party and the place was covered in our fingerprints. Even if we told them about David Curran, him alone, it was all very fishy. We were implicated, and a charge of first-degree murder would be one thing almost certain to prejudice Charlie Campbell against his new employee.

Nine

Before we left the flat we cleaned the place from top to bottom so there would be no fingerprints. I didn't have a police record anyway, but Becka said she had been arrested before for shoplifting, so we cleaned everything, even the walls, and the little handles on the windows. We packed up all our own stuff and put everything which had belonged to Lorna back just where we had found it. Then we got really paranoid about genetic testing, because, of course, there would probably still be hairs and skin cells and all of that shit on the carpets and in the clothes. And then I couldn't remember exactly what had been in the cupboards when I had first arrived at the flat, so we couldn't replace the contents exactly either. After that we had a long debate about whether to let Lorna's clothes out again so that they would be the right size, but we reckoned that if the police came it was less likely they would pick up a few alterations than unpicked seams down the sides of all of her clothes. Eventually, though, we pulled ourselves together and got ready to leave. The last thing we did was wipe David Curran's carefully plotted answerphone messages off the machine. No one was getting a free alibi here. If and when they found Lorna McLeish's body David would have to explain why he apparently hadn't got in touch with her and why he hadn't reported her missing. After we had done that we regretted it, though, because then he would know that someone had been in the flat, heard the messages and erased them. Though there was nothing we could do. We couldn't reconstruct them.

We had decided to go to Glasgow together. It was sanctuary. I still had three weeks before I was due to start at Charlie Campbell's and I could ring Trish and tell her that something had come up and that I wouldn't be in to Pagan McSwain again. She'd be pissed off and maybe I wouldn't get the last couple of weeks' wages, but hell, that was peanuts compared with what I would soon be earning. We needed to have a little time to get ourselves together, decide what to do, do it and say goodbye properly. So that was the plan, we would go to Glasgow for a week or ten days, then we would go our separate ways. It was a little Scottish holiday to sort things out. Becka was sure her parents would still be there and that we could hole up at their place for a while and sort out our heads. We were pretty shaken up and we were kids at heart. Our first instinct was to find a home. But only one of us had one of those. So to Glasgow we went.

At first we were going to hitch, because we didn't have much money between us, but we decided in the end to get a coach, and that we would eat when we got there. The coach went overnight. It left from Victoria Station at six o'clock in the evening and got in to Central Station in Glasgow at six o'clock the following morning. It was £12 each. A pound an hour. So as it got dark we climbed aboard like refugees, sure that we stood out from the crowd. In fact, everyone on the coach looked like they were a bit dodgy. But harmless enough. It put my mind at rest. We chose seats about half-way up the coach and settled ourselves as comfortably as possible into the spiky, blood-coloured, cropped-velvet seats. The coach smelt of petrol. It made me feel a bit sick. We rolled up our coats to use as pillows and sat in complicit silence until the engine started up. We knew we weren't going to discuss anything while there were other people around, we'd just let the whole thing sink in and try to get some sleep. I was surprised that we did sleep, actually. Becka had made a small potion from her magic box which we had downed on empty stomachs (we hadn't eaten all day) and it must have worked big time, because when we woke up it was still dark but we were about an hour from Glasgow.

I never realised how much colder it is in Scotland. I mean, you think of it as the same country and you don't take in just how much further north you are. When we got off the coach the first thing I noticed was the wind and the dampness in the air. It was kind of pleasant spring weather in London. A chill in the air, but nothing too serious. You knew the summer was coming. In Glasgow it was still winter.

'Cast ne'er a clout till May is oot,' said Becka inexplicably.

We pulled on extra jumpers and took stock of the situation. It would soon be dawn.

'I suppose we had better ring,' Becka thought out loud.

'How long has it been?' I asked.

'A year and a bit. I rang them at Christmas the year before last. Actually, I rang them last year at Christmas but there was no reply. They probably went away somewhere warmer.'

It made me wonder, really, how she could just leave her family behind like that. I would have given anything to get my family back again. Anything.

'Don't you love them?' I asked.

'Yes. I do,' Becka replied. She's just pragmatic like that – when she loves someone, she leaves. That's how

Becka copes with love. It's the only way she seems to have coped so far.

We dragged our bags to one of the phones which were dotted around the platform area. There was hardly anyone about yet, even the pigeons seemed still to be asleep. One or two pecked their way lazily around the ground, trying to pick up crumbs left the day before. It almost echoed as we walked. The station was vast and silent. All the shops were closed except the newsagents which was only just opening. A young boy in a blue uniform pushed up the shutters with a creaky rumble which reverberated around the empty station. He set himself to work and started to drag in the piles of parcelled newspapers which had been left bundled outside the shop. Someone else who had been on the bus with us was crossing the walkway, heading for the banks of red iron seats running parallel to the train lines. A couple of policemen crossed the concourse together in the opposite direction.

It took a while for Becka's parents to answer the phone, but when they did it sounded like they would be glad to see us. Becka was laughing down the phone line at them. Eventually she hung up.

'We're to get a cab, which will be underwritten by the Royal Bank of Mum and Dad. They are going to get breakfast ready.'

It was harder to find a cab than we thought. The rank was empty and the streets were deserted, so eventually we went back to the telephones and called one. It took ten minutes to arrive, by which time we had realised just how hungry we were. All the way to the house we were imagining larger and larger breakfasts upon which to feast our freedom. Bacon and eggs and sausages and toast and coffee and orange juice. A culinary delight! Becka's folks lived way out of the centre of town, a long way for a provincial city, but not so far to ride if you were used to the traffic in London. I suppose it took us ten or fifteen minutes through the silent streets. When we got there it was an enormous house built of stone. Mid-Victorian Gothic. Kind of like a miniature castle. There seemed to be streets of those houses. It didn't quite fit with Becka. I think I was expecting something more timid, something she could have escaped from. Like me. I wondered if that was what David Curran thought he had done – escaped from the horrid magnolia house in Drumcondra. I tried hard to remember whether Mrs C had ever mentioned David. I tried to imagine growing up in that house, with four elder brothers. I tried to imagine the politics of the place – the kids at school, what you'd have to do to belong there. Well he'd obviously decided not to belong – he'd left forever rather than be part of it. And the bastards had come to get him. That was the way I imagined it. In the end that's the way it was.

The taxi pulled up at Becka's. The garden was beautiful – there were banks upon banks of daffodils, which were by now out of season in London, but were just coming into flower up north. As we arrived up the gravelly path the dawn was lightening the sky and the air was fresh and dewy. The great, high, wooden front door opened and a plump lady in an enormous, fluffy, white towelling dressing-gown and little pink, flat-heeled slippers ran out into the driveway.

'Becka. Becka,' the woman was shouting.

Becka hurled herself out of the taxi door and flung herself at the woman.

'Mum,' she squealed.

I felt tremendously tearful as I watched them cling to each other.

Becka's father emerged from the doorway. He was a slim, clean-shaven man, wearing a bottle-green track suit. He paid the driver and held out his hand to me.

'I'm Libby,' I said.

'Well, I'm pleased to meet you,' he replied. His

glasses had steamed up because of the coldness of the morning. He flicked them further down his nose and peered over the top. 'Long-sighted,' he said, 'which is normal for my age and occupation. We thought you'd never get here. Come in. Come in.'

Becka still hadn't detached herself from her mother. 'I missed you. I missed you. I missed you,' they were saying to each other.

When we got inside, the house smelt delicious. Becka grabbed me and thrust me at her mother. 'This is Libby. She is my very best friend,' she announced. 'And we're starving.'

'Of course,' said her mother, who hugged me with enthusiasm. She smelt faintly of cleansing cream. 'Come in. It's lovely to meet you. Come in. Everything is ready.' We walked down the long hallway and into a huge kitchen. The table had been set with mugs and wooden boards. But the smell was coming from the glass-doored oven. We could see plates and plates of delicious breakfast – all we had imagined and more. We sat down and Becka's mum fussed. 'Now you must call me Mum, as well, dear. Please do. It's less confusing at my great age.' Becka's mother didn't look much over fifty. 'And you must tell me where you have been. All your adventures.' She set a big pot of coffee down on the table and turned back to the kettle on the sideboard to make a pot of tea as well.

Becka glowed with delight. 'It's so nice to be home again. It is so lovely to see you. Well now, where have I been? Oh, everywhere as usual.'

'Could have sent a postcard,' said her father with a mock gloomy expression on his face.

'But, Daddy, I didn't need any money,' Becka teased him.

The tea arrived on the table and Becka's mum turned herself to the task of getting the hot plates out of the oven. 'Careful now,' she said. 'You girls must be exhausted.'

'No,' I said, 'we slept on the coach. All the way. I did, anyway.'

Becka nodded her agreement. She had already started eating. 'We were just hungry, that's all,' she said as she swallowed. 'And I've wanted to come and see you for a while. And we needed a little holiday, so we decided to come and visit you for a week.'

'Well, it's just as well you did, darling, because Daddy is thinking of moving again,' said Mum.

'Yes. I've been offered a job back in the States again. Don't know if I'll take it this time. Money's tremendous, of course, but I wouldn't want to be so far out of the reach of my wandering daughter. Unless you would like to come and wander in a more hospitable climate.'

Becka shrugged her shoulders. 'I'll think about it. I'm not sure that life in the shadow of the brilliant Professor MacIntosh is for me,' explained Becka.

'I'd so like to have both my babies close by. Especially you, dear. Mothers and daughters. Toby is a pet of course,' said Mum, who was standing at the worktop making toast, 'but he is a boy.'

'Toby is my brother,' explained Becka. 'He still lives at home. Oh, after breakfast you'll meet him.'

The brilliant professor laughed a hearty laugh. 'Quite a bit after breakfast I should think. Usually presents himself about in time for afternoon tea. I'm not here, of course. I'm usually working. But I understand that is when he normally makes it downstairs.' The professor pushed his plate away, got up from the table and poured himself a glass of port at the sideboard. 'Just the thing in this weather,' he said, proffering the bottle towards us. We all shook our heads. He was not deterred. 'Just the thing. Lovely to have you home again, Becka.'

'Our layabout children,' Mum said wistfully from the other side of the kitchen.

'I beg your pardon,' Becka objected loudly. 'Don't lump me in with Toby for God's sake. I'm up and at 'em. Seeking my fortune. Living life to the full.'

Everyone laughed.

'I love them both, you know,' said Mum, finally sitting down at the table and starting on her plate of slowly cooling breakfast. I don't think anything could have been further from the Protestant work ethic which had come to me from my dad. It never occurred to me that I might not go out to work. That anyone wouldn't want to work. Ever. Not just a year off. Not just an interlude of madness. Just never working ever. Unless you wanted a laugh, for a bit of a change.

'Toby still building the rocket?' asked Becka.

'Well, he is building something out in that garage,' said Mum doubtfully. 'It looks like a rocket.'

'I'll be the judge of that,' said the professor. 'Of course, he would never have started on it if it hadn't had such pulling power with the girls. Science,' he mused, 'is very romantic.'

And we all laughed again.

After breakfast Becka took me upstairs to her old room. It was painted a peachy orange colour, which looked cold because of the harsh grey light outside. 'This room,' she said, 'faces south. In the summer it glows. Really. Golden light, you see. God, I had forgotten about it here.' She opened the wardrobe door and brushed the palm of her hand across the clothes still hanging there. 'Student's clothes,' she said.

I was surprised. I hadn't thought she had studied. 'What was your subject?' I asked.

'History. About as far from science as you can get. I drove the professor crazy.'

'It's a beautiful house,' I said.

'Yes. He bought it when we got back from Brussels.

They paid him a fortune there – he made masses and masses of money advising the European Commission. But he wanted to get back to Britain and to research rather than advisory work. He is a giant in the field of enzymes, you know.'

'He's lovely,' I said. 'They both are.'

'They kind of had to come back, anyway,' said Becka. 'I had a little sister, you see. She got meningitis. Annie. She died.'

I reached out and touched her. 'How old were you?' I asked.

'Twelve,' said Becka. 'Annie was eight.'

'We settled down on the enormous bed, and Becka fished around for a bit down the back of it and found a battered old panda. 'This is Giraffe,' she said. 'As you can tell by now, I was, and still am, an incredibly contrary child.'

I realised then why I had taken to her so easily. She had run away too. The difference is that she's running still.

It's not until you're older that you realise how important the things that happened to you when you were a kid are. Even things you can only half remember. Things still held behind a curtain in your memory – like being locked in a cupboard by your brother or scrumping apples over a neighbour's wall. Becka said she'd climbed into bed with her sister just before she died and held her as she slipped away, leaving just the empty shell of a body behind. She hadn't really been in that body for weeks – it was more like she was hovering nearby, already somewhere else, a place where the physical world was of no interest any more. It was as if she had deserted Becka before she died. She had left her twice. And Becka took it to heart. Perhaps it was the last thing that Becka ever took to heart, for no one and nothing else ever got so close again. I didn't know what to say. So I just sat there.

Ten

We ended up having showers and pulling on clean clothes from the stock of outfits in the abandoned cupboard. That meant jeans. All colours. And T-shirts and jumpers and colourful socks. Then we lounged again on the bed, nursing cups of coffee in our hands and watching the rain outside. It had started to rain not long after breakfast was over and now it looked set for the day. Mum was in her element. She was making a pot of soup in the kitchen, and nipped upstairs now and again to look us over. I think she thought that we would disappear at any moment. The professor had gone to work, for which no doubt the biochemical world would be eternally grateful.

'Does he discover things?' I asked.

'All the time,' said Becka. 'I can't believe he hasn't named any of them after me.'

Our adventures in London seemed a million miles away. There was an other-worldly quality about them. As if Lorna McLeish was only a flimsy figment of our imaginations and David Curran a misunderstood and essentially well-meaning kind of guy.

'So,' Becka started, 'tell me all about it. Where you live.'

'Lived. Well, the house is still there. It was all done up. At first I thought I would sell it, but you can't sell the sites of atrocities. It brought down the value of every property in the neighbourhood, you know. Someone told me it was by twenty per cent. Our house isn't worth anything much now. I'd be lucky to get £5,000 for it. Not as posh as here, of course. In immaculate condition too – they restored the whole thing. But who cares? I left Belfast to make my fortune in the big city. To put it all behind me. Ridiculous, isn't it?'

Becka just shook her head.

Then we talked for ages. Mostly about how likely it was that the Currans might be able to find out who we were and come after us. This was proving very unlikely. Becka had given a false name at the employment agency. She had used someone else's name and national insurance number. Someone she had known before and presumably hadn't liked. She said that she hadn't wanted to spoil her unemployment record and that she didn't like it when they could keep tabs on you. 'Once they know that you can type, you've had it. They go on and on about training schemes and God knows what, until you end up having to get a job just to get rid of them,' she said. My name, of course, was the stumbling block. There can't be that many Libertys knocking about and I had told him that I had a bank account at First Caledonian. But it was still under the old address. I could change my name if I had to. We were difficult to trace, then, we decided. David Curran might have a small chance if he was persistent and lucky. The police had no chance at all. Then we started to talk about Lorna McLeish and whether there was anything we could do.

'Well,' I said, 'we can't phone the police. They might trace the call. You've no idea – at home they trace all the confidential phone lines to the RUC, and once somebody knows who you are, or at least where you called from, you aren't safe from either side. There is a free flow of information. Maybe we could write. We could just write a letter, not involving the Currans or any of that stuff, just saying that she is missing. We'll post it somewhere else. Go to Newcastle for the day. Something like that. If they investigate, then the police are going to get hold of David Curran anyway – he was her boss and her lover. They could take it from there.'

Becka looked blank. 'She's probably dead by now. And we haven't done anything,' she said. 'I feel terrible about it.'

I nodded in agreement. 'Yeah. They don't have any reason to keep her alive. Well, none that I can think of. It's just a matter of logistics for them. I'd reckon they killed her that night I spent under the bed. The main thing is that we don't end up dead as well.'

We were interrupted. Outside in the hallway we could hear padding feet. Then manly, gurgling sounds came from the bathroom. Becka sneaked across her room and peeked out of the door. 'I'm going to get him. I am going to get him,' she said.

Poor Toby. As he walked unsuspectingly back down the long hallway, Becka jumped out on him like a banshee, screaming 'It's me! It's me!' at the top of her voice.

Toby screamed. Then he laughed. I could see him through the open doorway, swinging Becka around in his arms. He was a big boy, no doubt about it. Becka dragged him back into the room and introduced him.

'Well, girls,' he said, standing proudly there in shabby boxer shorts and nothing else but the straggly blond hair which came down to his shoulders, 'we had better get going or we are never going to get on the pool table at Old Ma Henry's. It's pay day at the dole club, remember, so the drinks are on me. I'm going to get dressed.' He had a lovely, soft English accent. No class in particular, just gentle.

Becka poked him amiably in the fleshy part of his stomach. 'Go on then, tubby,' she said.

He tripped across the hallway and back into his own room. 'That shouldn't take Toby long. As I remember it, his winter attire consists of a pair of jeans, some biker's boots and a big grey jumper,' said Becka. And do you know, she was spot on about that. The MacIntoshes were certainly a family you could rely on.

Eleven

We embarked on a carefree kind of adventure. To be frank, we didn't know what else to do. We'd gladly have handed the problem over to someone else. But there didn't seem to be anyone else to tell. Except the police, of course. Fat chance.

I rode pillion behind Toby. He had a great, big, metallic-blue, custom-built bike, which I think he must have made himself. Becka rode alone. She had jumped up and down with wild fervour when Toby had presented her with a small red moped from one of the leaky old stables behind the house.

'It's the Salient,' she had squealed with delight. 'Oh Toby you did it up for me.'

'Yeah,' said Toby, with good old-fashioned subservience. 'I knew you'd be a-comin' back, Miss Rebecca.' He threw the keys at her and we saddled up and set off, with Mum waving enthusiastically at us from the front door.

Old Ma Henry's was in Charing Cross, which I suppose is one of the trendier parts of Glasgow. It was an enormous pub, and popular, too. There were bouncers on the door. And it was only Thursday lunch time. It was packed already. Enormous it might have been, and popular it certainly was, but however much money they were making, they weren't ploughing it back into the pub, that was for sure. The walls were bare and the paint had been long stained a cigarette-smoke ochre, the lino-covered floor was worn to thread in places, and the bar itself was ancient and pock-marked. They weren't serving food, but no one seemed to mind that. It was a pub where people came to get drunk, play pool, get laid and meet their friends. Toby got us all bottles of Guinness while we put our names down for one of the pool tables placed at the back of the pub and then settled ourselves into one of the dark-red plastic snug seats banked up all around the walls.

'So what have you been up to, little sister and her friend?' asked Toby.

But before we could reply we were engulfed. Toby was a popular kind of guy. I ended up chatting to some sandy-haired bloke called Derek who was carrying a mobile phone. He said he was carrying it because he was a photographer. I must say, I didn't really get the connection. Anyhow, he placed my accent and that got him on to the subject of Northern Ireland. It never takes people long. He had been over there for a few weeks one time on an assignment for a newspaper. They had been working in Derry and one of his mates had got pulled off the street in the middle of the night and into a pub. The guy had only got out with his life because they realised that he had a Glasgow accent. They had made him name the whole of the Rangers football team before they would let him go. On the same trip to the North, Derek had seen one of his mates getting beaten up in a pub and had gone over to help. Everyone in the pub had told Derek he was mad – he had got punched.

'You don't get involved in fights in the North, do you?' he said.

'Tell me about it,' I enthused. So he did. In fact, I think those were the only words I managed to squeeze in edgeways and after a while I could cheerfully have punched him myself. He talked on and on for ages, during which time Toby, thankfully, liberally supplied us with subsequent bottles of Guinness. It was hot and smoky and after about an hour of Derek I was glad when our number came up on the pool tables. Toby played Becka first of all. It was like a childhood rite. I bet they had done this when they were kids all right. They were both great players and it turned out to be a long game – those scientific genes were coming out on top and they snookered each other all the time. Each shot was carefully lined up and thought about and played and relished.

I got chatting to some skinny bloke called Mike, who was somewhat held in Toby's thrall. 'Great guy, ken,' he said. 'You shouldnae be fooled by the name. Wanker's name, right? But he's a diamond.'

I declined to play pool. I had witnessed the devious devastation which Toby and Becka had sought to bring down upon each other and I knew I wasn't up to it. Becka had won in the end, though, so she got to play Derek.

Toby found us more drinks and sat beside me attentively. He smelt of burnt sugar. 'Let me guess,' he said. 'You two have been in London?'

'How did you know?'

'Your eyes,' he said inexplicably. And then, 'It's cut the edge off your Irish accent, though, hasn't it?'

I smiled. I mean what could I say? I asked him about the rocket, but he wouldn't talk about it.

Mike came over to us. 'This one is Irish, you know,' he said to Toby.

Toby nodded and sipped his stout.

Mike was not to be put off by Toby's silent indifference. 'Crackin' spirit, the Irish,' he said. 'Conquered and rose again. Never gave up. No' like oor peely-wally bastards. No soul left, you knaw. Just tartan troosers an' Burns' Night.'

'That'll be right,' said Toby, but Mike wasn't going to be shut up.

91

'Don't get me wrong. I mean, I know you're English and everything, but you're no' one of them. We will rise again. Scotland the brave. We'll get the money back. It's oor oil. The bastarts.'

Toby quaffed his pint deeply, but Mike wasn't quitting for anything. He was determined to get a rise out of Toby no matter what. 'He's jist so good-lookin', oor Toby. Jist gorgeous. Sends all the girls a-flutter, so he does. The strong and silent type.'

'Yeah, you can call me Apollo,' said Toby drily.

Luckily, just at that point Becka beat the pants off Derek. It didn't take her very long, either. Then Toby judiciously removed us from the pub. We walked up the road to an Indian restaurant. Charing Cross looked like you imagine some districts of New York must look. Old ladies were pulling their trollies along the pavement, nipping in and out of the shops to get their messages. There was a second-hand bookshop on every block and some nice-looking delicatessens and bakeries, with little coffee bars down one side where students were sipping cups of coffee and reading books. We passed a cheese shop where enormous, whole, round cheeses were stacked up along the grey stone walls. The door was wedged open and you could smell the cheese out on the street.

'You guys vegetarians these days?' Toby asked.

We shook our heads.

'Right, then I'll order us a feast.'

'Toby,' said Becka, 'how come you are doing this on the dole?'

'Well, little sister, dole is just my basic,' he replied. 'Hey, what do you think we went to the pub for? I wanted to make some money to take you out, little sis.'

'So, whatcha dealing, big boy?' Becka asked him with an evil glint in her eye.

'Nothing too heavy. Just jellies and dope. That's

about it, these days. Sometimes some E on the week-end. I do it for my family, you know.'

'Yeah. Livens things up for us, doesn't it?'

Toby was as good as his word and he did indeed order a feast of unrivalled splendour. The restaurant was about three blocks from the pub. It was nothing to write home about – just formica tables and pink and green plastic chairs. There was a geometric mural painted over the walls and a big telly mounted up nearly on the ceiling. The waiters knew Toby, though. They greeted him warmly, and an old Indian guy with a white beard came out from the kitchen and took Toby's plump hand in his long-fingered, loose, friendly grasp. Toby ordered lots of plates of curry which arrived with multi-coloured rice and yeasty, yellow naan bread and salad with a yoghurt-and-mint dress-ing. It was delicious. We drank pints of beer which appeared from the back of the shop and were served in clay cups. They evidently didn't have a licence. At the end of the meal it was nearly five o'clock and we sat back with our tummies pleasantly full, and sipped small cups of tea and toyed with delicate honey cakes, which our appetites were too sated even to taste properly.

'I love spicy,' said Toby.

'And creamy and tangy and downright yummy,' I replied sleepily.

It was still raining outside. Toby paid with a discreet little bundle of notes, and when we had taken our leave, we walked back up to the pub. The drops of water were coming fast and furious, and our skins were soaked. A big drip formed on the end of my nose. At least it was waking me up.

'I betchya missed the weather, hey?' said Toby.

'Ah,' replied Becka, 'rains in London too, you know. I'm looking forward to tonight, though. We'll listen to the rain on the windows while we are going to sleep. Always reminds me of home, that.'

There was a queue on the door at Old Ma Henry's, but Toby led us to the front and the bouncers let us go straight in. It was very crushed at the bar and they had started to play some background music. It sounded like Van Morrison. We squeezed ourselves in beside two very inebriated businessmen with pointed beards and shabby suits, who kept trying to catch my eye. One of them winked a long, lecherous wink at me. I ignored it. Toby racked up some shorts of whisky on the bar and we downed a couple each. Then he went off to the toilets and stayed there for about fifteen minutes, which, Becka pointed out, meant he was either dealing or wanking. He returned with a relaxed, big grin on his face in any case.

'We better get home, Mum'll be expecting us back,' he said.

'Oh, God, I hope she hasn't cooked dinner,' exclaimed Becka. Though we all knew that she probably had. We hailed a taxi, abandoning the bikes, because we were way too drunk to drive, and Toby said there was a big police campaign on and we might well get picked up.

If the dinner had been curry, it wouldn't have been so bad. It might have been possible to eat more of the same, but it was fresh fish and chips with a big, crunchy salad. We didn't have the heart to tell Mum that we'd already eaten, so we all just managed as much as we could. The puppy fat around Toby's middle attested to the fact that this probably happened to him quite often. I don't think Mum noticed anything. She was completely taken up with the fact that her babies were both home.

The professor arrived back in the middle of dinner. 'Damn day,' was all he said for the first half-hour, and he poured himself a whisky or two and toyed with his chips. Then suddenly he snapped out of it. 'Well,' he announced, 'home now, I suppose.'

Becka was talking about travelling on snow skis on the ice. 'I thought I might make it to Greenland or Iceland next. I could save up some money and buy some thermals and head off for the snow-spattered north. What do you think?'

It was odd to think of Becka going anywhere without me. I couldn't quite believe that there would be other adventures after this one.

Becka's mum was unperturbed. 'That sounds exciting, dear, you should take a camera with you,' she said. It was the first time I had heard her suggest something which might be construed as constructive.

After dinner we decided to go out for a walk. We needed some fresh air, to clear our food-addled heads. We wandered up the road, arm in arm, Toby lolloping along beside us, playing the fool.

He was humming to himself and every so often he'd burst into a snatch of some song or other – usually a football song. 'My old man said be an Arsenal fan and I said fuck off you bollocks you're a cunt,' he chanted joyously and we laughed. 'Oh it's all gone quiet, all gone quiet, all gone quiet over there,' he continued and then shouted, 'Better than nursery rhymes. Better by far.'

We got to the junction with the main road and Toby hailed a cab. Then he kissed us each lightly, sang 'Good-night, sweet ladies, good-night' and was gone.

'He'll come back with the bikes, I betcha,' said Becka. 'You just see if he doesn't.'

We carried on walking around the streets for a while. Becka said she had forgotten the greenness of her suburban home. 'It's so lush here,' she mused, 'maybe while you are up we should go north a bit and see the lie of the land up there. It's still the most beautiful place I have ever been.'

I nodded in agreement, but I knew somehow that we would never make it. It was a time to be comfortable. We still hadn't decided whether to risk our arses and report Lorna McLeish missing. We perched on a park bench under the shelter of some trees which ran along the boreen and we stared at the rain as it fell in white bullets past the street lamps all around us.

'My God,' I said, throwing my head back over the back of the bench and luxuriating in the leafy darkness, 'I envy you this.' Becka didn't reply. I don't think she noticed that I was crying, because I kind of knew there wasn't an easy way out of this one. I suppose I already knew we'd end up back in Ireland, but I didn't want to go. Sometimes, though, you have to go backwards to make real progress. And that's just the way of things.

Twelve

The next day we both woke up with an appalling head cold. Mum brought us up hot lemon and honey and a tray with toast and scrambled eggs, and she sat with us for a while. The professor was at work again. 'I'll go and ring your father at the office and let him know that you are unwell,' she said. I felt duly adopted.

'Oh God,' said Becka, 'he'll recommend some awful cure for a head cold and she'll make us take it.' She disappeared under the covers.

In the end, though, Mum came back and reported that he didn't recommend anything; then, on a short reconnaissance mission which we performed on the way to the bathroom, we ascertained that Toby had not come home the night before and that took over our attention.

'Does that all the time,' said Mum. 'Well, I can't be hanging about looking after you two. No. I'm going out today, to see one of my friends.'

She called out her goodbyes from the bottom of the stairs a few minutes later, and then the door slammed and the house fell beautifully silent.

'Well, looks like we are housebound,' said Becka after a while. 'My vote goes for TV, Kleenex and hot drinks after a very slow reveille.'

It was still raining buckets. Murky puddles, like tiny lagoons, had appeared all over the lawn outside the window and the once clean and bright daffodils were now battered by the incessant rainfall and spattered with mud. It showed no signs of letting up. The sky was a smooth, even, evil grey colour which loomed ominously over the city, hovering there, too low. Glasgow brought new meaning to the word 'overcast'. I turned back towards Becka and squirmed around under the covers until I was completely comfortable, then we turned ourselves to what was really on our minds – Lorna McLeish.

Becka spoke first. 'I have to do something,' she said. 'I can't just abandon her. It's not right. I just don't know what to do, though. And I've been negligent. It's been two whole days since we left London.'

I sipped thoughtfully from my mug. 'Yeah,' I said. 'We've been wallowing. It's just that I don't know exactly what we can do. Safely.'

That was the thing. Normal people would have gone to the police. That's what you are supposed to do. But the police can't protect you. I was living proof of that. And if we tipped them off, the very information would mean that the Currans might come looking for us. We were more than likely their only lead. Maybe they would find us and maybe not, but who was willing to take a chance like that? We were truly snookered. For me, it wasn't just Lorna McLeish either, it was Ma and Dad too. I was carrying them with me and it was a heavy weight. A decision was difficult, so we let it float on, waiting for something to happen. Waiting for a sign, or at the very least, a distraction.

Right on cue we heard the front door slam. It was eleven o'clock. We could hear Toby's big-footed lollop along the downstairs hallway.

'Looks like he got his rocket off, then,' Becka whispered to me. 'Betcha he tells us all about it.'

'What,' I joked, 'do you think he made it to the moon, or only to heaven?'

We giggled and he probably heard us. There was a short pause and then Toby ran up the stairs and finally peered cheerfully round the bedroom door.

'Tart,' said Becka.

'Layabout,' he replied with the air of a totally satisfied man about him.

'We are extremely sick, I'll have you know. Sick in an entirely different way from you, that is. So, then, tell us all about your nocturnal adventures.'

'Just some tart. A nice tart. Well. I had to do something to work off all that dinner. I'll make you something hot, then I'm going to work in the garage today. On my rocket.'

'So that's what it's all about,' said Becka, who was apparently now satisfied that the rocket was no more than post-coital relaxation.

Toby beamed.

Becka must have had an inkling then that we were going to leave. She was certainly one for arranging ample resources. Ever since I knew her. She eyed Toby as if he were prey. 'So, brother, exactly how much money do you make? Net profit,' she wanted to know.

'Depends,' he hedged. 'Some weeks I just stay at home. Other weeks I work my tidy little butt off. It just depends.'

'Cut the crap,' Becka snapped, 'and empty your pockets.'

Toby loved it. You could just see Becka as the bossy little four-year-old and Toby as the mischievous, but adoring, seven-year-old schoolboy. She must have run rings around him. Slowly he turned out his pockets. There was £200 or so, two condoms in a black-and-red box with 'AROUSER' printed all over it, some keys and a few sweets. Toby had evidently splashed out on a more expensive kind of condom.

'Did you buy a three-pack or what?' Becka demanded.

'Two three-packs,' he replied proudly. 'I am a love machine, baby.'

After Becka had satisfied herself that quizzing Toby further would yield nothing more of interest, he disappeared into his room to get changed into his rocket-building gear, which, when he emerged, turned out to be an orange boiler suit and greasy trainers. He lolloped happily downstairs and slammed the back door behind him. Becka waited for a moment, then she opened the window and leaned out. All we could hear coming from the vicinity of the garage in which the rocket was housed was the pulsing 'nying nying' noise of an automatic screwdriver working away for all its batteries were worth.

'We probably won't see him again for hours,' said Becka, closing the window. 'He used to be like this with cars. Well, at first it was stuff in the house, like the hoover and the washing machine. Mum never knew what was going to happen next. After Annie died, you know, he built this enormous ferris wheel out of Meccano. He wanted to put it on her grave. They wouldn't let him, of course. And anyway, now it is this rocket. I betcha it's a great rocket, though, because Toby has got better over the years and now he is only hot shit with machinery. I wonder if we could get him to name it after me? And you too, of course,' Becka added as an afterthought. 'The Good Ship Rebecca Liberty.'

I took a deep, long breath. Then we settled back down into a kind of silence, where we were both thinking like crazy about how we could possibly manage to clear our consciences of Lorna McLeish's cadaver and just get on with what we wanted to get on with.

'We could just let the bitch rot,' suggested Becka.

'Yeah,' I said unenthusiastically, 'I suppose we could.'

We weren't coming up with solutions.

Becka traipsed off to have a shower. She could take forever in the shower. I'm not entirely sure what she did in there – it doesn't take long to wash one medium-sized girl from top to bottom. She didn't sing or talk to herself or anything like that. She just stayed in there forever. I lay in bed and I knew that I had time on my hands. She would be fifteen minutes at the very least. I was in the process of making a big decision. I was deciding to go back to Belfast but I was hellish nervous about it. The Lorna McLeish thing was kind of showing me the light – you have to deal with things when they come your way and my instinct was telling me to go back to the Province. But I didn't want to. I suppose I was nervous because it made me so afraid – if I thought about it for long my hands shook, my toes twitched and my heart sank. I felt as if something was waiting for me there. Of course there was something. There was the house. There were the ghosts. I lay in bed, deeply distracted by my own feelings, and I nervously fingered Ma's ring, which still hung like a millstone around my neck. I didn't want to make the decision, you see. I'd have done anything to have the decision taken off my hands, so I made up my mind to call the shrink.

I got out of bed, crept into the professor's bedroom across the hallway and sat on the murky, camel-coloured carpet beside the dressing-table, looping the bottom of my pyjama trousers around my feet. I gingerly picked up the telephone. Directory Enquiries gave me a number and I dialled it and asked the efficient-sounding lady at the other end for Lloyd Baker. When he had said his goodbyes to me in the lobby of the hotel all those months ago he had said I could always ring him if I needed any help, or if I just wanted to talk. I wondered to myself if I should have taken the help when it was on offer. Maybe I was sick in the head. I would have expected more of myself than the disarray of purpose taking me over. With my background, hell, I should have been able to cope with one missing Bank Manager (presumed dead) and some poxy terrorists. I was hoping he'd take it all away for me.

Lloyd Baker didn't remember me at first. I suppose it must be hard for someone whose job it is to be a professional friend to remember all those passing faces who confide their deepest secrets. Somehow, I thought he must have remembered me. Well, he did. But only after prompting.

'Ah yes,' he said. 'Libby Lucas. Yes. What can I do for you?'

I pictured him drawing a finger over his clean-shaved, chiselled chin, as he listened.

'I'm lost,' I said simply. 'It's my parents. I don't think I'll ever forget them.'

'I don't think that you are required to forget them, Libby. I think you have to let go of them.'

'I have let go of them. They're dead. You can't hang on to the dead. But I'm so angry.'

'You should come in to see me,' he said. 'We can talk around the notion of forgiveness. You need some therapy, Libby. You are ready for it now.'

'I can't. I'm not in London. I'll be back in a couple of weeks,' I said.

'Come to see me then. Call the office when you get back. Don't beat yourself up about it. You are bound to be hurt.'

'I'm not just hurt, Doctor. It's not just that. If I saw it happening again, I don't think I could stop it. I feel powerless. I need to work it out. I just feel powerless. I'm so afraid.' I thought of that night I had spent, paralysed with fear, under David's saggy-bottomed bed. I thought of myself now, in Glasgow, with Lorna McLeish's murder on my hands.

'Forgiveness is the key. Believe me. Forgiveness,' he repeated again. 'I can give you a lot of time when you get back. You have to pack it up, forgive the people who did what they did and get on with your own life. How are things going, Libby?' My name didn't roll easily from him. He had been taught to use the first names of patients to make them feel at ease. He shouldn't have said it.

'I got a new job. I'll be starting in three weeks or so. That's not a problem. It's in my heart. That's where the difficulty is.'

'Forgiveness,' Lloyd said again. I got the feeling he might be reading something and not giving me his full attention. 'Don't worry,' he added. 'It's normal. You are perfectly normal.'

I hung up and lay on the floor staring at the ceiling in despair. Forgiveness was too civilised for me. Forgiveness wasn't powerful enough.

I pulled out the phone book from the bedside table and flicked through it. I looked at the long list of McLeishes in Glasgow. We didn't even know if she was from Glasgow or not. I closed the book and put it back, gently knocking my head on the top of the table.

'Shit. Shit. Shit. Shit.'

It was useless. I decided to go back to bed for a bit, so I slouched miserably across the hallway and fell on to the mattress. Becka came out of the shower much improved. She sat happily at the dressing-table and daubed her face with cotton wool and witch-hazel. 'I feel much better,' she announced.

'Maybe I should have a shower too,' I tried.

'No way,' she insisted. 'I think you are getting a bit wound up. I'm going to give you a massage.'

'Oh, that'll do the trick,' I replied sarcastically, pulling the covers up to my chin and curling myself into a warm little ball. 'We have to decide to do something. We have to decide now,' I said.

Becka wasn't listening. 'Massage is strong magic, you know. Really strong,'she said, bouncing her way over to the bed and diving under the cover. 'You'll see. Mum taught me. She gives Dad massages. It's how she retains control.'

I gave in to her. She laid me out on top of the bed and I complied. I was expecting her to mix up a magic potion from different kinds of oils so that the whole room would be tinged with the floweriness of it, like living in a great floral cloud. I was expecting a gentle, recreational kind of massage, after which I would feel loose and relaxed, and we would be able to have something to eat. We'd be able to talk. Becka opened up her box and took out a candle, a plain white one, which she lit and stood on the bedside table on a saucer. She told me to take my clothes off, then she composed herself, laying her cool palms on different places, feeling for the heat. One time she told me that the heat was where the anger was. It was like she was acclimatising herself to my body. Once she had mapped me out, she rubbed her palms with plain cooking oil, before laying her hands on for real. She didn't take them off again for nearly an hour. I just lay there with my eyes closed, or sometimes open and watching the flickering and guttering flame of the candle, while Becka's calm fingers worked their way all over my body. When I had my eyes closed I saw tremendous visions: not as vivid as real pictures – more ephemeral, like ghosts who sprang up before my eyes and then floated off. I saw my parents, I saw Lloyd Baker. I saw David Curran and I wanted to hit him hard in the face. There was one lump in my back, and I kept my eyes open the whole time Becka was working on it, because I was afraid to close my eyes and see what was there. I started to cry, not delicate little ladylike gasps, but great, heaving, sorrowful sobs. I couldn't stop. Becka said nothing. It was my voyage of discovery.

After the massage I sat up on the bed with my head lolling around my shoulders, in shock. Becka passed me a box of tissues so that I could dry my tear-sodden cheeks. She crouched at the foot of the bed and watched me like a dog watches its master. I caught sight of myself in the mirror on the other side of the room. I looked serene. We stayed there in silence for some time, until Becka got up and announced that she was going to make a pot of tea and bring it up on a tray. I stared out of the window into the rainy April storm which was raging around us and I not only knew that Lloyd Baker wasn't going to be any help, but I accepted it too. I didn't even want his help any more. Forgiveness be damned. I was going home.

Becka arrived back upstairs with a civilised-enough looking tray, with cups and saucers rather than mugs and a delicate, fine pot of Earl Grey tea. She slowly poured it out for us, as if she was measuring her energies, and then sat cross-legged beside me. 'So,' she asked, 'did you find your voice?'

I nodded. 'Thanks. You're a miracle.'

Becka leaned over and blew out the candle. 'Good,' she said. 'I'm glad.'

I was completely calm and composed. I had seen the light and I knew that no one was going to take anything off our hands. I think that's where people go wrong, you see. We could have fallen easily into that trap. We wanted to relinquish the responsibility and that's only natural. That's what I'd done in Belfast after all. I'd left it all behind. But you can't get away with that. The past hangs over you if you do – then it's always with you, waiting to be resolved. I stared at myself in the mirror and realised it was time to reckon with it; it was time for me to go back and sort things out. I'd have no kind of a future if I didn't.

'I think we had best get Toby to underwrite a trip to Belfast,' I said. 'I think I ought to take you home in order to figure this one out. This family thing is too surreal. Do you think he will give us the money?'

Becka smiled. 'Good call,' she said. 'We'll go as soon as we're better.'

And we shook on that. At the time I was kind of surprised that she wanted to come. If she had refused – well, I would have gone alone if I'd had to. But Becka just agreed. I think now that she would have jumped at any excuse to leave – she would never have been able to shoulder more than a few days at home, you see. She had to get out of there.

Thirteen

The last day we spent in Glasgow, we just hung out in the house and packed and did our nails, and that night we feasted on Mum's best recipe, which she called her 'Marry Me Salmon'. In her heyday, whenever she had cooked it for someone they had apparently asked to marry her. You could see why. It was delicious. Big chunks of salmon with asparagus wrapped around them, and then layers of pastry all around that. Mum made a dill and lemon sauce which made you beg for more. It was the first thing we had eaten all day. We had spent all afternoon in a daze, staring out of the window at the rain, and talking only now and then in words which would have seemed abstract to anyone else. The phone kept ringing but we hadn't even dreamt of answering it. About six o'clock Mum had come home without the professor, who had gone to a Faculty meeting. We had sat awaiting him with familiar jocularity, sipping our drinks around the kitchen table, until around seven, when Toby and the professor had arrived and cracked open a big bottle of bubbly.

'My "Marry Me" dish,' Toby announced, 'is my Banana Curry.'

'That,' the professor replied, between mouthfuls of the Salmon Divine, 'is not a "Marry Me" dish, it's a lottery. A "Marry Me" dish has to be one hundred per cent reliable.'

Then the phone went and Mum answered it. It was a girl called Monica, for Toby. 'She's a fool if she lets herself fall for the Banana Curry. Even if she had it on a good day,' she observed.

Toby returned to the table after the call, looking annoyed. 'You were in all afternoon, weren't you?' he asked Becka.

'Yeah,' said Becka, 'but we didn't answer the phone.'

'I'm never going to get rid of this bird,' Toby wailed. 'She's fallen for me hook, line and sinker.'

'Now, now, dear,' said Mum. 'Don't be so silly.'

Thinking back on it, the phone had rung at least ten times. If Monica was young, free and single, then Toby was in trouble. You have to have lost all your shame to ring more than three times of an afternoon.

After dinner we all lazed in front of the television and watched the nine o'clock news. There was no news from Ulster. Mum said that she found this reassuring, given our up and coming trip over the water. I didn't say anything. I didn't want to worry her. The marching season was just starting and that always meant trouble. Even the ceasefire wouldn't be able to stop that kind of trouble – men in bowler hats and orange sashes marching through Catholic areas of town all over the Province. It was kind of offensive and there were always fights about it. Especially in Belfast, which was a particular hot spot. The Orange March goes over the bridge into part of the city which used to be Protestant, but over the years has changed and is now Catholic. The marchers always say that they won't change the route because it is part of their history. The Catholics always say the march should be banned. If you're from Belfast, the Orange March always goes off like an alarm clock inside you. Every Easter right through to the end of the summer. I remember seeing this comedian one time who had a whole routine about the Orange Marches and what to do with your hands while you were watching one. I mean, do you clap? Do you clasp your hands behind your back? What causes the least offence? In the end he reckoned that it was best nonchalantly to hold a can of something fizzy. Fanta preferably. After all, it's orange. More people got beaten up in those few months – April till August – than all the rest of the year. It was a real high spot for wilful political violence. Nothing much on the news, though. Nothing reported. They probably did that because there was a ceasefire.

Fourteen

Toby said he would drive us to the ferry terminal at Stranraer. The professor and Mum turned out at the front door to wave us off on Saturday morning with packed sandwiches and a big bag full of clean clothes. They were in a good mood, facing the prospect of the weekend together.

The professor had a friend who was a lecturer at Queen's. He said he would ring and say that we might be in touch. 'No need to be shy,' he said. 'They will have you to stay if you need somewhere. They'll look after you. It's Professor Jackson. Professor Jackson. Physiology.'

Becka gave her father a knowing, I-can-look-after-myself stare. We promised to return soon. We reckoned it would only take us three days or so.

Becka had never been to Belfast before. This cease-fire was on like I said, and there was the most talk in years about making a lasting peace. The Westminster Conservatives had said that they wanted to have real negotiations to try to end the conflict. People were quietly hopeful. A lot of the military operations in the city had been, apparently, scaled down. They had taken down a lot of the barricades and the RUC had stopped patrolling the city in those scary green flak jackets. The number of road-blocks had been halved. There had been shootings, of course. Some guy who had tried to steal a car on the Shankhill Road had been winged by an over-enthusiastic RUC officer who was shooting to puncture, but missed. The IRA and UVF and all the others were battling it out for control of the drugs market. But there had been no bombs. So all in all, Belfast was in as relaxed a mood as the city could be during the marching season.

The crossing wasn't as rough as we had thought it was going to be. It might have been eternally windy and rainy in Glasgow, but we drove out of the bad weather and in Stranraer it was still enough and freezing cold, but fresh.

Toby took us to a roadside café and bought us great steaming mugs of tea and squidgy jam doughnuts. He gave Becka an envelope with a healthy sheaf of banknotes in it. 'You can bring back the change, you know,' he said, biting into his doughnut and firing a squirt of deep-red jam straight into his own mug.

'Yuk,' we all said together.

Toby stirred his tea thoughtfully, trying to incorporate the jam. He had put so much sugar in there, I supposed that jam might add a certain piquancy.

Becka discreetly ruffled the notes inside the envelope, as if she was counting them. 'Thanks, Toby. You're tremendous,' she said and gave him an enormous engulfing hug which made him spill his tea over the formica tabletop.

'Typical,' said Toby, with affected poor humour. 'You try to help someone and they knock over your tea.'

After another half-hour's drive we made it to the ferry terminal. It was a grey, grim, service-station kind of affair. We told Toby he could go back if he wanted to, but he didn't drive off until he was sure that we had bought tickets and that the Seacat would be sailing on time. We waved him away fondly. The boat was full of students who were returning to their college digs. I suppose that it would shortly be the beginning of the summer term. They played the slot machines and drank interminable hot chocolates to wash down plates of chips and steak-and-kidney pies. A group of lads took to the bar immediately and seemed to down a huge quantity of beer during the short crossing. They became more and more rowdy. The Seacat is the quickest way to get across the water – they must have been going some to get that drunk in an hour and a bit.

Becka and I sat by the floor-to-ceiling windows, on comfy velour seats. I was scared. My hands were shaking in fitful trepidation. But I was excited too. I wanted to get back to the house – just to live in it, see it again, if only for a couple of days. I had two copies of the keys – one which I had tied on a string around my neck the day before and the other, just in case, in a small pouch among my things. I was thinking about how the memory of home had faded. I couldn't remember the smell of the house – the smell of the way Ma cooked, or the musty, welcoming smell which pervaded the house when she wasn't cooking. I knew the smells had been there. I knew I would recognise them if I smelt them again, but I couldn't summon them up from my olfactory memory. I tried as hard as I could to remember other things – the colours of the rooms which I had chosen half-heartedly when the house had been rebuilt after the blast. The goods I had chosen for the kitchen. At first, I had planned to stay there. I didn't expect to leave. I could have had the cash otherwise. But even if I had known that I was going to go to London, I don't think I would have been able to take the money. I still would have rebuilt the place as a shrine to the family I had lost for ever. A house you could pray to and light candles in front of. A house which I kept because I wanted to hold on to something of them.

Becka stared soulfully out to sea, trying to catch a

first glimpse of the Irish mainland. She was really excited. She jumped up, pressing her nose to the glass at the first sight of land, and stayed there until we docked. The returning students collected their baggage and shuffled towards the exits and we followed them. There were Customs officials everywhere, but they let us through. I suppose we looked like students too. We caught a taxi at the ferry terminal, which was about fifteen minutes from the house. I had forgotten the ragged Belfast skyline, punctuated only by the dirty yellow cranes which towered over even the highest buildings. I had forgotten the grey of the city, which was unrelenting. It is the only city I have ever been in which is grey although the houses are often built from bricks. Belfast is even grey in the summertime. And the flags were out for the marching season. There was red, white and blue bunting strung up all over the place, and red, white and blue flowers on sale in the florists' shops and little grocery stores. The edges of the pavements were painted, though they already looked a bit muddy from being painted over and over with different colours. During the marching season gangs of small boys compete over the kerbside – it is the earliest sectarian game they play. Protestant kids paint red, white and blue; Catholic kids paint green, white and gold. And the streets on the edge of areas are fair game. They go out at night to paint and repaint their own colours on kerbsides of dubious political persuasion. Catholics learn young to scare the Protestants. Vice versa too, I suppose. And it was there in me as well. On the Ormeau Road we passed a freshly burnt-out car. I sighed to myself, genuinely down-hearted, because, you know, everything was the same as when I had left it.

Then I turned to Becka. 'Why did you agree to come?' I asked.

She shrugged her shoulders. 'I guess I must like you,' she said.

Fifteen

It's not that I expected the neighbours to be delighted to see me again. I just hadn't considered them much. Our arrival at Angel Avenue (for that was where I lived) was greeted by a frantic spate of curtain twitching. We walked up the little path and I delved into my shirt for the key. The house was stony silent and very cold. All the utilities had been switched off and the letter-box, ironically, was taped shut. It was like a show house. We walked into the little hallway and dropped our bags to the floor.

'Freezing in here,' said Becka.

I just nodded and pushed open the door of the living-room. I had evidently chosen mint green for the walls. There was a new suite which still had shop covers on it, and labels dangling from the side. The place smelt cold and new and still. It was spooky. Becka tried to turn on the lights, to no avail, so we walked on through to the kitchen like spectral shadows cast by the eerie cold light filtering through the plain chiffon curtains. The strange thing was that there wasn't even any dust anywhere. Nothing had entered the house. It was perfect. I sat down at the kitchen table and stared wide-eyed around me.

Becka followed suit. 'Well, here we are,' she said.

'Wow,' was all I could reply. I didn't feel unduly sentimental about it. This wasn't the house in which

Ma and Dad had brought me up. It was just a building of a similar type on the same spot. This was now an alien place. There was nothing in this house to tell any tales of who had lived here. No books, no music, no paintings, no clothes. Just shop-bought goods, chosen in a hurry to spend the money. I got up and walked around the house, as if I was being reeled around on a thread.

I was amazed by my own lack of emotion. It wasn't that I felt numb – I just felt nothing. This house, my home, had become an anonymous place. Except for one thing. In the room which had been my bedroom I had left a photograph of my parents. I had taken it one autumn when we had driven to Donegal for a long weekend. It was just before I had gone to Queen's. They hadn't noticed me with the camera as they sat on an old rug, laying out the picnic we had brought with us for lunch. The photograph glowed with the golden autumnal landscape and the light reflected in my parents' faces by the low and yellow September sun. The summer weather had continued up until October that year, and we had spent every free moment of the summer months outside in the good weather. Their faces were tanned and younger than I remembered them, although the picture was taken only just over three years before they died. I didn't remember them like they were in that picture, captured in one hundredth of a second: a time you would never normally notice, or even register. But there they were, captured and still, for ever. As if they had been tamed. When I remembered them I always thought of them as ani- mated people – the sound of my mother moving around the house, setting down vases of flowers, chopping at the old sideboard in the kitchen or engrossed in marking copy books in her chair beside the front window, her red pen darting over the pages and a smile playing on her lips at the mistakes the

116

children had made. I remembered my father carefully folding his jumpers and putting them into his wardrobe, or sitting at the kitchen table, fiddling with a screwdriver at something which had broken down and needed to be fixed. The people in the photograph weren't my parents – they were only a representation of them. An image, like the ghosts they now are, and I felt sad because it wasn't our house any more and there was no way I could touch them or feel part of them again. They were not the people who were alive any more, no, they were gone and my memory was changing them already. I had to change them so that they could still be part of my life – I had to bring them with me.

So, I was gazing, rapt, at that photograph on the wall and the next thing I knew there was a knocking on the front door. It was as if I awoke too suddenly. I had to shake myself to remember where I was and it took a few seconds to adjust back to the cold April light, filtering into the house like an opaque ghost. I blinked hard. Then I went to answer the door.

Mr McCaffrey stood on the doorstep with a sheaf of letters in his hands and an embarrassed but eager sparkle in his old brown eyes. He and his wife lived in the house opposite. 'Libby,' he said, handing me the letters and staring at me for clues, 'I took these in for you. A long time since. They taped up the box. But I kept them for you.'

'Thanks, Mr McCaffrey,' I said.

'We kept an eye on the house. A house empty that long is a target,' he said with the eagerness of a star pupil who doesn't have any friends.

I thought to myself that the house had been more of a target when there were people in it. I suppose he meant the contents, but I doubted that anyone would have taken anything. Therein lies the stuff of reprisals. No ordinary, decent criminal would have been caught near the site of an atrocity. 'Thanks,' I said again.

'Back for long?' Mr McCaffrey squinted into the darkened hallway. 'If you need any help switching on the water. Anything like that. I'd be glad to.'

'I think we'll be OK. Just came back for a short visit.'

'So, where are you staying now?'

'Manchester,' I lied inexplicably. 'I'm working for a bank there.'

Mr McCaffrey looked suitably impressed.

'Thanks very much,' I repeated helplessly. 'Thanks for looking after things.'

Out of the corner of my eye I caught sight of a bus wheeling into the Avenue from the main road. Buses never went down our street. It slowly chugged its way down the road, coming to a semi halt outside the house; then, as the driver saw us standing at the doorway, he moved on.

'Tour bus,' said Mr McCaffrey with lips so tight I thought that they might burst. 'Tuesdays, Thursdays, Saturdays and Sundays.'

'Touring what?' I asked blankly.

'The Troubles of course,' he replied briskly and turned back to his own house. I thought I heard him mumble 'Peace. I'll give them bloody peace' to himself as he was going down the path. It must have been hard for him right enough, being part of a living-history project four times a week.

'Oh, my God,' I said, half horrified and half laughing. 'Oh, my God.'

As soon as I closed the front door Becka wheeled around from her hiding place just behind the opening of the living-room. 'So, Miss Manchester of the year, shall we go for the ride? The Balaclava Boys' Tour,' she teased.

'Oh yeah,' I said. 'We have got to. Tomorrow. Sunday. The day of rest.'

We explored the rest of the house and made up the beds, removing the linen from the cellophane wrappers in which it had arrived from the shop. I thought the house was getting warmer, or perhaps I was just getting acclimatised. It was April after all. The cruellest month. But not the coldest. We found some candles and matches under the sink and laid them out ready for the darkness when it came. Then we decided to go out and buy something to eat. It was well after lunchtime. We walked up to the main road and took our bearings, then caught the first bus heading into town and made for Lavery's. I could see the changes in the city now that we were going to the heart of it. We didn't pass one soldier on our way. No road-blocks either. Saturday shoppers crowded the streets. It looked like a prosperous place.

We got off the bus and I pulled Becka in the right direction. I was surprised by the little coffee shops which seemed to have sprung up. People had invested in this ceasefire. Belfast was becoming almost cosmopolitan. It still hadn't become a city of pubs, though. There are really only three city-wide pubs in Belfast, that you would travel to go to – the rest are just locals. Lavery's was near enough the Holy Lands, which was where all the students lived, to let people walk home. But it also attracted young, working Belfast people. It was a great pick-up joint. Not that we were looking for that kind of excitement from the pub that afternoon. Lavery's served us up steaming Irish stew and pints of shandy, which we scoffed down eagerly, watching the news on the big, wall-mounted televisions as much as we were watching the game of darts going on on the other side of the bar. I reminisced to myself about the times I had spent in there as a student. There was a time when I could have come into the bar and sat at any one of a dozen tables. The pub had been full of 'how's about ye?' and 'how's it going?' and smiles and small talk.

I remembered one night when I had been sitting there with some friends from Queen's and we heard a bomb go off a couple of streets away. The whole pub had fallen silent, in a mutually depressed, down-hearted kind of way. Like a child at the top of the stairs, who has heard its parents having an argument in the living-room below. Someone on the other side of the bar had just said 'Damn'. And then, slowly, the talking had resumed, but instead of a babbling clatter it was more of a mumble. A bass tone of its former self. A couple of minutes later someone had come in the door of the pub and had slammed it hard behind him. It had made a resounding crash. People had jumped from their chairs. There was an instant of clear terror, then relief and everyone had laughed. It could have been us, but it wasn't.

'We could put our names up for darts,' said Becka. I nodded. 'Sure,' I said. I quite liked darts.

Then, as we cleared the last stewy smears from our plates, Becka tugged at my sleeve and pointed at the screen. It was on the news. They had found Lorna McLeish's body somewhere in Herefordshire and were appealing for information, and they thought it was a sexual killing. We gaped, disbelieving, then we called a cab and went back to Angel Avenue.

Sixteen

I slept all night. Soundly. It was as if a great weight had been lifted. We didn't have to tell anyone that she was missing. They knew. The next morning we got up early. Becka was worried, though. She'd been out for the morning papers. She came into my bedroom at half past eight and crawled into bed beside me, slapping them down on the bedclothes. Lorna McLeish had hit the headlines big time. There were pictures of her – mostly a head-and-shoulders shot of her in a navy suit. It must have come from the bank. The Currans had stabbed her and she had bled to death. The paper said it was a frenzied attack and she had been mutilated after she died. They didn't say how, but I knew. It had to seem sexual – that was what they wanted everyone to believe. Afterwards they had weighted her down and dumped her body in the River Wye. But she had been washed up on a sandbank and found by some campers who were following the nature trail through the Forest of Dean. I made an effort to concentrate on the facts. I tried not to think of her screaming as she bled to death. The news report went into detail about her family, her education and her job. Turned out she was from a small town called Haddington, somewhere near Edinburgh. Seemed she was an overachiever. They wanted to speak to anyone who had seen her, anyone who knew anything at all.

Becka laid the paper down on the bed and stared blankly at the photograph. 'We should tell them about the Currans,' she said very definitely.

'They will find David anyway. They might figure it out for themselves,' I replied.

'We should tell them,' she repeated.

I lay back on the pillows and stared furiously at the ceiling. 'Wait till you've been on the Terror Tour today before you tell me that you want to inform on the IRA,' I said. I suppose the intolerance must have shown in my voice.

'We should do the right thing no matter what,' said Becka.

'I already did the right thing and they murdered my parents,' I replied. 'Do you want to risk it?'

'We'd be risking us, no one else. Just us. There has to be a way we can do it.'

'I don't know. Maybe there is,' I conceded, 'but I don't know what it is.'

'They are terrorists. We are protecting them. It only hit home when I saw it on the news, you know. That's when I realised. We are protecting them.'

'No,' I said, with the wisdom born of experiencing survival, 'we are protecting ourselves. Besides, trouble like that and they will be long gone. Take it from me. These guys move around. They do their stint, then they leave. Anything goes wrong like that and they pull out.' This was the kind of well-known fact which had circulated as rumour when I was a kid. It was one of those things that you just knew.

The bus left from City Hall at one that afternoon and we were on it. We had walked the long way into town, passing Ian Paisley's church on our travels, where there were queues outside for the Sunday service. The congregation were real hard-liners – mostly ladies in ugly hats – and they had stared at us as we passed on the other side of the street. We had stared right back at them in insolent silence and continued into town. Then we had eaten a small early lunch at one of the new coffee shops which we had found open. Coffee shops open in Belfast on a Sunday were a strange sight indeed. The flower shops did a roaring trade. People went to visit their dead on a Sunday, but the demand was almost non-existent for pubs and coffee shops and off-licences. Most of those places usually closed. You never felt that you were missing much in Belfast if you had to stay in of a Sunday.

'We are only trying this. To assess the demand,' the girl behind the counter had told us, with her definite Belfast accent. 'I don't think we'll be keeping it up, you know.'

She was probably right. The place was empty.

After lunch we made for the bus. There were quite a few people taking the Northern Irish Tourist Board's Tour of the Troubles. There was a group of students and some couples who were presumably visiting the city. I noted that no one was local – the accents were English mostly. We paid our money and we took our seats. A cheerful lady from the Northern Irish Tourist Board was welcoming us all. She told us her name, though I can't remember it now, and she was wearing a green linen uniform with a kind of peachy orange scarf, which we thought was quite diplomatic since wearing the colours of one side, without the colours of the other, might have made her a potential target, given her high profile. She was also wearing more lipstick than I have ever seen anyone manage to keep on before – it didn't so much as smudge during the hour and a half we were with her. The Tourist Board had been prudent, she explained, they were an unbiased body and she was about to take us on a tour which would show us the main sites of the Troubles, with equal emphasis placed on the dreadful atrocities committed by both sides. She wanted to assure us that although many of the awful things which she was going to tell us about had happened in the very recent past, there was a ceasefire currently in operation and there was real hope in both communities that this ceasefire would, in time, provide a lasting peace in the North. She had the disquieting habit of pausing and smiling after statements like these, of which there were many. The Northern Irish Tourist Board obviously wanted to get the tone just right. She read everything she said word for word from a file which she held open in front of her. At the end of each paragraph she looked up and smiled the big-toothy, lip-glossy smile. I stared at her as she spoke. Her teeth looked fluorescent against the shiny lipstick. Her lips moved like slithering, shiny, pink eels. There is a magazine in the North called the *Ulster Tatler* and she looked just like the overdressed ladies in that. She would have loved to have been photographed at a fund-raising do for wounded policemen. All she needed was a man with a dinner-jacket and she would have been away.

As we drove off, the commentary started. She paced herself as she launched into a paragraph or two about Bloody Sunday and the riots – background for what was to come. We started off the tour proper on the Falls Road, then up the Shankill. From there she took us up and down a few of the streets where bodies had regularly been dumped and pointed out the video cameras which had been installed on the last brick house of each street to record the grisly scenes for posterity, or rather, for the RUC. She pointed out the murals. Whenever she had given details about an atrocity she would tell the tourists how many people had been killed, who had claimed responsibility for the killings and whether anyone had been caught, tried or jailed for it.

I kept wondering how many people had died like

Lorna McLeish, because of the Troubles, but would never be recognised for it or form part of the statistics.

Our house came near the end of the tour.

'The Troubles have reached even the quieter suburbs of the city,' the lady explained. 'Only a year and a half ago this house was the subject of an arson attack by the IRA. As a result of the fire the building blew up because of a fault in the central-heating system. Two people were killed. The father of this family was a senior official in a non-sectarian company which undertook work for the army on more than one occasion. No one has been apprehended for the crime. The house has been rebuilt.'

'It's my house,' I said under my breath. I was sure that they had picked it out because there was nobody living in it. Most of the bombsites we had seen were empty, just the shells of structures long gone, abandoned shops or meeting places blown up mostly by the IRA, but occasionally also by the UVF. The rest of the tour schedule was either made up of public buildings or else took the form of a more general description. This is the Falls Road where all the Catholics live, and this is the Shankill and the Protestants live round here. The annual Orange March takes this route, she told us confidently, and the March passes this building and that building. She would detail the number of troops and RUC men who were deployed at the time of the March. Then she briefed the tourists about who had been kneecapped where, and how the City Hospital had developed tremendous expertise in the field of gunshot wounds of all kinds. That kind of thing.

The bus turned back into town and drove past a popular pub which had been the subject of a bomb attack when I was a kid.

'The bombing was claimed by the IRA. A gunman and bomber named Liam Curran was arrested and convicted for the atrocity in which nine people lost their lives. The court ruled that he had not acted alone, but he would not divulge the names of his co-conspirators. He was incarcerated in the Maze Prison in 1979 and, having served his sentence, was freed some thirteen years later.'

Becka and I stared at each other. We turned in our seats to catch the last glimpse of the now derelict pub. I counted the years out on my fingers. Liam had not been long out of prison when I had met him at Mrs C's. Hence, I supposed, all the talk about freedom around the house at that time. But the Northern Ireland Tourist Board had not allowed time for such recollections and we were on our way back to City Hall, where the lipstick lady finally pointed out the Linenhall Library which had taken a blast in which no one had been killed. I remembered it. I remembered the guy who had been in charge of the library coming on the news report and the reporter had been anxious to talk about the loss of valuable manuscripts which the blast had caused and all the library guy could say was 'at least there was no loss of life. That's the main thing.' But the reporter kept on at him. The terrorists weren't just blasting people any more, they were blowing up knowledge and history – robbing the Province of its heritage. The library guy was relentlessly sensible about it. 'But no loss of life. That's the main thing,' he kept saying. And he was right. My mind raced with the confusion of memories. The bus pulled up to a halt.

The lipstick lady thanked us all for coming on the tour and hoped that we enjoyed it. Then she did a short paragraph about the Northern Ireland Tourist Board and how great it was to come and holiday in the Six Counties and how you could get information about so doing. We shuffled down the stairs and through the door in a stunned mood and walked instinctively over the road to the Linenhall Library. It was closed on a Sunday, of course.

'I suppose that was one of the brothers,' said Becka.

'Yes. I suppose so. Second eldest I think,' I replied. 'We should come back here tomorrow,' I continued. 'They have lots of records – old newspapers and stuff. I think we should see what we can find.'

The first glimpses of the fire of revenge were in my eyes, then. I'm sure of it, but we neither of us said anything, just walked back to Lavery's and played darts for two hours solid. We played doubles and beat a couple of guys who said they were some kind of champions. After we had been playing for a while they decided that they ought to check us out. They tried asking which schools we had been to and then they tried asking which football team we supported. We gave nothing away.

'So, what d'ya reckon about this ceasefire then?' one of them asked, in a desperate bid to clarify where our sympathies might lie.

'Don't give a shit,' I said, scoring a double twenty and putting us safely in the lead.

The guy eyed me with suspicion. He wasn't giving up. 'Is that Protestant don't give a shit, or Catholic don't give a shit?' he asked.

That was the high point and we didn't think we'd top it, so we decided to leave and make for Angel Avenue in a taxi. We stopped off and picked up a couple of pizzas on the way.

'Pizza by candlelight,' said Becka. 'Very romantic.'

The cab driver looked worried. He didn't want to carry any sexual deviants in his car – hell no. He'd heard about lesbianism and by God, it sounded awful.

'She's only joking,' I leant over and confided in him.

'None of my business,' he said gruffly and dropped us at the front gate.

Seventeen

The Linenhall Library is more like a club than anything else. The library stands on three storeys just opposite City Hall. I think it was endowed by the Linen Trade. Hence its name. It's scruffy and friendly and kind of nice. You need a membership card to get in. I told the doorman that I had had a card, but that it had been blown up. He looked at me suspiciously. It was the truth. He took my name and said he'd have it checked against the records, then he grudgingly waved us through. We climbed the big wooden staircase up to the first floor. That is where the coffee shop is. The Linenhall Library isn't like a normal public library. The clatter of the coffee shop is right next to the reading rooms. It's like being at home. The first floor is painted a very pale blue which has gone shabby over the years. There are big mahogany tables and comfortable old wooden and leather chairs for reading at. When you first go into the Linenhall Library you think that the books aren't catalogued properly. The volumes look like they are just flung up on the shelves. When I was at school I had competed for a social history prize and I had chosen to do a project about the Belfast Royal Opera House. I was really diligent. So, I had tracked down the old files to the Linenhall Library and I went every day after school for weeks. In the end, I got chatting to one of the librarians who had taken me up to the attic. There were boxes and boxes of old papers about the Opera House up there. There were posters and signed programmes dating right back to when it had opened. The librarian let me sit in the attic and wade through it all. 'Shouldn't leave you here on your own. We haven't catalogued it yet. But I can trust you, can't I?' she had said amiably. That was when it had struck me that the haphazard shelves downstairs were catalogued. They just didn't look it.

Right in the middle of the first floor of the library there is a photocopier, which stands out like a sore thumb. Then there is the coffee shop which sells home baking – it makes the whole of the first floor smell of freshly baked cake. The second floor is painted a well-thumbed coffee colour and the walls are lined with leather-bound volumes of old newspapers. We headed for the newspapers and took seats opposite a plump, shiny faced old man wearing a bowler hat.

Becka read for hours. I was fidgety, distracted by the old sash-and-case windows which creaked in their frames. There was a little storm going on outside – a short-lived April shower, as if the weather had suddenly lost its temper. We looked up the newspapers around the time of Liam Curran's trial. They didn't tell us anything much, except that Liam had refused to speak anything but Irish in the dock and they had had to have a translator in court. There was one picture of Mrs Curran leaving the courtroom in tears, after he had been sent down. She didn't make any comment to the press. She was probably relieved that only one of the boys had been caught. Becka looked up the papers around the time I had built the Maze. First of all, there were pictures of me at the opening of the Maze, with the Lord Mayor and people from the Arts Council and the Provost of the University. Becka read everything. Then came the pictures of me at the funeral. And after that no pictures at all; and the news items got shorter.

We went downstairs for coffee.

'You think that it happened because of all the stuff you said about peace, don't you?' said Becka.

I stared out of the grubby window on to the shopping precinct below and just nodded. Tears were coming into my eyes.

Becka reached out her hand. 'No one else made that connection. Maybe there's a reason. Lots of people have spoken out about the Troubles and it didn't happen to them.'

'I said that you have to be prepared to give up everything for peace and they set the house alight. Dad had been working at that company for years. It was the day after I had said it. It's my fault. I know it is,' I replied.

The Linenhall Library is perhaps the one place in Belfast where you could talk in public like that and people wouldn't stare or even listen. The coffee shop was full of members sipping their drinks and reading the newspapers. Mostly people were on their own. The tables were set out for four, but there would be two people sharing them, each reading a paper and smiling at the other if they happened to turn the page at the same time, but not speaking. In any case, the jangle of coffee cups being stacked and plates being put out for the lunch-time rush meant that you probably couldn't listen in to a conversation if you weren't concentrating on it.

Becka reached out with both of her hands held up to me, and I met her fingers with my own. 'Close your eyes,' she said, 'and just breathe. You're alive. You have to see the light inside yourself. It wasn't your fault, Libby, really it wasn't. Don't remind yourself of it. You have to get away from that. Get away from it.'

I closed my eyes. It wasn't a white light, in my mind's eye. It was a red light. I suppose I was still angry. 'I want revenge,' I said. 'I want freedom.'

'Let's get out of here,' said Becka, pulling her hands away. 'Let's go for a walk.'

That's Becka to a tee. Passion is the one thing she is scared of. Passion is love making itself over. It's reconciliation. It's what she can't handle.

We abandoned our mugs of coffee and tripped down the stairs and outside into the fresh April air. The sun had come out. We walked up Donegall Pass without so much as looking in the windows of the famous antique shops. The wet pavements shone like mirrors beneath our feet. And when I looked up there was even a rainbow.

Eighteen

After wandering aimlessly for some time through the web of the city, we ended up near the University, so we decided we'd try to go and find Professor Jackson at the Department of Physiology. I was familiar with the buildings, it was only just a couple of years since I had left. I expected to be hailed as soon as we went near the place – to see people who had been at college with me, even though I knew, of course, that they must have left at the same time as I had. There were the kids on bikes, the lovers holding hands, the people running, late for something, clutching their folders tightly to their chests, with bags swinging at their side. They looked like I should have known them. But I didn't recognise any faces. We tramped our way to the Department of Physiology and were met by the department secretary. The offices were Dickensian. But someone had tried to modernise them. The modern stuff sat uneasily with the ancient. There were formica shelves mounted on the walls from floor to ceiling. Modern fluorescent files stacked uneasily on the lower of these shelves and above them great hefty leather-bound tomes were catalogued on the sagging upper shelves. One good sneeze and it looked as if the whole lot would tumble on to the immaculate new charcoal-grey carpet. There was natural light from a very small window to one side, but it wasn't enough to read by, so fluorescent strip lights had been raised to the ceiling. Around the edges of the ceiling there was some plain cornice work. Right in front of the door, there was a Victorian oak desk with an enormous grey IBM computer perched precariously to one side and behind the desk sat the nervous department secretary, Miss Rogers, her name emblazoned in white letters on to the formica name-plate before her.

Miss Rogers suited the office so well, it was as if it was her natural habitat. She kind of had the appearance of a Dickensian caricature. She was a very thin lady, but you felt she was sturdy, somehow. If you had jumped on top of her from even the very topmost of those formica shelves, she wouldn't have broken. Perhaps the impression of a certain toughness in her nature came more from her clothes. Miss Rogers wore heavy, utilitarian clothes – tan-coloured brogues, woollen tights and a khaki corded dress. Anything more soft and feminine and she would have looked consumptive. She had a long, red-veined nose with an opaque whitish patch of skin at the end. You couldn't be sure it was skin, it could have been snot. She took a handkerchief from the pocket of her navy cardigan and wiped her nose as we entered the office. It must have been skin. It didn't move.

'Hello,' she said, and smiled. She had kind brown eyes. They were laid back a bit into her face, but they were there.

Becka beamed at Miss Rogers. 'We're looking for Professor Jackson,' she said.

Miss Rogers looked worried. 'Well, dear,' she said softly, and there was some gratitude in her voice as well, 'he isn't here. He's over at the science block.' She turned her swivel chair with unexpected swiftness to consult the timetable behind her. 'He'll be in 4013 until just after two. You could catch him there,' she said.

133

So Miss Rogers gave us directions and we set off to Room 4013. It was already half past one.

The labs were state-of-the-art prefabs. We waited outside the door, leaning lazily against the tubular steel railings, in between the padlocked bikes. The sun was winning through and we basked in it.

'We should see if we can get him to take us home for dinner,' said Becka.

I nodded my silent agreement. 'Provided we like him,' I replied.

And of course, we did like him. Well, at first we did. He was a great, big, friendly bear of a man with the kind of powerful, floppy, expansive way of expressing himself which would have just wreaked havoc on Miss Rogers's carefully but precariously balanced office. He flung his arms around Becka when he realised who she was and boomed at her, 'Well, you've grown up a lot. Don't expect you even remember me, eh? And who's this?'

I stepped forward and introduced myself.

'Liberty,' he shouted. 'Well, it's always a good thing as far as I am concerned.'

The students were packing up their notes and leaving the lab in dribs and drabs. Professor Jackson turned to wipe the board clean of his scribbled notes.

'Just let me finish up here, and we'll go over to my office. I'm working on a newish project. The craniosacral system. It's like a tide sweeping through your body, you know. Beginning to look as if its function is vital for recuperation after illness. Relatively new stuff for conventional medicine. Going on for years in the alternative community but near as damn it unexplained by scientists. We're continuing where Stone left off – working with the core energy relationships of the cranial process. Actually, I have been collaborating with your father about it. I'll be in Glasgow myself next week. Well now, we'll have to have you home, of course. Dinner tonight. Moyra would kill me if I didn't.'

Becka sat up on one of the benches placed all round the room and swung her legs beneath her. 'We'd love to,' she said, 'it's my first time in Belfast.' She jumped down and wandered casually up and down the room, stopping finally beside the store cupboard, near to Professor Jackson himself.

He threw her a key across the workbench. 'Go in there and fetch the blue folder on the shelf by the window, will you,' he said.

Becka did as she was bid.

'Not like it was when we first came here. Height of the Troubles, you know. This ceasefire seems to be working, though. I hope that something good will come out of it.'

Becka locked the cupboard door smartly behind herself and delivered the file straight into his out-stretched hands.

Professor Jackson moved like a great, blundering whirlwind towards the doorway. He was carrying two brown portfolio cases and he had a white lab coat thrown over one arm. When I say he was carrying these things, I suppose my impression was that he didn't carry things as much as they were attached to him like magnets. It was as if he scooped things up and they clung to him. Really quite extraordinary.

'Come on, then,' he said. 'Keep up.'

And so we followed him all the way back to the Victorian building from whence we had come. It took us some time to find anywhere to sit in his office. It was miles away from Miss Rogers – on the other side of the building in fact, and right up on the top floor, like a garret. 'More light up here,' he said joyfully. Eventually we uncovered some chairs and sat down, and Professor Jackson found a phone and rang his wife, who said she would love to have us for dinner. Things were going to plan.

'So,' said Professor Jackson, 'what are you doing in Belfast, young MacIntosh?'

'Well,' Becka started, 'Libby lived here for a while, and I had never seen it, and we wanted to see what it was like now the ceasefire is in effect. So we caught the ferry.'

'Just Belfast? Why not Donegal? Why not Derry? We'll see what we can do, eh? This is the opportunity for a real adventure. Ever been down to the South? Dublin? Kerry? It's beautiful. Just beautiful.'

We smiled at him. I don't think it would have mattered too much what we said – he was on a roll.

'We have an extra car just now, you know. Young Jake has gone off on his travels without it. You can borrow it if you like. The open road and all that.'

Becka beamed at him. 'Thanks,' she said. 'We might just take you up on that one.'

Professor Jackson drove us back to his place. It was a big, posh house on the Malone Road. The Troubles hadn't done anything more out here than disrupted someone's shopping trip. Mrs Jackson emerged from the kitchen as we entered the front door and laid our jackets and bags on the two chairs set out at the front of the hallway. She was much younger than the professor, with a scrubbed, clean kind of face and a body so thin it was hardly there. The professor gave her an engulfing but childlike hug. I could see her tiny face appearing in the crook of his arm. She looked all squashed up and uncomfortable.

'This is Becka.' He gestured towards us. 'And Liberty.'

'Of course. How lovely to see you again, Becka. Please call me Moyra. And Liberty. Welcome.' Moyra detached herself from the professor's embrace and advanced, with a blithe kind of grace, towards us up the hallway. She kissed us both lightly on the cheek. 'Are you vegetarians?' she asked. 'Do you eat meat? I made us a game casserole, then I had this awful thought that you might be vegetarians. I can make something else, though.'

We assured her that we were dedicated meat eaters.

Then the professor led the way into the kitchen. It was a large room and it was entirely white – everything from the walls, to the cupboards, to the painted kitchen chairs, gleamed with the antiseptic shine of absolute cleanliness. There were shiny white tiles behind all the work surfaces and pristine formica on the floor. Here and there were touches of colour on the bleak and snowy landscape – a green tea-towel or a crimson tea-cosy, but these travesties were few and far between. I thought to myself that having dinner in that room would be like eating in an operating theatre. The table was already set out for the meal. The professor opened a bottle of wine and started to pour glasses of it for everyone. The liquid looked deep and dark against the brightness of our surroundings. The glasses were like chalices of blood. We sat ourselves down at the table and the professor proposed a toast to our great adventure, and we all drank to it with fervour.

The casserole smelt delicious. We hadn't really eaten properly since we left Glasgow. Pub food never quite feels nourishing enough, and apart from pubs we had only eaten in coffee shops. My mouth watered at the prospect of some home cooking. The professor was telling us about his travels the previous year to the Ukraine. He had taken some of his annual leave to go there and advise on a hospital which was being built. A couple of his research students had gone with him for the ride and they had all stayed for a week deep in the countryside on a farm, near the site of the new hospital. The students had been vegetarians and their host couldn't understand why they wouldn't eat the meat on the table. It had been killed especially for them. The professor mimicked the farmer, booming, in a mock Ukrainian accent, 'Why not? Why not eat this meat? I knew this pig. He had a good life. Eat him.' The students had caved in after a couple of days of nothing but pickles, black bread and vodka. We giggled amiably with the professor, who slapped Becka on the shoulder as he rocked back and forth to the sound of his own hearty laughter. After a few of these stories and some glasses of what was an extremely rich red wine, the stark whiteness of our surroundings became more of a splendour than the assault they had first seemed. Having lived in Angel Avenue for two days, where darkness fell absolutely at seven o'clock and was relieved only by the gentle light of the candles we had found under the sink, it was like sitting in heaven, having dinner with the Archangels.

Moyra brought the casserole dish to the table, but it sat there for a while unopened, with one small jet of steam piping ferociously out of the side of the lid. We agreed to stay overnight. The hot showers in the morning would be a treat and a house which was warm and light was too great a luxury to turn down. The wine flowed freely and we listened to the professor's stories of travels abroad, of students who fainted at the sight of blood and of the day that he had been winged when a building on Donegall Pass had blown up only half a block from where he was standing. He described noticing the windows bulge only an instant before the blast, as if all time had slowed down for him and he could see in fractions of a second, the way you have to watch things if you want to catch a magician doing a trick. His right arm had been bleeding when he rose again to his feet into the confusion all around.

'You can't blame them for blowing things up now and again,' said Moyra wistfully. 'It must be so frustrating.'

'Yes,' the professor sneered at her sarcastically, 'those poor political activists. I personally find it satisfying when children die for the cause – what about Warrington, Moyra? Want to go over there and tell the parents that their kids died because some poor, war-torn terrorist got a bit frustrated?'

Immediately, Moyra's face was transformed. It was as if someone had torn open an old wound. Her eyes flashed furiously at her husband and she snarled, her teeth the ivory white of animal teeth and the soft fleshy parts of her mouth all red from the wine. It looked as if she had been eating raw meat. Any vestiges of her meek appearance had disappeared and she was taken over by a profane and fundamental fury.

'You are such a Brit,' she snarled. 'No backbone, no integrity, only stubbornness. There are innocent victims in any war. Look at what your people have done to this country. Centuries of it. What about those innocent victims? Oh, I forgot. They weren't innocent, were they? They were Irish. Don't you feel any shame? I can't understand why you don't feel any shame.'

Becka and I locked eyes in disbelief, but the professor was too drunk to be embarrassed at what I expected he thought of as an unseemly display of temper. 'So,' he said calmly, 'I suppose you think it is a great idea for the soldiers to pull out, against the wishes of the majority of the people in the Province. To hand the Counties back to a country with a vastly inadequate social welfare system. To hand the Counties back to a country where there is no divorce and no abortion. A country with an appalling record in the field of women's rights.'

'It's our country and it's changing,' Moyra snapped. 'I want to help it change. I want to vote for change and I want to campaign for change.'

The professor cut in on her. 'I'm sure you would find

it a bit frustrating, don't you think? All that campaigning. But then they would probably forgive you if you blew up a couple of Battered Women's Hostels in the name of change. You could bomb the Registry Office in protest against the anti-divorce legislation. After all, heaven forbid you should be frustrated.'

I felt I ought to say something, but Moyra recovered herself at this point. She backed off. It was as if she had remembered we were there. 'There will be divorce in the South. They've just had a referendum about it. And I know it's gone to the High Court, but hell, it's going to be difficult to talk the High Court into ruling against the wishes of the majority of the people,' she said calmly and eagerly sipped her drink.

'You think that the wishes of the majority count for something in the South, but they don't count for anything up here, do they? Most people here don't want to be part of the Republic. Most people want to stay just where we are. But then, I almost forgot, you think that the poll should be taken of the whole of the island, don't you? Well, you would probably win in that case. But then why not make the poll for the whole of the UK too? Oh, I don't know.' The professor contemplated his own glass and shrugged his shoulders. The storm had passed and they had decided the argument was over.

'Let's eat,' he said, and took the top off the casserole dish, thrusting the serving spoon into the stew beneath and leaning down to smell the meal properly. 'Jesus, Moyra,' he exclaimed. 'It's a bit brown looking. Not very appetising.'

Moyra's eyes had become calm as soon as attention had been turned to the meal, but now they flashed again. In a furious instant she had reached into one of the pristine white cupboards and come out with a little tin of something. She petulantly thrust her arm out in front of herself and poured the entire contents of the tin over the top of the casserole.

It was the first and only time I have ever had stew with hundreds and thousands on top. The granules melted into the juices of the meat, leaving little puddles of pastel-coloured sugar dotted all through the meal. It wasn't as bad as you might think and after all, you had to kind of admire her for it.

Nineteen

The next morning Becka and I woke up late. It was very quiet on the Malone Road and the bedrooms were at the back of the house, so the noise of traffic, which usually stirred us, was missing. I suppose it must have been eleven o'clock or so. It took a few seconds for us to remember just where we were. We had been put down, after two more bottles of wine and another small hooley, in Jake Jackson's bedroom. Becka said she kind of remembered Jake Jackson from when she was a kid. They had been seven or eight years old and they had been allowed to go out on their bicycles up and down the street together. She remembered that he'd been smaller than she was, tiny, in fact, with skinny little ankles, which worked themselves into a blur on the pedals of his bike, that sunny day they had spent together in the Seventies. In his room we found a photograph album. He had grown into a strapping lad. Perhaps it was all the stew. We fell into his enormous bed and happily drifted off to sleep in the early hours of the morning.

Now we sat up again in that same bed and surveyed the room in daylight.

'What are we going to do?' asked Becka.

'Take the car,' I said. 'Go for a little road trip.'

'About Lorna McLeish,' Becka said helplessly.

The beginnings of an idea had been forming inside

my head ever since we had come back to Belfast. It was my teenage rebellion, I suppose. Better late than never. It was because of David Curran too – I mean he was involved in it, he was playing the game, even if he didn't want to. He did it because he was scared. I had heard the fear in his voice. I had listened to him cry himself to sleep. He was scared and he wasn't going to stand up to that. Not really. Not for anything more than show. To me, though, it wasn't the fear that made you a good person or a bad one. It was what you did about it. I realised that I had been scared all of my life. Most people I knew in Belfast were scared. Some were brave and some were cowards, but everyone was scared. You looked to the police to protect you, or to the gunmen to protect you, depending on what area you lived in. You looked for other people to make a peace for you, for someone else to negotiate a ceasefire. And then you had people like Lloyd Baker to help you clean up the mess it made of your soul. You thought it wasn't your problem. You just weren't part of it. Perhaps you held certain views of one kind or another. Perhaps you even went so far as to express those views. I had built the Maze, after all. But when it came right down to it, you were scared. I was scared. And I decided, then, that I wasn't going to be scared any more. I wasn't going to let anyone else take responsibility for me any longer either. I was going to take responsibility for myself, and what's more, I was going to prove to myself just how responsible I could be.

'We're going on a road trip. We're going to find out where the bastards are,' I said to Becka, and as I said it I thought of Lorna McLeish's body and of my parents, and I was angry. But I was in control and that was the difference. I had changed. So I waited to see what she would say and, like most people on the mainland, Becka didn't have that natural inbuilt fear in quite the same way that people from the Six Counties do. That's why the bombing campaigns on the mainland were never as successful as they were in the North itself. People on the mainland would inform if they saw anything dodgy – there aren't any reprisals over there. Well, none that you hear about. And the hearing about it is the thing that puts you off. If they saw something going on, most people in the North would go back into their house, make a cup of tea and not do anything about what they had seen or what they thought they had seen, because they didn't want to end up dead. Nearly 4,000 people have died because of the Troubles in the years of conflict since 1969. Many more thousands have been beaten up or kneecapped, or told to leave the country or die. Everyone in the Province has been intimidated in one way or another, to the point where, if you did see something going on which you knew had something to do with the paramilitaries, you didn't want to become any more involved than you already were. And besides, if you did see something, chances were you were kind of on the side of the particular men of violence you were in a position to inform on. The UVF didn't prepare themselves in a Catholic area, and the IRA didn't have safe houses anywhere that was Protestant. Whoever you saw, even if you didn't agree with what they were doing, was doing it for a cause in which you probably did believe. You sort of even despised people who informed on the terrorists in the North. You despised them if they informed the RUC or the army, that is. If you did happen to see the other side's terrorists stashing arms or making bombs in the back shed, you would probably inform your own terrorists. Now that, at least, had some strange kind of integrity about it. But to inform the RUC that something was going on didn't really cut the mustard. You might want the RUC to protect you, but you weren't going to do anything as goody-two-shoes as tell them what you knew. People thought that was a cowardly thing to do. Marching for peace was one thing, dobbing people in was quite another. Like I said, people were scared.

Becka didn't have it, though. That particular brand of scaredness was missing in her. 'I don't get it,' she said. 'I mean, what if we find out where they are? What do we do then?'

'I don't know,' I said. 'I'm not sure yet.'

Actually, I think even then I was sure about what I wanted to do. I just wasn't prepared to say it, because I knew it was wrong. I wanted to kill them. I wanted to fight my way out of the fear. Snuff out the trembling flame of terror inside me at the same time as I killed someone who was the very symbol of all I had been afraid of all of my life. I had never gone along with the they-deserve-to-be-hung lobby. I don't think I could ever condone the formality of that kind of procedure. I am anti-establishment to the point of neurosis. You've probably noticed. But they deserved to die. I wanted to kill them. Bastards. And I was proud of myself for deciding that. It took a lot to let myself do it. You can't sit on the sidelines in a conflict like the Irish war. Perhaps that's what freedom is all about. Participation. You can't sit on the sidelines. It destroys you if you do. But I didn't tell Becka anything. She guessed herself, later, in any case. And Becka was very amiable. She agreed to come along. I think something about my new confidence inspired her. If I had an aura, it had turned whatever the confident colour is. I would never need to ring Lloyd Baker again.

When we got downstairs Moyra Jackson made us all a big pot of coffee and some toast.

'You were amazing last night,' I said. 'Do you fight about the Troubles every evening?' I had meant it as a kind of joke. A bit of a dig.

'Yes,' she said sadly, 'I suppose we do.'

I was immediately sorry for what I had said. I wanted

to make it up to her. 'I think you're right, you know,' I told her. 'Maybe for different reasons than you have. But I think you're right. I'm not sure a political solution can work, either. In Britain, politics is too much of a game. They are juggling with opinion polls. There's nothing they like quite so much as a bit of a war to get all their ratings going. They are real Tories that way. I don't understand how they can say they want peace and not admit that there are wrongs on the British side too. It's like they think they're some kind of martyrs to it.'

Moyra nodded sadly. 'Well,' she said, 'we'll see how much he wants peace now.'

'What do you mean?' I asked.

'There was a bomb last night in London. They blew up a block somewhere in the City.'

'Oh my God,' was about all I could manage.

'That's it,' said Becka, laying down her toast. 'I'm going to the police.'

And Becka was as good as her word. Moyra Jackson gave us the keys to Jake's old, beaten-up Vauxhall Astra and waved us off. We promised to come back in about a week. We told her we were heading South to sample the delights of Dublin, but before anything, Becka insisted that we drive into town and I gaped in wide-eyed disbelief as she walked, barefaced, on her own, right into the police station and confidential phone lines be damned. I watched her as she went, but it wasn't in me to go with her. My revenge was a private affair. I wanted to find my own path towards freedom and the RUC were, to me, as much of an enemy as any terrorist in the territory. Becka was OK about it, and she had agreed not to mention me. Going to the security forces is the next best thing to going to the Loyalist paramilitaries. RUC and British military covert intelligence operations know few boundaries. At one time the only way they felt that they could tackle the IRA was to almost support the UVF. Not

146

openly, of course. But somehow the forces had felt that they were hampered by the law and they couldn't seem to deal with the Republicans in any other way. An eye for an eye and a tooth for a tooth. There was a big hullaballoo which never hit the British headlines, of course, when Amnesty International expressed its concerns that security force personnel were taking part in Loyalist death squads, passing information to Loyalist paramilitaries and turning a blind eye when need be. The IRA responded with all its most vicious military tactics. Informants were key targets for murder and torture. The IRA has its own disciplinary procedure, which is set out in a document called 'The Green Book'. Basically the accepted drill is to kidnap offenders, interrogate them (and that certainly includes torturing them) and summarily execute them. People don't come back after the interrogation stage. That just doesn't happen.

They had dismantled the sandbags and a lot of the barbed wire around the police station on account of the – now broken – ceasefire. The IRA used to lob shells over the perimeter wall there. I remembered it from my schooldays. It used to be a little fortress. Now it looked more like a derelict building than anything else, with the windows taped up and the doorway all dark and cavernous. Becka emerged from the building just over an hour later. I had expected to have to wait for her till nightfall and beyond, but they took her information and just let her go. She said it was pretty grim inside there, but didn't give out anything much else about what had happened.

'You're safe,' she assured me. 'That's what matters. I just told them that Lorna McLeish was abducted by the Curran brothers and that they were the ones who killed her. I gave them the names, though I don't expect they needed them. Let's go, then.'

And that was it. She wanted to drive straight down to Dublin there and then.

'But didn't they interrogate you? Didn't they want to know how you knew about it?' I asked.

'Course. Said I had worked in the office after she had left. Said that I had overheard a telephone conversation between David and his brother. Then I saw it on the news and put two and two together.'

'And that's it?'

'Yeah.'

'Rock on.'

I expected that we would be followed, but as far as we could tell, there was no one on our tail, although it was possible that they were trailing us by using the video cameras on the street corners. Most of Belfast is available on film. Still, I cut down side-streets, which remained deserted in our wake. I scanned the skies for helicopter surveillance, but the only things up there were the clouds. I couldn't quite believe that we had got away with it. I suppose that the cops might have checked the plates on the car and tracked them down to a house on the Malone Road. That would have put their minds at rest. Becka came from the mainland, of course, and that helped too. Maybe they were too busy organising security for the Orange March – there was one due the following day. But still. Even so. I noted to myself that there was really nothing to connect Becka and me. We had met by chance. If anyone tracked her down, they would have to track still further to get to me. There was no obvious link. My main concern was the information which was routinely leaked from the police to the terrorists. The IRA was unlikely to make reprisals against some itinerant, hard-to-trace Scottish girl on holiday in the North and soon to go home. Someone from Belfast, though, that was a different matter. If they knew, they might get to me. But no one knew. The connection between us was vaporous and insubstantial.

Becka was unaware of all this. She sat in the front seat, looking kind of righteous after her ordeal at the cop shop. 'How long will it take us to get there?' she asked.

'Three hours or so,' I said. 'If there aren't any roadblocks on account of the resumption of the bombing.'

As we headed out of Belfast on the big motorway to the South I noticed it was three in the afternoon. We still weren't being followed. By my reckoning we would be there by six.

Just in time for tea.

Twenty

The road running between Dublin and Belfast is not the road of a united country. On the British side it is a pristine multi-lane motorway. On the Irish side it deteriorates rapidly into a winding, single-lane nightmare, punctuated by white signs with an ominous black spot in the centre. Mum used to joke about it being where Robert Louis Stevenson got the idea for the black spot in *Treasure Island*. Once the pirates had given you the black spot you were doomed. It was kind of the same on the road to Dublin. Seven people have to die at the one place on a road. Then it qualifies as a black spot. The signs are usually erected on the more winding roads, where you can't see what is coming and have to be particularly careful not to deviate from your own side of the roadway, or to speed. The black-spot sections of the road are kind of scary – even if you slow down and behave, you never know what is coming the other way. I heard that the Irish Government got loads of European money to build a motorway from the border to Dublin. It came under a measure for the promotion of peace. But the new motorway wasn't finished that day when we went down to Dublin, so I had to negotiate the old road.

Becka sat eagerly in the front seat and sang Blur songs out of tune, while she hammered on the plastic dashboard. It was the most annoying thing she had ever done. I tried to talk to her, really just to stop her singing, but it didn't work. In the end I had to come clean. 'For Christ's sake, stop singing, would you?'

She banged out the dull thud of a drumroll on the side window. 'Sorry,' she answered. 'You should have said.'

'I am saying. I'm saying it now.'

We lapsed into silence and I felt guilty for snapping.

'Sorry,' I said, after a couple of minutes.

'No, it's cool. Police station spooked you, huh?'

'I suppose.'

'They were OK really. I was expecting these monsters, but they were just normal, dim-witted policemen. Well, they gave me a policewoman. I think it was a woman. She was in a skirt, anyway.'

We laughed.

'What I'm really after wanting to know,' I said, lapsing into the sleepy drawl of the South, 'is why they didn't follow you, or hassle you, or keep you longer.'

Becka shrugged. 'Look, I came into the station honestly. I told them what I knew honestly. What is the big deal?'

'People usually get kneecapped, you know. Or worse than kneecapped. For going to the police honestly and telling them what they know honestly. That's the big deal.'

'Scare me, why don't you.'

'Sorry.'

I think, you know, that Becka liked me better when I was kind of nasty to her.

We got through the border with no hassle. In fact, I didn't realise that we had gone through until we were a few miles into the Southern state and the road got worse. What I did notice was the despondency about the towns on both sides of the border. This was the front line. If the bombs started again, these were the towns which would be most routinely affected. We tuned in to the local radio station which was a mêlée of farming reports and local news items and comments about the bomb in London. Three men had been killed in the basement of a nearby chemist shop. There were over one hundred people who had been wounded, in one way or another. None of the wounded were in a serious condition, though. Just glass cuts. The building had been totalled. There was an ongoing debate on the radio between Unionists who thought that the ceasefire had only been a sham, and Republicans who maintained that the IRA had grown tired of waiting for further action on the peace and wanted to get around the table and stop being messed around by the Brits. Everyone talked about how much the people wanted peace. None of them seemed prepared to compromise, though. We switched it off after about half an hour and sat in contemplative silence, until we decided to stop in Dundalk for a cup of tea in a café. We turned off into Dundalk at the bridge by which you can bypass the town.

'Another hour,' I told Becka before she had the chance to ask.

We found a suitable café, and ordered a pot of tea and scones with butter, which were brought out with the measured, calm pace which is the undercurrent of all activity in the Southern part of Ireland. It is one of the benchmarks of a culture I always think – the pace at which it operates. A good way to measure it is to order a taxi and see how irate local people get if it is late. In London you would be on the phone within five minutes. In some parts of Belfast you would ring as soon as it was supposed to be there. In Dublin, though, you wouldn't ring until perhaps half an hour had gone by. That's the pace of the South. They don't take traffic lights too seriously either. There are a few seconds' latitude on either side of a red light which are kind of up for grabs. Things happen slowly, though you always reckon that when things get wherever they are supposed to be, they will be wonderful. It's a very seductive way to be. All that calm confidence is very attractive.

Becka poured out the tea for us and bit eagerly into her scone. 'Do you think it was them, in London?' she whispered, her voice lowered so that the jolly-looking lady behind the cherry-red formica counter on the other side of the room wouldn't be able to hear us.

'How am I supposed to know? If it is, though, I mean if they stayed on in London after doing Lorna in, then they will have to get out now. And quick. The IRA will have a few people operating in England if they have decided to resume over there. There will be more than one cell in London. That's how they operate – in cells. They group up in teams of five or six or so, and the people in one cell don't know who makes up the other cells. Only the head people know that. That way, if the soldiers on the ground are caught they can only give away their own cell. The most people they can lose is five or six at a time. No one knows the whole plan, either. Like the army might catch one guy, and he might talk, but all he can tell them is what he was told to do and who he was involved with. There might be three or four plans of attack involving three or four cells, so they can switch if anyone gets caught. It's like gambling. Hedging your bets. That's why the Brits have had real trouble catching the guys, you know.'

'Wow,' said Becka. 'How do you know all this stuff?'

I just shrugged my shoulders. Everybody knew.

I stared out of the window at the grey, ramshackle Dundalk streets. The sky was dimming right down, like it does before it begins to get dark and it was cloudy, so you couldn't see the sun. I was looking forward to hitting Dublin again. It was a place of golden memories for me and I just wanted to have the kind of fun there that I had always had before. As well as trying to track

153

down the Currans, of course, which, I imagined, gave me a dark and measured purpose – the kind of reason I had never had before for visiting the city. It was the first time in my whole life that I had a reason for going somewhere. I knew I was doing the right thing.

After the scones we hit the road again and sang our way southwards into the black, velvety cloak of the night, and it wasn't long before the countryside gave way to the smattering of houses which were the first signs of the big city. On the way in, as we passed through Fairview and Drumcondra, I decided to leave the Currans until the following day. We weren't tired at all, and Mrs Curran would want to feed us and put us to bed. We were excited, though, and after the silent constraints of Belfast we were certainly ready to let our hair down.

Once we were through the suburbs, I turned off the main road and cut down through Mountjoy Square, following the hill to Custom House Quay. The car had Northern plates, and in this area, I decided, it might not be smart to leave it on the street overnight, though, admittedly, the quay looked a lot more up-market than the last time I had been there, when I had had my bag stolen in a cheap greasy spoon café near the train station. Two guys had just come in, picked it up from where it lay at my feet and legged it towards O'Connell Street and into the crowds. The waitress at the café had been unsympathetic. I think she thought it might have been a ploy on my part to get a free bacon butty and a mug of tea. The guards found the bag in a litter bin on George's Street a couple of days later, and it had been duly returned to me, devoid of my purse which had contained £50 in cash and some credit cards, but with everything else intact.

Things at Custom House Quay looked much more up-market now – the burgeoning office developments were taking their toll, property prices were rising and the tough guys were moving on – even a couple of years can make a big difference. But I decided to go over to the south side of the city, where things were traditionally much safer. We passed the bus station and crossed the river, winding around the back of the Trinity College campus in all its leafy green certainty, up past the Dáil and finally coming out on to St Stephen's Green. I parked opposite the Shelbourne Hotel, knowing there would be staff on duty there all night, and if they saw anything they would ring the Gardaí. We were near enough the Dáil to get immediate attention for anything suspicious.

The air was cool as we got out of the car, and the moon was as thin as a mouse's whisker. We walked round the Green. It was as beautiful and shabby as I remembered it, the Georgian brick tenements on the Green still having the great majority over the newer buildings. There was a time, not so long back, when modern architects in Dublin were almost considered vandals. The wreck of Georgian Dublin was an architectural scandal on an international scale – the historic country houses and Georgian terraces of Ireland rotted and there was a mad, macho kind of frantic development going on all over the country. I suppose that perhaps they wanted to get rid of the buildings that they regarded as relics of the British occupation. They thought the buildings weren't really Irish. The developers went for that big time. They sent in the demolition teams and people joked that Belfast suffered less from the bombings than Dublin did from the developers. But then the Government wised up to tourism and the money it could bring in, if the country could deliver enough in the way of historical interest, so they introduced tax incentives and strict planning guidelines and, architecturally speaking, it was said that the city became truly European – as European as Barcelona. They restored the Four Courts and the Custom

House whereas ten years before they would have torn down buildings like that. They were careful what they rebuilt. The place began to look more like a capital city again. That was something that always interested me. Belfast just looked like any wealthy provincial city in Britain. But you could tell Dublin was a capital. Anyway, Stephen's Green had escaped the vandalism stage and benefited from the kickback against it. It was beautiful. The evening air was icy and refreshing. It felt glorious to be back again.

'Whatcha fancy?' I asked Becka.

'Boys,' she said. 'I feel really in the mood for some boys.'

Maybe her success at the police station had turned her on. Uniforms do that for some girls.

Twenty-one

Boys aren't so hard to find in Dublin, but personally, I wanted to eat. We had most of Toby's money left – still well over four hundred pounds there – and I wanted to go somewhere and have a truly great meal. We headed down Grafton Street, then cut through into Temple Bar where we stopped in at a pub for a quick drink. We had decided to go for Mexican food. Dublin is one of the youngest cities in Europe – more young people live there than old ones. The only other statistical fact I know about Dublin is that the average age at which people get married is pretty high. It's something like thirty-five. That's because there is no divorce, you see. It came as no surprise, then, to find that the pub was packed with single young people not entirely unlike ourselves. We ordered pints up at the bar and carefully carried them up a short flight of stairs at the back of the pub, to an open room with only about five or six tables in it, where we found a seat not too far from the small fire burning in the grate right at the very back. The atmosphere of the place was tremendous. It's something you can always count on in Dublin, this kind of relentlessly hip atmosphere which makes the general shabbiness of the place quaint. I suppose I make it sound like Dublin is all shabby and old, and in some places that is true. The other thing that goes to make up the hip atmosphere is some of the most forward-thinking initiatives in Europe. In Temple Bar the faded, age-old, nicotine-stained pubs stand amid projects like the Eco Friendly building, internet cafés, modern galleries and state-of-the-art sound studios. It's the same kind of mix you find in the people – hip young kids, who are wild and free, mingle with Catholic fundamentalist housewives. Serious Republicans, the kind of people who blow stuff up, hang out with that rare soul in Britain, the European believer. The EC is popular big time in Dublin – the South is poor and it gets a lot of money from the Community. A lot more money than it puts in. All these people get on. It's part of the culture to get on with everyone in the pub. On the easygoing surface, in any case. It's a heady, mad, creative cocktail and no mistake.

It didn't take us long to get chatting to people. It was just a matter of diving in and gabbing away, really. Most people were there in order to meet other people so it was pretty easy. Becka turned to one table on her right and off she went, so I kind of shrugged my shoulders, took it on the chin, and off I went to the left. We heard about a club which would be on later that evening, further along the river at an old warehouse. There was a real buzz about it and we decided to go there much later on. After a bit we quit the pub and went for dinner together at a restaurant nearby, where we toasted ourselves with jugs of margharitas – heavy on the tequila with crushed ice and easy on the strawberries – and feasted ourselves on chicken fajitas for two hours solid. We decided we loved Dublin. The more tequila we drank, the more we loved it, and we had plenty, plenty tequila before we staggered joyfully out on to the cobbled streets again, and I somehow managed to lead us to the famous Grogan's, to take a small one (for our health) before closing time. It was a freezing cold evening, at that stage, and Grogan's was packed to the gunwales. I had often gone to Grogan's in the summertime, when the crowds spilt out on to the pavements and into the pedestrian arcade at the side entrance to the pub. That pinched and freezing April night, I think there were probably just as many people there as in the summertime, but they were all stuffed inside the pub together. It was nearly impossible to move. At this point, however, we had had so much to drink we hardly noticed the crush and we moved quite easily among the crowd, slithering through the cracks in between people and ending up at the bar. Becka ordered us two whiskeys and I think it was when the whiskey hit my bloodstream and mingled with the tequila that I could no longer really be responsible for my own actions.

I am entirely unsure of how we got to the party. I really can't remember anything of the journey there. Anyhow, we ended up at this party back down on the docks in a night-club which was really an old bonded warehouse. It was the one we had heard about earlier. The party roamed around over three floors. On the ground floor there was mostly just drinking and some background disco music with mellow, subdued lighting to match. We passed on upwards. On the first floor there was a DJ who was kind of stuck in the Eighties. I quite enjoyed it, actually, but Becka pulled me on up the stairs and towards the heavenly top floor, where there was a cracking, live indie band and the crowd frolicked, barefoot, like hippies from beyond time.

We danced for a while, then we got split up and I went out on to a little balcony which was marked 'Fire Exit', where I sat on the cold iron grating with my legs swinging over the edge. Below was the infinite. The freezing air should have sobered me up, but I didn't feel a thing. A lanky, good-looking guy meandered out and sat next to me. He talked at me kind of aimlessly for a while, and I listened as I sipped from his Bacardi and Coke. Then he stopped talking and shambled off. It never occurred to me that he might come back, but he did. This time he brought a small supply of Bacardi and Coke – four glasses full, in fact. He talked at me some more and then he kissed me with a thin-lipped kind of kiss from which I was saved by a bouncer, who came to tell us that we were blocking the Fire Exit and had to go back inside. Somehow, I lost the lanky guy on the way back into the throng and miraculously found Becka, who wasn't feeling too great. We headed for the toilets where she threw up for at least half an hour.

'I'm never, ever eating Mexican food again,' was all she managed to say once it was over. I nodded surreally, in solemn agreement, and we went back down to the ground floor where we found some comfortable seats and ordered mineral water and some chips from the bar. The indie band, which had finished its set, had also come downstairs, and sat at the table next to us drinking beer. I still had very little grip on how much of what was happening was real and how much was only going on inside my own head, but I do know that Becka and I ended up at the table with the band, and that, after a while, we ended up outside, sitting on the carved stone steps which led down to the Liffey, necking with the bass player and the lead singer. I didn't even feel the chill of the night air, I just found it exhilarating to be back in Dublin again. This was what I remembered. The letting go. The lackadaisical fun. The forgetfulness of it all. The snogging.

I got the bass player. He had a tattoo of a rampant lion on his back. That's what I remember most. He showed it to me. Becka got the lead singer, who had peroxide hair. I know that I had sex with the bass player, but I don't remember it. We definitely had sex, though, because we booked into a seedy hotel over on the other side of the Liffey. Becka and the lead singer came too. We got a taxi which took a circuitous route via Donnybrook. We had laid down the law: no chocolate, no sex. So the taxi driver disapprovingly took us to the all-night store on Donnybrook Road and we stacked up piles of Crunchies and Whole-nut bars, then headed back to the hotel on the north side of the river. I don't know the bass player's name, but he signed us in as Mr and Mrs Neilson. I remember that bit – I hid my naked wedding finger from the guy on the desk who handed him the key. I don't remember much about the sex, though.

When I woke up it was after ten o'clock and there was blue biro scrawled all over my hand: 'Meet Becka at the Elephant and Castle in Temple Bar – NOON.' I hoped that we had had the foresight to write the same on Becka's hand. I hoped she hadn't had a hot, bubbly bath at any time before she went to sleep – before, during or after the throes of passion. I headed for the shower and made the same big decision that Becka had taken the night before.

I was never going to eat Mexican food again either.

There are some people who have to eat lots after a night on the town. I know people who sit down to a gargantuan full fry and a hot chocolate. I am just the opposite. I can't face a thing. The bass player – and in the cold light of day he looked quite magnificent – was still out cold on the bed when I finally got out of the shower and pulled my clothes back on. Everything still smelt of cigarettes and beer. I resolved to get a change of clothes as soon as I possibly could, but realised that first I ought to check the car. I left a goodbye note on the dressing-table, along with all the chocolate that was left over from the night before, then left the building. The skinheaded young concierge looked perturbed to see me go. I expect that he thought I might be absconding without paying for the room. He was too thin and kind of nervous, though, and he didn't even try to stop or question me on my way out. I took a brisk walk over to St Stephen's Green where I fed the parking meter with change from my pocket. It is true, you know, that the Lord provides. I didn't usually carry any money when Becka was around. I must have been sent up to the bar to buy something the night before. Or maybe it was change from the chocolate. Anyway, it was handy. It was eleven o'clock by then. I took two sets of fresh clothes out of the boot of the car – one for Becka and one for me – and I walked over to the National Gallery where I changed in the ladies toilets. I threw the old clothes out, stuffing everything into a sanitary disposal unit, which was the only bin. Then I wandered around the gallery for a while, letting the cold and splendid paintings soothe my befuddled brain.

At a quarter to twelve I made for Temple Bar. The Elephant and Castle is the height of urban chic, but sadly, that week they had a Mexican Special. There were little flowering cacti on all the tables and a great big sombrero installed over the service bar. The Gypsy Kings were playing energetic music, with much banging of guitars, over the stereo system. I ordered some mineral water and a pot of tea. I wasn't able to eat yet in any case, but the combination of the music and the smell of chilli and nachos was really upsetting me.

Becka arrived late, and in total disarray. She went to change in the toilet and, to my complete disbelief, ordered an Aztec Corn Soup when she returned to our table. 'I think,' she admitted, 'that it wasn't the fajitas last night, it was the tequila.'

You couldn't argue with that. Tequila is made from cactus, after all. It's bound not to be so good for you. I found myself wondering if they removed the spikes from the cacti before they fermented them, or whether they fermented the tequila with the spikes in it and sieved them off later.

Becka was oblivious. She tucked into her creamy

soup with gusto. It didn't take me too long to feel a bit better myself, and by quarter to one I had managed to give up on my great internal debate on the subject of the fermentation of cacti and had ordered a club sandwich and a Coke of my own.

Twenty-two

I don't know how many times I had driven to Mrs C's the morning after the night before. Plenty times. But somehow, this time I got lost. I made it to Drumcondra all right. Well, you can hardly miss it – it's on the main road leading northwards out of the city – but once we got there all the streets looked the same. We drove around for a while, until Becka realised that we were lost. She made me go to a petrol station to buy a map, then we slowly made our way to the house, constantly consulting the street guide. It looked just the same – magnolia pebbledash and a deep-red door. When we had first come to Dublin, at the very beginning, the door had been painted a bright sunflower yellow, but someone had told Mrs C that it looked a bit showy, and the next time we arrived down it had been painted claret. And claret it had stayed.

We rang the doorbell, but there was no answer, so we sat on the doorstep and waited for half an hour, until Mrs C returned, resplendent in an electric-blue pair of nylon trousers, a white blouse and a pair of navy walking shoes. She had been down at the shops.

'Liberty, dear. My, oh my, Liberty. Well gracious me, how are ye?' she said and ushered us inside.

The Catholic thing was kind of a culture shock for Becka. The hallway was a little shrine. There were statues of Our Lord and some of the saints, and there was even a little phial of water from Lourdes, where Mrs C had gone at one time, to seek Our Lady's help with her sciatica. Mrs C suffered from many mysterious complaints, which meant that she almost always 'ought to be resting in bed', although I had never seen or heard of her actually going to bed and resting at any time. She had most bother, allegedly, from what she called 'stomach troubles'. She had a hearty appetite, though. She ate anything. Myself, I thought that there was more likely something wrong with her womb. Mrs C would never talk about something like that, so, I figured, she had convinced herself that she had these terrible 'stomach troubles' so she could tell people about them in all honesty, when she had to explain the little brown bottles of pills ranging across the ledge in front of the kitchen window.

She made us all a big brown pot of tea and disappeared behind a small hillock of tupperware in the corner of the room, from which she brought out a fruit-cake and some scones. I told her that we wanted to stay the night and she said that would be fine.

We had to go for what we had come for, though. I nodded to Becka, who nodded at me and pointed out a photo of the Curran boys over the mantelpiece. 'Gosh,' she said innocently, 'are those boys all yours, Mrs Curran?'

'Five sons,' Mrs C admitted proudly. 'All away from home now, though.'

'Are they still in the Gaeltacht?' I asked.

'Oh, all over,' said Mrs C. 'You never know when they might turn up, those boys.'

'You must miss them,' said Becka.

'That I do. I miss them terrible. But you know, when they have grown up you have to let them go. If you let them go, you know, they'll come back. Visiting. I was thinking, though, that this summer I might go down to Galway myself. Just for a week, like. To visit.'

'That would be lovely. You can pick a week when the weather is nice. I've heard that Galway is lovely in the warm weather.'

'Ah it's beautiful any time, now. Just gorgeous. The light always changing. That's why all the great painters go there. I suppose I will go in August, though. It's the nicest time.'

'Do the boys stay very far from town?' I asked.

'Ah,' said Mrs C, her eyes going all misty. 'I've never been there myself, but I know it is out beyond the Twelve Pins. The middle of nowhere. Their father, God rest his soul, had land out there before he came to Dublin. It was bad living in those days. Bad living out the Gaeltacht.'

I remembered that one of the Irish Sunday papers had sent a group of journalists out to Connemara to live off the land for a week. Ireland has ruralism deeply embedded in its culture. Most people don't come from the city – if they do come from the city themselves, then their parents or grandparents came from the country. Consequently there is this idea that people belong in the country. It's a kind of rural idyll embedded in the soul of the nation – you should be living in the country, where you can be poor, but honest: in the country close to nature and close to God. So anyway, this newspaper had cashed in on it and had sent a squad of journalists off to the countryside to live out the nation's dreams. They had set up a good, old-fashioned camp and they were supposed to catch rabbits and things. Anyhow, they sent back a long report, in which they stated that they had caught and killed a sheep, which had supplied them with ample meat for their week of hardship. There was an outcry in Dublin. Sheep do not roam wild around the Gaeltacht. They hadn't caught a sheep, they had stolen one. Public opinion demanded that the owner be found and reimbursed. The theft of a sheep in the Gaeltacht was a serious matter. Two rival farmers had come forward claiming ownership of the stolen animal, and two damages claims ensued. The nation was on tenterhooks and the whole matter blew up out of all proportion. The journalists were recalled to Dublin where, after a few days of questioning and even some police involvement, they eventually admitted that they had made up the whole story about the sheep. They had, they claimed, genuinely spent their first day in Connemara trying to bait food, but in the end they had given in to their hunger and had eaten each day at the Bed and Breakfast about a mile from their camp. But they had still had to produce the article for the newspaper. They had decided, all together, on the story about the sheep. It made the co-ordination of their story easier, since if the animal was large enough, they would only have to make up and stick to one story about its capture and slaughter, and they would be able to claim the meat had lasted for the whole week. The fraud had had a profound effect on my imagination. Now when people talked about living off the land in the Gaeltacht, I was always kind of suspicious. I had heard, though, that the IRA didn't pay its soldiers much. The top guys were doing all right, but most of the money went on equipment. So maybe it was possible that the Curran boys were telling the truth. Maybe the lads were living off the land, roughing it, after all.

Mrs C was fair away with herself. 'We'll go into Galway, of course. For a Sunday lunch at a nice hotel. They have to move around all the time anyway. For the food. Last summer Liam went as far as Ballyvaughan, down in County Clare, to catch fish off the pier there. No fish left in Galway town. The Corrib was empty, what with all the tourists. They love a nice bit of fish, my boys. Once Conor told me that he had gone to Galway in the night and killed a swan there. Beautiful swans they have on the Corrib in Galway in the summertime. Hundreds on the water, making it glow at night.'

'Handsome boys,' mused Becka, who was staring at the photographs.

Mrs C beamed.

After tea we sat in front of the television, while Mrs C battered around the kitchen for a while. At seven o'clock we told her we were ready for bed. The night before had taken its toll. She put us into the pristine twin room next to her own and we arranged to have breakfast the next morning at eight.

'I can't believe we are in bed at half past seven,' said Becka. All I could see of her in the dark was a slightly luminous face, like the moon, appearing over the top of the pale-green duvet cover. Mrs C had 'done over' all the bedrooms when the boys had left. I expect that before they went the rooms were blue and black and full of boys' things. She had made them all green and peach. The house was a great source of pride to her.

I giggled at Becka. 'Aren't you tired?' I asked.

'Yeah. But half past seven.'

'You don't have to sleep. Tell me about last night.'

'His name was Seamus,' said Becka.

'You're doing better than me. I know he told me his name. I just can't remember it,' I admitted.

'What else can't you remember?'

'Anything that had a chance of being good. I wish I had been sick like you. I'd do better then. Focuses the mind. Gets rid of the alcohol.'

'Are we going to the Twelve Pins, then?'

'Yeah. I'd like to.'

'Me too,' said Becka. 'But first, tomorrow can we go to Thomastown in Kilkenny? Seamus is singing there.'

'You have to be joking.'

'No. It's nearly on the way, isn't it?'

'No. It's not.'

'It is nearly. Come on.'

'Do you know where they are playing?'

'In a pub with a courtyard. There's a marquee.'

'I can't believe you are such a tart! Of course we can go.'

'I can't believe you are such a square. Anyway – it's not being a tart. It's being a groupie.'

We lapsed into good-humoured silence for a while, and I was just about going to sleep when Becka sat up in her bed. She had obviously been pondering for a while just why we were looking for the Currans. She sat up as if she had had an epiphany. It was kind of startling. 'You want to kill them, don't you?' she said.

I turned over and opened my eyes. 'I don't know. I think so.'

'The odds are against them having killed your parents, you know.'

'Yeah. Way against that. There are enough psychopaths in Belfast to have managed it all on their own. No, I know that. I suppose they might have. Or they might not have. They killed Lorna McLeish, though. All of them did, no matter who pulled the trigger or whatever they did to her to finish her off. They must have killed other people too.'

'Poor Lorna McLeish,' said Becka.

'I think it's because they would have killed my parents. If they had been told to do it, that is. They are just as responsible. In any case I think they are.'

'How do you want to do it?' Becka asked.

'I'm not sure. We could pick them off one by one. I wonder if they've got guns.'

'I have a kind of idea,' said Becka. 'I think I know what to do. Do you think, though, Libbs, that we could get our hands on this money? The money David Curran's transferring. The IRA stuff.'

'If we went back to London. Maybe. If he can transfer it in for his brothers, maybe he can transfer it out for us.

If they haven't used it yet. We'd have to kill him, though. And knocking people off in the middle of nowhere is one thing, but knocking off a bank executive in London is another. Don't know if I fancy it. It'd be crazy. Stealing money from the IRA. They'd slaughter us.'

'My God,' said Becka. 'I never dreamt we'd be like this. I never dreamt.'

Neither had I. I was shocked at Becka. She was the one who had gone to the police, after all. I hadn't expected her to agree so readily. I had expected her to try and talk me out of it. Now, I suppose, it gave her a good reason to stay with me. A reason other than friendship. I hardly noticed then how keen she was about the money. I was too caught up in my own thoughts. I stared into the dark silence of suburbia and realised that the comfort of that silence had been taken away from me for ever. I don't mind that, though. I have new comforts now.

After a while I went to sleep and the whole conversation just became part of my own dreams of freedom. The last thing I remember thinking of, before I finally did go under, was wondering to myself why it was that Mrs C had never mentioned David. The boys maybe were out the Gaeltacht, sure enough. But David certainly wasn't. He must have been living in London for a while. She never mentioned him, though, separate as he was. Different from the others. She never singled him out. It niggled for a while, then finally the haziness of sleep overtook me.

Twenty-three

Mrs C laid on a great breakfast. She fried everything up in an enormous pan, which straddled all four rings of her cooker, for she was used to the appetites of five growing lads. We were starving after our long sleep, and we dug in with some gusto and made not a bad showing, for two puny-looking girls.

'Where are you off to today, then?' asked Mrs C, who was cramming toast with butter and marmalade into her mouth with alarming enthusiasm and washing it down with great, unladylike gulps of strong tea.

'Back to Belfast,' I said definitely. 'We have to return the car to a friend of Becka's father. We only borrowed it. I have to get back to England, too. Just a holiday this time. We had fun though, didn't we Becka?'

Becka nodded.

After breakfast we packed our things back into the car, paid Mrs C and drove off.

'They're her sons,' said Becka.

'Yes,' I replied. It didn't really change the way I felt.

The road to Thomastown, Kilkenny is made up of half European-funded motorway, which you can fly down at a great pace of knots, and half old road, which, when you come upon it all of a sudden, means that you have to slow down at a ferociously dangerous pace. I'm sure more people must die on the rough and smooth roads in Ireland than in places with just the old roads.

It's the mixture that's dangerous. You never quite know what's coming next. It was a gorgeous, sunny spring day, and we drove through Kildare and stopped off along the way to stand in the sunshine and watch the horses in the roadside fields.

'We're so lucky,' said Becka.

'Yeah.' I was beginning to feel powerful. I had made a decision.

'It's only one day,' Becka carried on, as if she knew I just wanted to get on with it. 'It's on our way.'

I hung my head back, taking in the spring sunshine, and I felt free. 'It's OK,' I said. 'I'm quite looking forward to seeing what's-his-name.'

The gig wouldn't start until early in the evening and we had no intention of showing ourselves up by being too early, but we didn't have anything much to do. Becka said she couldn't face lunch. I had to agree. That breakfast would keep me going until tea-time. We cut off the main road and just drove around for a while, taking in the derelict old cottages and the modern bungalows with the satellite dishes outside, which had replaced them. I suppose that is something which always interests me about the country in Ireland. The need people have to rebuild. They eschew these beautiful little cottages and build new, with a complete disregard for history or tradition. Maybe they are eschewing their colonial past along with the buildings. I don't know.

After a while we came to a little town, where we stopped off and wandered aimlessly around the shops. There was a pottery there, and we were more or less the first tourists of the season.

'Will you have a cup of tea?' the old lady who was looking after the pottery shop said insistently. 'Ah, go on, now. You will. You will.'

She beetled around in the back and came out with big, bold mugs of tea. Then she was unrelentingly nice to us for over quarter of an hour. We knew we were going to have to buy something. In the end we decided to go for the mugs themselves (£7.50 each and made on the premises), and we wandered out into the street, still sipping tea as we went. It was a nice enough little place. Further down the road we found a shop selling little bits of jewellery and cheap incense oil and bubble lamps and all sorts of other things that you don't need. Just waffle, really. We left laden with different coloured sun-glasses and silver and gold nail varnish, and we wandered around for a while and finally sat out on a wooden bench in the sunny summer square and Becka made me try on all the different coloured glasses to see how they made me feel. I stared at the town rosy-eyed, and blue-eyed and green-eyed, but nothing made the day less sunny; nothing made me feel like we were on less of an adventure than we were.

'Keep trying,' said Becka, who had herself gone for the orange glasses all along.

In the afternoon we stopped off and lay in a field just outside Thomastown. I fell asleep while Becka studiously painted her nails with uneven gold and silver zebra stripes. When I woke up again her nails were done and she was grinning from ear to ear. Well, she was sitting smoking a joint. It took a second or two for me to realise what that meant.

'Oh my God,' I said, 'you brought drugs over the border. If they had found that we'd be in big trouble, you know.'

'What, like we will be when they find the bodies of those Curran boys?' she parried, passing me the toke.

Becka's so reckless. I suppose that's what I like about her. The lack of pretence. The spirit. The danger. The disloyalty.

I took a long, deep draw and decided not to make a big issue of it. It was just after four o'clock and

Thomastown was only a few minutes away. We would have to find something to do. Dope never works for me. Well, it never has yet. Acid and Ecstasy and mushrooms all make me happy and high and full of the beans of wonder and love. Cocaine makes me speed up – I dance fast and I think fast. I am the wittiest girl in the country when I am on coke. Alcohol makes me slide easily into adventures. But dope just makes me cross because it never works for me. I handed the joint back to Becka and said I wanted to go back into the car. We drove the last leg into Thomastown looking for inspiration. And there it was. I pulled up the car outside the ladies' hairdressing shop. In fact, I was very taken with that shop. We had been messing around with the way we looked all day. But if the nail varnish wasn't for me, I was going to get professional help with something else. We needed to change our appearance. We were on our way to commit a crime. Later, there might be descriptions. Oh, it all made sense.

Around seven o'clock, when Becka and I both came out of the shop we were blonde. Not strawberry blonde, mind, or dusty blonde, but peroxide blonde, and I had had my eyelashes and eyebrows dyed a deep, blue black. It was the most outrageous hairdo that Thomastown had seen in a while and no mistake. You'd be amazed what blonde can do for you. I had been mousy all of my life. We changed outfits in the back of the car into the pastel shades that blonde girls wear best with jeans and then we chose our coloured sunglasses with fastidious care and headed for the gig. It was the first time in my life that I walked into a pub and people turned to look at me. We were truly stunning. I had never felt so powerful before. I had never realised that the way that you look has such an effect on other people. Take my advice, if you want lots of attention, go blonde. White blonde. Even if it means a wig.

'This is a bad disguise,' said Becka. 'It makes us a bit distinctive.'

'D'ya think?' I asked, looking, rapt, at myself in the mirror.

The indie boys liked it, though. We walked out of the main pub, through to what was a kind of tented coach-house courtyard at the back of the building. We walked right in on their sound check, watching for about a minute as the singer flung himself around the stage, led by the tambourine which was shimmering before him. Then they noticed us.

The bass player jumped down off the platform and walked eagerly across the bare boards of the marquee towards me. 'Wow,' he said. 'Whatcha do?'

'Had a shock. Bad shock. Terrible.' I laughed.

'Looks great,' he said.

Then Becka's lead singer called him back on to the stage and we arranged to meet up with them after the gig. They weren't playing until nine. As we were on our way out, we noticed two girls right at the back of the marquee. They looked at us with those-are-our-boys daggers in their eyes. They were kind of too skinny – the sort of dissolute, desperate girls who hang around indie bands all the time.

When I was growing up and I started to go to Dublin on weekend trips, I always wanted to be one of those kind of stunning girls who'd grunge around the place in old clothes and just look amazing. They knew how to flirt, all right. I could never quite believe that I wasn't one of them. I was amazed when I caught sight of myself in the mirror. And pissed off. I had thought I was taller. Those girls were usually pretty. And manipulative. And calculating. I knew of one girl, one time, who had tried to kill herself over a guy in a band who had dumped her. She became a bit of a legend on the Dublin scene for a while. She had called the ambulance before she had taken the pills.

But now, all blonde and dressed in Becka's old clothes, I was truly gorgeous for the first time in my life and the girls at the back of the hall were just fishbait which had been too long in the water. I dragged Becka over to them.

'I'm Libby,' I said. I figured we might as well be civil, seeing as how we were going to win anyway.

'Yeah,' Becka said. 'I'm Becka.'

The groupies looked a little bit shocked. No one from the band had blown the sound check when they came in.

'I'm Rolex,' said the darker one. She had been dancing around, like a black-haired banshee, when we had first arrived. 'This is Peach.'

'You know the boys, then?' asked Peach. Straight to the point, there.

'For years,' said Becka. 'Really old friends.'

I was beginning to enjoy immensely the power of being pretty. I had never been considered a threat before.

'Well,' said Rolex, who couldn't have despised us more, 'I guess we'll be seeing you around.'

'Not for long,' I said, allaying her fears on the one hand and winding her up on the other. 'We won't be around for long. We're working in London just now. For the BBC. Have to get back there, you know. New series starts in a couple of weeks.'

This was a breeze. Girls like us won hands down over girls like them, once we had had our hair done, that is.

We sauntered out of the marquee and back into the pub, fuelled by our own giggles, and ordered mineral waters. This time I wanted to remember my night with the bass player. After that we decided we were hungry, so we left to go in search of the chip shop. We just followed our noses around the other side of the square to the shop, where one of the hairdressers was serving behind the counter with her cousin. It looked like the family owned half the town. We chatted jocularly and introduced ourselves round.

'Can't thank you enough. You are so brilliant. We have just got more attention than we would have thought possible.'

The hairdresser beamed and gave us extra chips. 'Looks fabulous,' she said. 'I said that to my mother. Just fabulous.'

We sat out in the square eating our supper with greasy fingers and swigging red lemonade from the bottle. And then, at nine, we sauntered back to the pub, just as we heard the sounds of the band getting into its stride.

The gig passed quickly as if it was only one long song. After the set, during which the lead singer dedicated two songs to Becka and me, we camped with the boys, down by the river. We were all tired, but high. We had danced for the whole of the gig. Danced barefoot, like the possessed, without stopping for breath. Perhaps that's why it had gone so quickly. Then we had walked together in the inky black countryside around the town. They had already set up tents and built a campfire, and we all sat around and sang as the bass player strummed on an acoustic guitar. I think there were about ten of us. Becka got hold of the tambourine and covered herself in glory. The drummer brought out a pair of bongos. We sang for over an hour. Rolex and Peach skulked, but they clung on like terriers none the less, abandoning the comfort of their Dublin beds, waiting for the moment when we would leave and they could pounce again.

We told them all that we were just going on a road trip. We told them that we were going to drive all the way around Ireland – all the way around the coastline. We told them we would be camping, just sleeping in the car, or staying in the odd Bed and Breakfast joint.

We couldn't have sounded farther from Thelma and Louise if we tried. We were charming. Becka pulled out two bags of marshmallows which she had appropriated at the chip shop, and we toasted them over the fire on sticks. Then we settled. It must have been after two in the morning, and the air was so chill that even bundled up together by the fire, we still felt cold. It was cosy, though. I had expected to while my way into sleep as I had for the few nights before, fluttering on the wings of my new freedom. Imagining my revenge.

'I don't know your name,' I whispered to the bass player as we pulled his sleeping bag over ourselves and settled down beside the glow.

'Mike,' he said. 'Mike Curran.' And he kissed me.

It caught my breath. It was like a knife, that kiss.

Pictures of the Curran brothers flashed before my eyes for the whole long night. I didn't sleep a wink.

Twenty-four

All over the world, when they train anti-terrorist troops, they teach them a very interesting thing. If you are a soldier and you are faced with armed, dangerous terrorists, and you get into a shoot-out, you are trained to shoot the women first, and to shoot them to kill. That is because women are considered more vicious than men in that particular situation. Once they have dedicated themselves to a cause, women will fight to the end for it. No holds barred. The men, however, are more likely to give themselves up once things seem truly hopeless. That cold Thomastown night, I mused on that particular fact. It was one which had always interested me. I realised that I wasn't playing a game any more. I had a purpose and it was one I had taken on with a selfishness I hadn't seen in myself before. I didn't want to piss around any more. I was dedicated – truly dedicated – to killing the Currans. I wanted revenge. Not for Lorna McLeish (God rest her soul), not even for Ma and Dad (rest theirs too), but for me. I wanted the satisfaction of not being afraid any more. It did occur to me that perhaps I had turned into a terrorist myself – I was prepared to kill for something rather than trust it to justice. I was not participating in society in the way I had been taught was right. I knew that. But it didn't matter to me. I knew what I wanted too. And what I wanted was more important. I think that everyone has something that they will kill for. It's just a matter of how far things have to go until you get angry enough. For some guys it's having beer spilt over them in the pub. For others it's someone muscling in on their drugs territory. For normal people, though, it's different. The thing that makes you violent is probably something which would never happen in the day-to-day run of things. It's something difficult to imagine, that thing which would hurl you over the edge of the moral abyss. Imagine if someone gunned down your children in cold blood. Would you kill him? Imagine if someone kneecapped your brother. If someone raped your wife. Held a sawn-off shotgun to your mother's head? Really imagine it. Imagine it like it had happened and scare yourself with the power of your own fear.

That's what living in the North does for you every day of the week. I knew a guy one time who watched horror movies. Hundreds of them. He came from Ballymena. Horror movies were his life.

I watched the bass player as he slept and I knew that the phone books of Ireland were full of pages of Currans, running into their thousands. I knew that they weren't all related. Not nowadays. I knew that the bass player didn't look anything like any of the big, bad Currans – the ones that I was after. But I also knew that I wouldn't ever be able to see him again. Just because of his name. I was dedicated to my cause.

At six in the morning I slid out of the sleeping bag and crept over to where Becka lay hot with sleep and motionless, curled into a ball in the arms of the lead singer. I nudged her.

She crawled out of his sleepy grasp.

'What is it?'

'We have to go before they get up.'

There must have been something particularly authoritative about my tone of voice. She didn't question it, even though I know she would like to have stayed. We walked up the river bank to the car, started it up and then we drove for half an hour before either of us spoke.

'Oh, my God,' I said. 'We're on the wrong road.'

'Fate,' replied Becka.

I had thought we could cut across the country, north-west across Kilkenny, through Tipperary and up into County Galway. Of course, we didn't have a map. That hadn't helped. I had made it into Tipperary all right, but we were heading towards Limerick, which is to the west, rather than to Galway, which is almost due north. There was no way that I was going back to try and find the right road, and besides it might be a slightly longer route, but we'd still get there.

Limerick is the biggest town on the whole west side of the country and it has a reputation for being particularly tough. Every springtime they have a Festival of the Visual Arts in Limerick, much to the bemusement of the majority of the locals. The festival brings about a thousand artists from all over the country to the town and they have an enormous bash for about a week. The opening party is famed. Limerick bouncers have particular difficulty dealing with hordes of (admittedly) scruffy Irish artists. They are used to tough guys, but tough guys who wear suits. After a couple of years, they had to start bringing bouncers down from Dublin for the party. The ones from Limerick treated anyone in jeans as if they were criminals. The Minister for Culture (casually attired) only gained admittance when one of his bodyguards pushed the point. Two other particularly important people in the visual arts were stopped and searched for knives. You can't entirely blame the bouncers for that, though. After all, it's the town that the 'Limerick smile' comes from. In the Eighties there were big gangs in Limerick. Really ferocious bastards. Anyway, when they mugged you in Limerick they would cut you with a knife, just at the corners of your mouth. Then they would kick you in the stomach until you screamed. When you did scream the whole of your face ripped open. The scars which were left (and it generally took over a year to heal the gashes) made it look like you were smiling all the time. The town got such bad press that the Government set up an urban regeneration committee – and one of the things those guys had come up with was the Limerick Festival of the Visual Arts. So I figured that maybe Limerick might be a good place to start. It certainly might be a good place to buy a gun.

'How much money have we got left?' I asked Becka.

She dived into her pocket and brought out a sorry array of notes. 'A hundred or so,' she said.

'Shit.'

'What's up?'

'How are we going to buy a gun?'

Becka beamed. 'We don't need one,' she said. 'I have got a plan.'

She wouldn't spill the beans, though, until we had had a shower and some breakfast. So I decided that we would stop before Limerick – when we made it to Tipperary town. We were there by half past eight. We decided to head for the new sports centre. It's crazy, really, a town the size of Tipperary having a sports centre. I suppose in the summer plenty of tourists make the long Trip to Tipp. Perhaps it is particularly well used in the summer. We sat on the steps and waited. The place didn't open until nine. Then we paid in and had a shower and a steam bath, where we lolled around on the smooth white banquette and saw who could catch the most drips from the ceiling in her mouth. Afterwards we plunged into icy showers and at last, duly refreshed, we got changed and walked up the main street to buy some breakfast in the little hotel there. It was a cold day. Becka didn't feel it, though, and she lent me her jacket. There was a pair of men's boxer shorts in the pocket.

I drew them out slowly. 'What on earth is this?'

'They're Seamus's. I stole them,' she said, with the proud look on her face of a cat who has brought home a dead pigeon.

I didn't ask how she'd done it.

When we got to the hotel, we decided that we were exhausted and I must say, we both looked particularly peaky against the demanding colour of our new hair. We decided to take a double room and rest up for the day, make our plans, then head up through Galway to Connemara. Becka had about a hundred pounds' worth of Ecstasy tablets which we could sell if we needed the extra money, which it looked as if we might.

'Happy I brought my little box now?' she said.

'Ecstatic,' I replied, settling down under the floral bedspread for a good day's sleep. 'So tell me this plan of yours.'

'We can poison them. I have got some poison.'

'What?'

'I nicked it from Professor Jackson. From the lab. The cupboard,' she said, and threw a small bottle with a yellow label on to the bed. Becka's kleptomania was burgeoning, and she was good at nicking things too – the knickers off an indie star and the poison from under a scientist's nose. I decided I had better start checking my pockets regularly.

'You are one dodgy babe,' I said.

Becka beamed again. 'Not my father's daughter for nothing,' she replied.

'Well, Lucrezia Borgia, the only thing is,' I pointed out, 'that we will have to get pretty close to them to be able to poison them.'

'No we don't. Not really. We could nip it into their pints in the pub.'

I laughed. 'In the Gaeltacht? You've got to be joking.

Wait till you see it. We'll stand out like a sore thumb. Unless you happen to speak Irish, of course. And we dye our hair back to normal. How is your Irish?'

'*Amachas an Dáil anois,*' said Becka.

'That's it?'

She nodded.

'Me too,' I admitted. 'That and *tiocfadh ar lá* of course.' Our Irish then, was limited to campaign slogans and marching songs.

Becka was not to be put off. 'We'll think of something,' she said cheerfully. 'Anyway, we have to find them first. And that'll take some doing. The Curran Brothers, Somewhere out by the Twelve Pins is not much of an address to go on.'

'True. Let's sleep on it.'

And I fell into dreamless slumber to the sound of Becka picking her way through the mini bar, eating all the chocolate and peanuts and washing them down with miniature bottles of rum.

It would cost us the same to stay all night in Tipperary as it would if we decided to leave at six o'clock, which is when I woke up again. So we decided to stay. Becka had been up all afternoon, watching TV, and now she was the one who was tired. We had more showers and went for a walk around Tipperary, which looked particularly pretty that April evening. We called in to the pub for a drink and Becka noticed that there was a night-club on that evening at the sports centre. No sooner had we seen the poster than we decided to go. There wasn't much else to do. Walk among the cowfields. Eat more. Drink more. We figured we might as well dance. And dance we did. Until midnight. Becka sold most of her Ecstasy tablets and netted £20 more than she had reckoned. Prices in Tipperary were inflated and she was undoubtedly the most popular girl on the dance floor. She even managed to get rid of the rest of the magic mushrooms, at

184

£5 a pop. The youth of Tipperary thought that the Big Wide World had come to visit in the shape of two fast-dancing, drug-dealing blonde girls, who claimed to be from Dublin. Part of me was worried about being spotted, perhaps even arrested. But the Gardaí in Tipperary didn't know any more about drugs than what they had read in the tabloids.

We slept up at the hotel, had a big breakfast at seven in the morning and zoomed out of Tipperary, all the richer, on to the Limerick Road. We hit Limerick town mid-morning and had a picnic lunch by the river. Then we made our way north towards Galway, gunless as planned. I drove straight into the city through the quays and parked down by the Spanish Arch, where we sat for nearly an hour, contemplating the smooth-flowing river, duly bedecked with swans, just as Mrs C had described. It was still quite early, but we decided that we would sleep there beside the arch in the car that evening in any case.

Galway is the last town before the Gaeltacht. At one time clocks in Galway ran twenty minutes behind clocks in Dublin. To tell the truth, it's still a bit that way. In the summer, when the place is a morass of festivals, it's full of hippies and travellers. They come for the Arts Festival. The Oyster Festival. The Galway Races. The tall sail ships which race around the coastline of the west coast in the summer. In the winter the town is battered by the biting winds which come across the Atlantic and break on to Galway with a howling ferocity. The tourists disappear and the place is awash with farmers and local wide-boys. In the summer, though, it just rains mostly. They say if you stand on the beach at Galway and you can see the Aran Islands then it's sure to rain. They also say that if you stand on the beach and you can't see the Aran Islands, well, it's already raining. It's a small town which has made good and there are plenty of locals who are ready to make a quick buck out of that. They are an ignorant, vicious type – the tourist sharks. But mannerly – in Galway they are nice to you as they take your money, though it's really only the money that they care about. It's an attractive town, though: it has a river and the University and the old quarter with the cottages of the Claddagh and the terraced, winding streets and the Long Walk, which runs all up one side of the river. It's popular – plenty of people have a reason to go there. For one thing, it's a good place for rich people to retire or keep cottages. It's only two or three hours from Dublin, and right on the cusp of the most remote and arguably the most beautiful countryside in Europe. That's heaven for rich folks who want to get away from it all. It's also dole heaven for burnt-out hippies. There are tourists in season, and students out of season. And the land around the town is quite cheap, so it attracts people who want to get out of the rat race if they have some capital – Galway is surrounded by oyster farms, and organic gardens and handmade cheese factories. It has the highest proportion of vegetarians in the country. So, apart from the tourist sharks there are nice people there too. On Saturdays there is a famous market, beside the old quarter of the town, where all the local producers come and sell their cheese, bread, vegetables, oysters, pots, knitting, wooden toys, or whatever it is that they make. It is a kind of enchanting place, and no mistaking that.

We had arrived right at the beginning of the season, when the weather was still crisp, and no summer blow-ins had yet arrived to camp illegally on the banks of the Corrib. They say that takes up more police time than anything in Galway at the beginning of the summer, until about mid-June when the police just give up trying to stem the flood of campers with nowhere else to stay. I told Becka about a trip to Galway I had made one time, when a long weekend in Dublin had turned

186

into a lost fortnight. The Galway Arts Festival was on and we came across country to watch the street theatre and drink pints out in the summer sun. We had discovered the delights of Salthill, which is the holiday resort to the west of the city. Some of the shenanigans in Salthill put Blackpool to shame. There were slot machines and donkey rides and everything shimmered with neon – even in the afternoon. We had spent our afternoons in Salthill on the shore, then headed back into town for the evenings. Salthill turned into Tacky Disco Central by eight in the evening. We had preferred to sit out the balmy August night, beside a great, open campfire by the river, and sing and drink whiskey out of the bottle. It turned out that the guy with the whiskey had broken into a little restaurant further along the quay and had stolen a whole case. The guards came and arrested him very early one morning. They left the rest of us alone, though. I suppose they figured that we hadn't known and, after all, there were about twenty people around the campfire that night – too many to accommodate in Galway's small police station on account of twelve bottles of stolen whiskey. There were a few really rough guys those weeks that we hung around Galway. Guys who slept in the open without a tent and stole whatever they could. Guys who got into fights when there was no need. I remember one of them had been refused entry into a pub – he was fighting drunk already and had only wanted to go in to use the toilet. He had pulled his dick out of his trousers and peed all over the bouncer's shoes. We had left Galway and camped out in Connemara. We visited little villages, with just one pub and a post office which doubled up as a shop; we swam in the reedy, freezing rivers and lay out on the rough hills of the Gaeltacht until, after a fortnight or so, we had run out of money and, worse, we had run out of drugs, so we had headed back to our grey Belfast lives.

Belfast, in one way, is extraordinarily orderly. Most of the trouble is political – and the terrorists curb the freedom of the kind of people who would chance peeing on a bouncer's shoes. It has the lowest incidence of domestic violence in the Western world, you know. We headed back to Queen's, high on the fun-filled freedom of summer. But Galway had really impressed me. I was glad to be back.

Becka and I decided to head up to Quay Street for a pizza and a pint. It was that kind of time of day. We made for the Quays, which was the most famous pub in Galway, and settled down to our Guinness in rough wooden seats made from old barrels. The Quays had tremendous character. It had been bought over about twenty years ago, when it was just a dirty quayside brawl bar, by one of those Galway entrepreneurs. Now it was the trendiest pub in the county. The regulars sat up at the bar, sipping their pints with measured precision and greeting each other with a nod of the head. It was four o'clock in the afternoon. The pace in Galway is slow, even by the standards of Southern Ireland. It's where tensed-up Irish people go to wind down.

'I've got it,' said Becka. 'I know how to do it.'

We were close enough together to be able to talk in low voices without anyone else hearing.

'If they really are trapping wild game, it'll be easy. We'll poison the animals in their traps. They will cook 'em, eat 'em and that'll be that. Untraceable. There's no way anyone could know it was us.'

'You sure this stuff is deadly enough to kill them? All of them? Even a small amount?'

'Hey,' said Becka, 'trust me. When it comes to chemicals I have the world's most inclusive education. The professor taught me everything he knows.'

'It's never like this in the movies,' I pointed out.

Becka glanced around the shebeen. 'Looks like a movie to me,' she replied.

The easygoing nature of the West sank into us, and we gradually finished our pints and ordered some more as the pub filled up with students. It was the beginning of the summer term. Mostly they were carrying clip files bulging with notes, and they were complaining to each other about how much work they had to do. There seemed no sign of anyone doing any work at all, though. The Quays just got fuller and fuller until the seats ran out and it became difficult to make it to the bar, through the burgeoning crowds of customers, to reorder your Guinness. We got chatting to a lad from London called Simon, who was waiting for his friends to arrive. He had wild, weird hair which flopped irregularly over his shoulders, and a little scar down one cheek. He might have looked menacing had he not been wearing lime-green dungarees and purple Doc Martens. Simon was studying law. Now what use on this earth an Irish law degree might be to a cockney called Simon in lime-green dungarees I have no idea, but he was very amiable all the same and told us about a club that evening in Salthill. At first I didn't really take him seriously, but it seemed that someone had rented out one of the tacky discos in Salthill and was putting on an ambient house gig once a week. He said that the place was packed and people came from all over to it. There were kids driving from Country Clare and hitching over from Dublin. The party was called 'Mercedes Heaven' and it happened at the Golden Cow Ballroom. Becka had half a dozen tablets of acid we could get rid of and Simon said he could get us into the club for free, so we arranged to go. Eventually his friends arrived. One was a beautiful girl, who came into the pub on roller-blades. She was wearing pink hotpants and a tiny tank top and she had the body of a model, but all the dreamy-eyed wonder of a believer. The other was a surly-looking guy who didn't say anything much for about half an hour, until he had downed some beer. Once the alcohol hit his system there was an astonishing transformation and he turned out to be a DJ called Michael.

'So,' Becka asked him, 'how addicted to alcohol are you, cheery boy? Do you wake up in an absolute heap on the floor and not know how you got there?'

Michael almost went back to looking glum again. 'Big time,' he admitted. 'No doubt about it. I'm getting better, though. For a while it took Bolivian Marching Powders to get me going in the morning. I think I'm gradually cleaning out. Now it's only a couple of shots of Rambling Turkey.'

We ended up chatting about football. The girl with the roller-blades was a big fan of Manchester United and we eagerly swapped our best examples of terrace chants, though the edited highlights of Toby's collection won the day. We had been planning to go and fetch some pizza, but in the end the pizza came to us. By about ten o'clock there were a couple of lads who wandered round the pub with trays of hot snacks at a pound a pop. There were spicy stuffed naan breads and squares of pizza with mushroom topping and baked potatoes which had been mashed up and refilled with a kind of herby butter through them. We stuck with the pizza and another pint before we started the long, windy walk out to Salthill. It was refreshing, to say the least. The temperature had dropped down below zero and the wind had come up something vicious.

When we got to the club we were some of the first people there. We breezed past the pay-in desk and made for the bar. The whole dance floor was overhung by at least a hundred small glittering balls. You know the kind, the ones made of mirrors, which feature in *Come Dancing*. Well, they were just like that, but smaller. The music boomed, and one solitary brunette was going through her paces out there on the boards. There was an air of frantic expectation about the place. And gradually it did fill up. Within about an hour and a half it was packed way beyond what might be classed a reasonable fire risk, and you had to fight to get close enough to the bar to get your drinks in. The crowd were of Ireland's coolest, but it really was too busy to stay for long. Becka had fought her way to the space just in front of the DJ's box and sold her wares off and we decided to go back to the car.

Outside we hopped into one of the waiting taxis which left us back at the Spanish Arch. Our car was the only one left in the car park. I slept in the front and Becka laid herself out in the back. Out of the wind it wasn't as cold as I had expected. We piled on a couple of jumpers and stared out through the windscreen at the stars. The swans paddled delicately in the water. It was a really beautiful place. There was a peace and serenity about it which left your soul soaring.

'We'll head for Connemara tomorrow,' I said.

Becka mumbled her agreement. 'I know why they came here,' she started. 'I mean it is a great place to hide. It's so sleepy. We should come back again. In different circumstances. Another time.'

'Yeah,' I said. I counted up on my fingers the number of days we had been away from London and the number of days I had before I had to get back there. Ten days. Only just over a week. Charlie Campbell seemed more than a million miles away. More than a planet away. Another cosmos. I thought about buildings. The ramshackle streets of Galway suited me just fine. Architecture. Structure. Your life is a very private thing. There are general rules to follow, of course, but the real decisions are personal. Different things seduce different people. Different people want different things. And that's the trick. To be honest, I mean. Right at that moment, like Becka, I suppose, I could have

191

stayed beside the Corrib for the rest of my life, listening to the plash of the swans, watching the stars in the stormy sky and easing myself into the lull of forgetfulness for ever. Letting go and copping out all at once.

But the thing I had always wanted, and the thing I really wanted still, was to build tower blocks into the sky. To make the soaring crystal day-dreams of my happiest moments into the diamond skyscrapers of tomorrow. To triumph not only over gravity (which you cannot see or touch or smell), but also over the musky earth of nature which you can throttle with your bare hands if you are willing to squat in the dirt. I wanted to triumph in just the same way over the soft clay of my own nature. I wanted to fire it with revenge. I wanted to mould it until it showed how powerful it really was. I wanted to build myself into an icy tower of achievement so that I could point to myself with pride. My dreams weren't enough any more. I wanted to build them too. And because of that I required freedom. So I would never know retreat again.

I watched a big debate one time on TV where they were arguing about whether dangerous adventure sports should be legal. On one side of the audience there was an array of rock climbers, sky divers, bungee jumpers, free-fall enthusiasts and professional stuntmen. On the other side there were people who had been paralysed in tragic accidents and the families of participants who had died in the course of one sport or another. There was a man from the British Safety Council and a lady who had given up being a jockey when her kids were born. It was an interesting debate. A lot of the people in wheelchairs said that they wouldn't have it any other way. They reckoned that you were dead already if you didn't take risks and experience the adventure of your life. You had to conquer your fear. You had to climb your own mountains, whatever they might be. The whole audience ended up arguing against the poor guy from the British Safety Council, who said he was all for life, but thought that foolish risks were unnecessary in the course of experiencing it. It reminded me of Cervantes, who wrote a lot about passion and taking risks and being alive. His works were banned from the main school library, available only to the sixth form in their final summer term. We had hidden the books, still sharing them as we had been taught to do. But till that moment in Galway I had never really understood what an adventure life could be, if you followed your heart and did what you really wanted to do, which is what we must all do in the end.

And now, it seemed, I was engaged in what was probably one of the more dangerous adventure sports on the planet, and whenever I wondered just what I was doing I had only to close my eyes and remember the gentle laughter of my parents which I would never share again. I realised that only a very small part of my spirit, of me I suppose, was there with my body in the car. The revelation came like the clear, bright moonlight, an intense, engulfing and unyielding epiphany. Part of me still lived in Angel Avenue and always would. Part of me basked in the memory of my parents, in the blinding, bright light of a way of life which was dimmed for ever and dimmed too soon. I had to be faithful to that.

I glanced over at Becka, who was fast asleep, and decided I wanted to make progress. I wanted to get on with it. So I quietly pulled myself up into the driving seat and drove out of the city through the well-heeled streets of Taylor's Hill and into the vast and silent blackness of the Connemara night.

Twenty-five

When we woke up, we were at the Twelve Pins. Well, we could see them. It had taken me over two hours to drive there, in the all-consuming darkness, on the single-track, stony road, which prevails all the way to the coast once you are a couple of miles out of Galway town. The villages along the way had thinned out, the first three came every twenty minutes or so, then one after half an hour, until at last there was nothing for over fifty minutes. Not even a cottage, well, not one with a light on in any case. At three in the morning I had pulled over to the side of the road and closed my weary eyes, knowing first light would wake me in only a few hours.

Actually, it woke Becka first. She got out of the car and gazed in disbelief at the cloudy dawn. 'Where's the river?' she said.

'We moved on. We're in Connemara now.'

'Did we bring any food? I'm starving.'

There was nothing to be seen for miles around, and I hadn't brought any food or water, but I knew that we weren't that far from Clifden, where we would be able to fill both the petrol tank and our stomachs, as well as procure some supplies. So we got back into the car and drove on along the winding road.

Becka pulled her jumper close around herself, hugged her knees to her chin and stared, bleary-eyed, out of the window at the vast and empty countryside. 'You know,' she said eventually, 'we are never going to find them here. It's huge.'

Actually, it's not that huge. On a normal-sized map of the country you can more than cover Connemara with your thumb. But still, on the ground it's a lot of land to get through. People would think you were crazy if you just went to a big city, say New York, to find someone without an address. The difference being, of course, that there are hardly any people at all out in the Gaeltacht. Maybe a few thousand at most over all that area. And only a few buildings and still fewer pubs, though probably more pubs per capita than in most places in the world – but still, very few. I reckoned, myself, that the pubs were the key to finding the Currans. Living off the land or not, they were sure to be calling in somewhere for a pint and a packet of fags from time to time. The way that Mrs C had been talking about 'past the Twelve Pins' cut at least half of the area out of the question in any case. It wasn't even as much as a thumb-print on the map. No, it was more as if you turned your pinkie on its side and only counted the very top part of the finger, and even then you got some sea and a couple of islands.

By the time we got to Clifden it was spitting raindrops, although there were shafts of softly coloured sunshine breaking through the clouds. We filled the car up and bought our breakfast at a B and B. Just up, outside the village, we could see the plush great hotels which commanded a view of the coast. These were five-star, serious establishments with helicopter pads and cordon bleu chefs. A Curran-free zone. It was a really beautiful place, though. With breakfast inside me, I could acknowledge that at last. The light was stunning and the land remote and unspoilt, arid in places where the harsh wind had eradicated everything except the low-lying, dark plant life. It was almost lush in other parts – not lush green, but lush none the less. Rich in its texture and its scope of colours – heathers and browns and khaki and of course, green too.

We had bought a local map, which Becka was studying carefully in the front seat of the car. 'We need to have a council of war,' she said, as I climbed into the front seat. 'We need to make a real plan.'

We drove out of the village a little way and switched off the engine.

'We're never going to find them here,' said Becka.

'Yeah, we will. Look, I think we should concentrate on the pubs. It's going to be difficult, because we can't really draw attention to ourselves. We can't ask anyone about them. But they'll be calling in for a drink somewhere. There can't be more than fifty or sixty pubs in the area. That's tops.'

Becka looked at the map. She drew a line around the whole of Connemara with a blue biro pen and handed it to me. 'It takes three hours, maybe more, just to cross it, the roads are so bad.'

I took the pen from her and drew a vertical line through the Twelve Pins. 'They are past the Twelve Pins, remember? As the crow flies, the area is an hour wide at most and an hour and a half long. I think we should concentrate on the coastline.'

'I'll give anything a whack, you know that,' said Becka. 'I'm just not too hopeful.'

I made up my mind to be straight with her. 'What I want to be sure of is that we don't allow anyone to make any connections between them and us. I want to be sure that the stuff you nicked from Queen's will work. I want to be sure that we can get away afterwards. And I want to be sure that you are not going to steal something from them as a little souvenir which will connect us to them after the fact.'

Becka cast down her eyes. She pulled Seamus's boxer shorts from her pocket and threw them out of the car window. 'Don't worry,' she said. 'Don't worry about anything. Especially not the poison. That'll definitely work. It's not a nice way to go, strychnine, but it works. You get convulsions. It's a very stable compound. It's an alkaloid. It's like arsenic – it just won't decompose. We can inject it into any raw food we like and they can cook whatever we put it into and it won't be any the less deadly. They won't be able to smell it and they won't be able to taste it. The only thing is that the police will trace it in the autopsies. But we'll be long gone by then, and the stuff isn't traceable to us. Strychnine isn't so hard to come by. It's common enough – it's in rat poison for God's sake. Anyone who really wants it can get their hands on it, though you can't buy it pure over the counter.'

'Terrorists don't use it much,' I said, thinking of the IRA's Green Book and its catalogue of kneecappings, executions, interrogations and other prescribed tortures. 'It's not a great cover. It's definitely the work of someone outside the organisations most likely to want these lads dead.'

'They'll know that they have been poisoned, right enough. I mean, they will know that someone has poisoned them deliberately. Strychnine doesn't occur naturally in animals, that's for sure. You got any other ideas? Hey, if we started a fire wherever they are, I mean, we could burn them after we do it. That would cover the evidence all right. No question of that,' said Becka.

I thought for a moment. 'No, a fire out here would attract lots of attention. Too much. People would see the smoke for miles around.'

'That's true,' Becka conceded. 'You have to decide what's your poison, so to speak.' She pulled a bar of chocolate out of her pocket, opened it and offered me a bite.

I shook my head. 'Becka,' I asked, 'why are you prepared to do this?'

Becka just shrugged her shoulders. 'I don't know exactly,' she said, her teeth all smeared with the chocolate. 'I don't know. Because you want to, maybe. If you decided not to, I'd go along with you. It feels like the right thing to do. They killed someone else, after all. Probably more than one person. And there's the money. I want to get the money from London. I want to have a whack at that. It's not like I have anything else to do.'

I thought to myself that if I was about to steep my soul in the blood of the damned I might as well get some fiscal advantage from it. Becka was right. There is more than one kind of freedom and lots of money is one way to help ensure that people don't fuck with you. That and being tough. And tough I was definitely becoming. I was tough enough to put my life on the line to win my own freedom. And fuck them – let them come after me if they wanted to try.

'I think we should drive right along the coast for a start,' I said. 'Then we can cover the ground inland. As far as anyone is concerned we are tourists. They are used to tourists out here.'

'Fine by me,' agreed Becka, licking the last vestiges of melted chocolate from her sticky fingers. 'Let's go.'

We found nothing at the coast. It took us a day and a half to drive all the way around from Clifden to Killary Harbour and then overland back south to Cashel and up to Clifden again. On our way, we called in to every pub for a small drink of something and a packet of cigarettes. The back seat of the car was piled up with Marlboro boxes and cans of Coke – a little red and white monument to our failure. We considered taking a trip to the islands, but we reckoned it was unlikely that the Currans were permanently based offshore. Mrs C had talked about trips over to Galway and down to

Ballyvaughan. These were not the rambles of someone living on an island off the coast – people living on islands were more inclined to self-sufficiency. No, these were the travels of itinerants living on the mainland. We stopped off whenever we saw a fishing boat, and once or twice we stood in the harbour and watched the pink-faced, oilskin-clad fishermen unloading their fresh cargo as the hungry gulls swooped in loops over the brackish waters around them. The men were keen-eyed and strong, and they mostly spoke Gaelic to each other. Once, when I got close to one – for I was straining to see the lobsters he was unloading – I could smell the cigarettes and the salty fresh sea air as he moved. Becka and I were careful not to talk too much. To let the fishermen nod first at us, and start any conversation in their gentle, lilting English. They talked about lots of things – the kind of boats they worked on, the nets they used to harvest the bounty of the sea in great numbers, or the lines and hooks which caught smaller quantities of fish without damaging the flesh. We were invited on board to see the cabin, or just to smoke a cigarette leaning against the still, rusty chains which bound the great nets to the winching system. It was during one of these sessions that we heard about a fishmarket which took place two evenings a week in a huge warehouse at Tully Cross. That was where we spent our second evening. If any of the Currans were working on a boat, it seemed likely that they might also be working the market.

We stood out like a sore thumb, even with dark woollen jumpers and navy hats pulled hard down over our hair, we were the only women there and the youngest people by at least ten years, or possibly more. The place wasn't refrigerated, but it was freezing cold and the whole floor of the warehouse was covered in huge plastic boxes of fresh dead fish, laid out for bidding in lots of different kinds. It was odd – the place didn't smell so much of fish, more of a kind of salty, scented seaweed. At first all the men were inspecting the lots haphazardly, picking up fish and checking them for freshness and quality. Then all at once the auction started and everyone moved around after the auctioneer in a huge gaggle, bidding on the lots at a frantic pace. There were guys there buying for local restaurants (they usually went to the highest price). They would bid up and up on a huge lot of fish and only take one box of the very best fish at that price. Then the bidding would have to start again, so that the exporters and fish shops could take the rest of the boxes for less. The exporters carried mobile phones. They wore designer glasses with thick black rims, and thick, lined, long leather jackets which came down to the middle of their thighs, and were tied against the cold with stout buckled leather belts. They looked like men with some power. The local fishmongers wore anoraks and trainers, and they stamped their feet against the cold. Any kind of unusual produce in a box caused a great deal of excitement. One lot was a kind of fish that I don't know a name for, but it looked kind of exotic. The bidding went on for five minutes on that box, and there were only three sorry-looking fish in it.

Becka and I gave up on the auction after half an hour. It was colder inside the warehouse than outside. We decided to go for a walk – away from where we had parked with all the other cars. All down the other side of the structure there were vans, parked up with open doors. The drivers were waiting to pack the catch of the day in polystyrene containers with large chunks of ice and seaweed to keep them fresh, so they could be loaded into the back of their vans. Some of them were set to drive all night, to make it to the airport, so that the fish could be on the tables of the best London restaurants the following evening. We decided to go down and have a look at what was going on. That was when I spotted him. I couldn't be sure, of course, that he was a Curran. I had never met this guy before. But it was something about the way that he was smoking his cigarette – it reminded me of Conor. And when I observed him closely I could see the shadow of Mrs C beneath his rough, pock-marked skin. We wandered around the vans, casually staring out into the endless starless sky above us.

As we reached his van, I decided to talk to him. After all, if you want to catch a fish, you have to bait your hook. Besides, I wanted to see if he had a Dublin accent. I looked up at the sky, down to the ground and all around me, as if I was bored. Then I raised my eyes, as if I was only just realising that he was there. Becka shifted uneasily behind me. 'Does this go on late?' I asked. It was an open question, but one cast in his general direction.

He looked at me with a kind of offensive indifference. Maybe that was only in my mind. 'Depends what you are buying,' he replied.

'Oh, we just came to have a look. We met some of the fishermen unloading over at Letterfrack and we thought we would come to see the auction, you know. Do you work on the boats?'

'Sometimes,' he said.

The van behind him belonged to a fish shop. There was a Galway city address and phone number emblazoned down one side, with the logo of a jumping salmon, in blue, over the top of the lettering.

'Do you work in the shop, then?' I asked.

'Nah. I just help out, like. From time to time.'

'The sea here is so wonderful. All the little harbours. It's beautiful,' I rambled, casting my eyes skywards once more and tugging Becka's sleeve gently, so that we could move on as one. We wandered along

nonchalantly until we turned the corner of the warehouse, and we heard behind us the sound of men's
laughter. The laughter of men sharing a joke at our
expense once we were safely out of sight.

'You sure?' asked Becka. 'It's one of them?'

'Yes.'

We made our way back to the car and started up the
engine. Then we drove back into Galway town. It was a
long way in the pitch-black night. Well over an hour.
We didn't speak to each other at all. We had found one
of the Currans and now we were switching ourselves
on to automatic pilot for the rest. We made it back into
Galway at nine o'clock and we parked around the
corner from the fish shop, near the old stone-built mill
on the river.

'Do you think that they'll come back here tonight?'
asked Becka.

'Yeah. I think so. I mean they will want to drop it off,
won't they? They might not prepare it tonight, but
they'll drop it off so that it can stay refrigerated till the
morning.'

'Is this the only shop they've got? I mean they
wouldn't go anywhere else, would they?'

'It was the only address on the van. If he doesn't turn
up, at least we know who he's working for.'

The shop was the second from the end of the street.
We stationed ourselves around the corner of the
opposite side from where we could see the glass and
marble façade with 'Fishmonger' painted in orange and
gold over the window and the same line drawing of a
jumping salmon which had graced the side of the van.
The row of shops backed on to the river, so there was
no possibility of the van arriving to the rear of the
buildings. The only way in was the main entrance on
the front street. This side of Galway, where the locals
shopped, seemed still and silent as the grave. There
were no pubs on this side of the town, and the old mill,

which had been converted into a restaurant long ago, seemed deserted, although the flickering light of table candles glowed from its tiny windows. It was hard to imagine there was anyone inside those thick grey stone walls.

'What do we do?' asked Becka.

'Wait till he gets here. Follow him when he leaves.'

'No, I mean. Oh, I don't know,' Becka fumed.

But I did know what she meant. We were conspicuous as hell – two girls driving a car registered in the North, following a guy around the dark, silent Galway streets.

We settled down into our seats and pulled our clothes around us as the temperature inside the car cooled right down to that of the night outside. It was after eleven o'clock when the van finally pulled up, its headlights jerking us to attention as we snapped out of our day-dreams. Our man jumped down from the driver's seat and pulled open the van doors. A car pulled up behind him. There were now three men. One Curran, one guy whom I recognised from the auction – he had been bidding – and another. They unlocked the shop door and began to unload the boxes of fish from the van. It didn't take too long. There were only, perhaps, a dozen big boxes. Then they closed up the shop, and the guy who had been bidding got back into his car and drove off. The Curran and the other man got back into the van. I started our engine, but didn't switch on the headlights, or move, until the van had laboriously turned in the street and was heading back down for the main road and almost out of sight. We followed them, hanging well back. The main road was quiet, but not entirely deserted, and I wasn't too worried. The road was pretty straight, and once you got out of town it would be easy to spot tail-lights for some distance ahead, so we wouldn't have to stick too close to them. The main thing was that they didn't realise we were following them. I was ready to tail them to hell and back, but they stopped almost immediately; in fact, as soon as they made it to the main strip in Salthill they pulled up outside one of the late-night bars on the waterfront, and both men jumped out of the cab and wandered inside. We pulled up a little way back along the main road.

Salthill was all a-glimmer as usual. The fast-food restaurants along the main drag pumped out the smell of frying chips, which hung around the place like a cloud of enticement.

'Jeez, I'm hungry,' said Becka, right on cue.

She jumped out of the car before I could reply. I thought she was heading for the chip shop, but she walked right over the road towards the van; then I had scarcely blinked and she was inside the cab in three seconds flat. Becka was clearly a girl with some history. I was kind of amazed that she hadn't done any time. Anyhow, she got in the cab, had a good root around, slipped back down on to the road side of the van, picked up some chips from the shop nearest us and hopped back into the car to report.

'Two fish on the front seat. Wrapped in paper, and in plastic bags. Presumably one each,' she said, offering me the chips.

I realised I was hungry too, but I could feel the heat of the little packet from where I sat and didn't want to burn myself. I gingerly proffered clasped fingers. 'We can do it now, but if we poison both fish we get the other guy too, and maybe a family. Kids and everything.'

The chips were salty and delicious.

'I'm going to have a look inside the bar,' I decided, emboldened by Becka's undeniably selfless bravery. I pulled off my woolly hat and jumper and applied some lipstick with care. I looked like an entirely different girl.

The bar was pretty seedy and no mistaking it. A kind of sticky film engulfed the formica top of the counter, which was crowded with grubby glasses not yet cleared away. There were tinted mirrors running all the way around the room behind a façade of wrought ironwork which was attached to thick strips of cheap orangeish wood at the floor and the ceiling. The place was packed out. I stood for a moment at the door, to get my bearings, walked over to the bar and bought a packet of cigarettes at the machine there. I caught sight of the men at the back of the pub, sitting at a small table with glasses of whiskey before them. They had made a little oasis of calm around themselves, in the frantic atmosphere, as people edged away from their no doubt fishy clothes. I lit one of the cigarettes, ordered a Coke, and continued to observe them. They sat there until well after one in the morning. I popped out to reassure Becka a couple of times. The bar began to empty out after twelve as people left to go dancing in the brash discos further along the front, but the men still sat there, sipping whiskey, or sometimes bottles of stout off the shelf, as they talked. At last they seemed to be getting ready to go, and I made my exit, diving back into the car, where Becka lay sleeping. I didn't want to wake her up. I started the engine, and watched as the men climbed back up into the cab of the van and pulled out from the kerb, turning off to the right, shortly after the end of the block, into one of the suburbs behind Salthill. I followed. Again, they didn't go far. They parked the van on a tiny street only two minutes away from the bar where they had been drinking. They jumped down again, and the other man took a key out of his pocket and let them into one of the tiny houses. They didn't put on the lights. I stopped the car at a vantage point further down the street and waited. Nothing moved. Were they watching me from inside the darkened cottage? I knew no fear. I was foolishly emboldened. I got out of the car and walked right up to the dark glass of the front windows and I was lucky. There was nobody there. They must have gone to bed.

I decided to walk back to Salthill, betting that the men were settled for the night at least. When I got there, I had an idea. I took a phone book from one of the telephone boxes on the front and hauled it back to the car. There was no way that I would be able to sleep. I was too, too excited. By the ginger light of the street lamp I strained my eyes to scan the listings for the right address. It took over an hour, but I found it. Feeney, J., 24 Claddagh Terrace, Galway. Obviously Mr Feeney was a friend of the Currans. I wondered if the two red-faced, ageing men might be more than friends, perhaps even lovers. The idea amused me, that even at that moment they might be rolling around together, rough-handed and fishy, in a bedroom somewhere to the rear of 24 Claddagh Terrace. But the Currans stuck together. I was sure of that. If we could only follow this man, he would lead us to his brothers. It would be more difficult in daylight. And with these thoughts jumping around my mind, I finally fell into a fitful slumber some time near three in the morning.

Becka woke before me and had fetched us rolls for breakfast. I pointed out the cottage to her and we ate in silence, sipping on a shared can of Coke and never breaking our gaze. That was seven o'clock. There was no movement until ten, when the men appeared at the darkened doorway, Feeney there to wave Curran off. He left with the fish tucked under his arm and walked along Claddagh Terrace, turning down towards the main road.

'What do you think?' whispered Becka to me, as we crouched down in our seats until Feeney had closed the door and disappeared back into his house.

'He has to be heading out west, doesn't he. He's got paid, he's got his fish, he's heading out west.'

'How will he get there?'

I started the car and pulled off, heading for the main street through Salthill. 'Well,' I said, 'there aren't any buses. A taxi would cost a fortune. He doesn't seem to have a bicycle and he doesn't have a car. I'd say he's hitching. I'd say he'll walk a little way out of the town and then he'll stick his thumb out.'

Hitching is common in Southern Ireland. It's an accepted, normal way to get around. Particularly down in the country. Up North, of course, you'd be mad to hitch and even more mad to pick anyone up. Like I said before, up North even the taxis don't stop if you hail them in the street.

'I think,' I said, 'that we shouldn't pick him up ourselves. It's too obvious. Let's wait until he's had time to get himself set up out on the main road and then pass him. We'll stick to the main road. Then we'll go on out, say, as far as Maam Cross and wait. When we see him pass in another car we'll follow it.'

'Hey, you're tricky,' Becka teased.

I grinned. 'Years of paranoia,' I replied. 'It's great training.'

Twenty-six

What made everything so easy I will never know. Perhaps doing the right thing always feels easy. We were tired, dirty and kind of hungry for a decent meal, of course, but we did what we had planned and followed him across country, ahead for part of the way, then behind some stranger's car, until we got out as far as Ballynahinch on the main road. There the car dropped him off, just past the end of the Ballynahinch Lough, and he disappeared on foot into the woods. We stopped and parked a little way ahead and, scrambling to put on jackets and stuff supplies into our pockets, we waited for nearly two minutes before we followed him. I knew how close we were to finding them. I knew that he could have just changed cars and hitched further had it been any long distance to his destination. There was a side-road to the south, before the woods started, and he could have been dropped off there. He'd chosen to go on foot for the last part of the way.

The woods at Ballynahinch are famous among the cognoscenti for their game and among the youth of Ireland for the proliferation of magic mushrooms which grow wild there during the autumn months. I had never been there before, but I knew it from the map, which we had now been poring over for several days. The woods ran, a mile long and half a mile wide, on the hills above a scattering of loughs. There were three rough roads skirting the area. The first ran around the coast (we had already covered that one) and it was far away, the second ran through the woods to the west (the turn-off that he had missed) and the last one, which ran well south of the woods, was built on a natural land bridge dividing the loughs into a smattering to the north of the road and a more generous sprinkling to the south. If he was on foot, I guessed, he must be heading for somewhere in the northern and eastern portion of the wobbly circle created by the roads. It was a tear-shaped area, dropping down from the main road, and it was tiny. Any other place, I reasoned to myself, he would have made his way by road.

It was quite sunny as we set off into the woods. That would change later. The weather moves quickly in Connemara. It's the first land mass after America and it is subject to the full force of the unhampered winds coming off the Atlantic. The sky can become unrelentingly cloudy in a matter of seconds and the rain can torrent down on the sunniest days with no warning whatever, drenching the hillsides and bringing out all the colours of the wild landscape. The woods were damp, the moisture of the long wet winter held in the mossy bracken and the earth beneath it all muddy. The foliage on the trees blocked out most of the light. It took a few seconds for our eyes to get used to it. We walked slowly back towards where he had entered the trees and looked for his tracks. They were pretty clear. We waited a couple more minutes – there was no point in sticking close to him and risking discovery when we could trail him easily all through the wood without seeing him once. I suppose it took about an hour to get through the trees and out on to the open ground, and by that time it was raining. Most of the drops collected up at the top of the trees until the weight of the water made a leaf give way and a deluge splattered down to the ground. Becka got hit a couple of times, but I was luckier. Anyhow, we got out of the woods and looked down on to the array of loughs which lie to the south-west of it. I pulled the map from my pocket, blinking even in the oblique sunlight which was filtering down through the clouds. There was water as far as the eye could see. Lough Conga, Lough Fadda (the Long Lough), Lough Scanive, Lough Barrowen, Lough Maumeen and Lough Bollard were the only ones named on the map, though I wasn't sure which ones we were looking at. There must have been easily another fifteen smaller pools, which lay unnamed by the ordnance survey team, and then hills in the way, to boot.

Becka thoughtfully pulled a KitKat from her pocket and started to eat. 'Wow,' she said. 'It's beautiful. They look like fjords.'

'You ever seen a fjord?' I asked her distractedly.

'Suppose not,' she admitted.

The ground became firmer as we walked away from the woods and the tracks were more difficult to follow. The hard grasses and heathers just sprang back where you walked on them.

He was gone.

'We are going to have to sweep the whole area,' I said.

'Yeah. Sure.'

We set off. There aren't many houses there – it's fairly remote all right. Back up near the road there is an enormous five star hotel (I think it used to be a castle), which owns shooting rights to the surrounding area. The cottages near the hotel which were once used by the estate farm workers (and there aren't even that many of those cottages left) are now used to house the hotel staff. We were further south than that, though.

'We should go south and westwards first,' said Becka, peering over my shoulder at the map. 'That isn't

too far until we hit the road, then we can work our way
back if we haven't found them.'

I nodded in agreement.

We walked all day, crouching down low whenever
we saw anything of any interest and watching patiently
like the shadows of stalking Red Indians, until we
knew exactly what was going on. We found two
cottages – one which seemed to be an empty holiday
home and the other a tiny, one-roomed affair, which
was inhabited by an old woman, who, apart from a few
chickens, was alone. She was out working in the
garden. At nightfall we went back to the holiday home
and broke in through a window. Becka made us some
dinner from the tins of food stocked in the kitchen
cupboard and we slept that night in borrowed, unmade
beds.

In the morning we started again, working our way
back towards the east. We passed a couple more
cottages – this time abandoned and open to the skies.
In the end, it wasn't their cottage we found, it was
them. It was eleven o'clock in the morning and they
were digging peat to the west of Lough Conga. There
were three of them, working out on the open hill,
piling up the turf on to an old, rickety wagon. Turf is
still the main source of energy out there in the
Gaeltacht. In fact, lots of people still burn it up in
Dublin, just for nostalgia's sake. But out in the Gaeltacht there is no piped gas and in some places no
electricity, and the peat is a way of life. We watched
them for an hour and a half, then followed them
northwards for perhaps half a mile until we came to
their camp. They had put up a couple of fluorescent
orange tents inside the skeletons of two abandoned
cottages, and had built a campfire out to the front of the
tent flaps. We didn't get close enough to distinguish
them, but I was pretty sure that the man we had

followed wasn't with the peat cutters. We lay down on the high ground behind the tents and waited.

'We should watch them for a good long time,' I said. 'I want to know what they are doing. Everything. Exactly.'

Becka nodded back at me. 'How far are we from the car?' she asked.

We consulted the map, poring over it carefully.

'I suppose it's six or seven miles – a couple of hours at most.'

Down below us we could make them out, stacking the peat in the long-abandoned fireplace to one side of the cottage, where it could air out. You really want to dry the peat a little before you burn it. Otherwise the smoke that comes from the fire is a bit overpowering. When the peat is dry, you get the oaky, woody, light smoke which smells like pipe tobacco. It's a safe smell. I never met anyone who doesn't love it. We watched them all day, hanging out there. Away from the eyes of the world, well away from whatever they had been doing in London. Connemara's a great place to hide, remote and wild and free as it is. And what people there are wouldn't bother you, especially if you spoke Irish. The fourth brother arrived back at the camp in the middle of the afternoon. He was carrying a tin of fresh milk and he had a couple of loaves of bread stuck in his pockets. Two of the others went off to check and set traps off to the west. Becka tailed them while I stayed up on the hill and watched the last one as he had a swim in the lough. He was a brave man, it must have been freezing in there. In the evening they sat around the fire while their supper cooked in a big pot, and they smoked cigarettes and we could hear their laughter, although we couldn't make out any of the words of their conversation.

'OK,' said Becka. 'Time for a plan of action.'

She was quite right, of course. This was absolutely

no time to be infirm of purpose. It's just that I had been watching them living all day. I had kind of got used to it. Becka pulled the box out of her pocket and took out the strychnine and a syringe. We got down to the nitty gritty and decided that we would poison the game in their traps. The rabbits were going to get it, but, we agreed, there was no way that we were prepared to murder animals in cold blood. We wanted the rabbits to be dead already. Besides, if we did murder the game it might show signs of its unnatural demise and alert the Currans. We headed westwards. Becka led the way – she had seen them check the traps early that very afternoon and knew where they had been laid. They had caught only two rabbits, which they had skinned and gutted, and these were now stewing in the big black pot over the fire. When we checked their traps we found only one dead rabbit.

'You sure?' Becka asked me. 'Absolutely?'

I nodded. I was sure, you see. I am sure still that it was the right thing to do. I had to weigh things up – all the odds – the possibility of getting caught, the possibility of regret and the possibility of purging myself of my past. I had decided not to regret it, no matter what. Becka was standing there with the little bottle in her hand and I stared straight at the yellow label, which was marked with the skull and cross-bones, and a whole load of medical-looking letters.

'Yes. I'm sure,' I said, and Becka did the honours and injected the strychnine into the rabbit's hind legs and on both sides of its back, along where the fillet meat runs in a strip. I only watched her. We both kept our ears open for anyone approaching through the bracken, but we weren't really scared. We were past that. And besides, we could hide easily before anyone could come upon us. We decided to sleep rough on the hill above the camp and check the traps again in the morning. We also wanted to check that all four of the brothers would be staying in the camp the following day. The last thing we wanted was to kill three of them and be left with one avenging angel on our tail. Not that we would be easy to trace, but still, you never can be too careful.

I didn't sleep much. It was freezing cold and we had no cover. And besides, there was a dreadful feeling pressing down on my heart heavily enough to quash any relaxation. I stared at Becka as she slept and I realised that I was afraid of her. Just because she was the one who had done it. She was the murderer. I wondered if I wielded the syringe the following day if I would feel more light-hearted. But already the ghosts of the Currans hovered overhead in the dark night and I had a strong feeling that they would be with me for ever more. It was as if I was collecting spirits to follow me. Ma and Dad. The Curran brothers. Who knew who might be next? But no regrets. I wondered if Becka would be prepared to murder me if we got our hands on that money. It was an unfair thought. But it did occur to me none the less. I mean, if the money was the only reason she was doing it, why should she share it with me? Just before dawn I had a really strong urge to run back to the car alone and disappear somewhere. But I resisted. I really did want to see them dead, you see. I know I did. I had my own reasons. I had decided against regret and I stuck with that. However much the spectre of my haunted future hung over me, I knew that my pride, my self-esteem and my freedom of spirit depended on this. You have no future when the past rules you. I had to break with the past. And, after all, it was what I had decided to do. It was swift justice. It was revenge.

The lads rose early. Becka was still asleep. They stoked the fire and went down to the lough to splash their faces. One of them brewed up some tea, which they drank from tin cups as they stood around the fire.

They brought out a radio from one of the tents and switched it on. The tinny sound of radio music wafted up the hill at me. I nudged Becka awake and she rolled over and watched them too. Two of them were staying in the camp all day – they would check the traps and keep the fire going. The other two were pointing at the flatlands to the east. They were going that way to do something or other. Perhaps to go to the nearest cottages for supplies. Perhaps they might be gone all day. We decided to set off to check the traps again. We were going to carry on with our plan, regardless. If there were no signs of the two travelling brothers returning, we would nip over to the traps, whip out the rabbits and bury them. If they were going by the same routine as yesterday, they wouldn't check the traps until after two o'clock in the afternoon in any case. Or thereabouts. They had caught two more animals. This time I insisted on doing the honours myself.

'Partners in crime,' I said to Becka, and we smiled at each other as I squeezed the deadly liquid through the point of the needle. The ghosts of the night before were gone.

I was a bit over-enthusiastic with the syringe and we ran out of strychnine. That was OK, though. We ate the last of our chocolate beside the final trap and then walked back to the vantage point on the hillside. There were four men again. They were sitting on the lough-side drinking what looked like short bottles of Guinness while they were fishing, and there was no sign of them moving. At one o'clock we did a final tour of duty. There was one more dead rabbit, but we just removed it and reset the trap. We wanted every piece of meat in the stew to be tainted. We got back to the hill in three quarters of an hour, and just as before, around two o'clock, two of them went off to check the traps and we watched them return triumphant. They hung the rabbits up, though. They had caught two particularly vicious-looking pikes from the lough and that was what they were intending to eat that day. One of them took a knife and scaled the fish into the river, then gutted them. The others sat around the fire and drank more tea.

'What do you reckon?' Becka said.

'Well, they've got the rabbits now. We can't get them back. But I think we should stay and empty the traps again. If those rabbits are the only thing they have to eat, they will have to eat them tomorrow.'

It's amazing how sneaky you can get. It's amazing how easy it all was. I'm kind of surprised that the Brits don't have agents doing that kind of thing all the time. Under cover. The only real difficulty was that we were getting very hungry at that stage. But still we stayed and watched them eat the pike, and get riproaring drunk on whiskey. Then we passed another night on the hillside. We didn't sleep much. We were too hungry for that and it was freezing cold. We huddled close together for the warmth and we talked.

'I got panicky last night,' I admitted.

'Me too,' said Becka.

I had thought that she had slept as soundly as I ever saw anyone slumber. I wondered if she had thought of running away, like I had.

'I'm not good at getting this close to people, usually,' she said. 'That's what happened in London. When I met you. We had fallen in love. So I left.'

'Is that why you travel? I mean, your family. You're hardly there.'

'I suppose.'

'It's cool,' I said. 'It's just the way you are. It's OK. Look at what a basket case I am and you don't complain. You wouldn't even be here if it weren't for me.'

'I might be,' replied Becka, defending her independence. 'I want to go back to London and get the money.'

I suppose that is really where we differed. I don't mean the money. I mean in the way that I had lost people and was desperate for love. Becka had lost someone and never wanted to risk her heart again.

'We'll be this close, stay or go,' I said. 'It's eternal.' I really didn't want to lose her.

Becka looked troubled. Maybe she'd have stayed longer if I hadn't been so understanding. I should have been more of a bitch.

Just before dawn we checked their traps again. Nothing. Then we decided that we wanted to check that the four of them would be there for their last meal. Not that there was much we could do about it at that stage, but all the same, we felt we ought to make sure. Once it looked safe enough, and they had spent all morning with no signs of anyone leaving the camp for the day, we emptied the traps for the last time and decided to go back to the car and get out of there. We were going to head back to Belfast to return Jake Jackson's car to his parents. We were going back to real life in London. It was difficult to leave when the job wasn't really complete. But we realised there was nothing left for us to do. We couldn't go down and inspect the bodies after all – we'd leave forensic evidence. And we didn't really relish the thought of watching as the men died, convulsing, beside the lough, as the poison broke down their nervous systems. It really was better to get out of the country. Besides, we couldn't go for much longer without eating something ourselves. It was difficult to leave, though.

'I never saw anyone dead. There wasn't anything left of my parents,' I said.

'They'll break down. They'll convulse. It won't be a normal death,' said Becka.

I glanced over at the direction we had to take; then

217

back down the hillside at the peaceful ignorance of the Currans' camp.

'I saw my sister when she died,' said Becka into the silence. 'I had climbed into the bed with her in the hospital, but she hardly knew I was there. She was very ill. Poor bastards,' she said then, jerking her head towards the camp.

I nodded. But I knew that was the price of principles. Let them die. Let them die a horrible death. It was in front of me when I closed my eyes. In front of Becka too. We couldn't stay.

We made our way back up on to the main road and got into the car. We didn't speak at all. I drove. We went a little way further along the main road and stayed with it as it turned north. We didn't talk for over two hours, until we got to Westport where we got out of the car and bought fish and chips. We must have looked a sight – we hadn't washed in four days and we were ravenous. Then we got back into the car and headed inland through County Mayo, County Sligo and finally, through Leitrim. As we approached the border there were squads of Irish soldiers. It's really odd. The British soldiers to the north side of the border always look like real, lean, mean fighting machines. The hedgerows to the British side of the country bristle with machine-guns wherever a road-block is in operation. To the south side the soldiers look as if they are practising. Even when they are actually holding a gun they look as if they wouldn't really know how to use it. They are plump, too. Becka became a bit panicky about the soldiers. We still had incriminating evidence in the box in her pocket. We had planned to burn the syringe and the poison bottle, but we hadn't done it yet. My palms were clammy with fear, but I looked the soldiers straight in the eye. They waved us down to stop the car and asked us where we were going.

'Belfast,' I said, putting on a strong Catholic Belfast accent.

They waved us on and we breathed again. Afterwards I found out that the road-blocks were there to stop farmers smuggling sheep over the border. There were inspectors from the European Commission in the country to verify numbers of livestock, and farmers were borrowing flocks of sheep from each other, in order to maximise the subsidies they could claim. On the British side, the soldiers checked my driving licence. They asked where we were going.

'Belfast,' I said, putting on a strong Protestant Belfast accent.

They waved us on. There is no end to the games you can play with your accent at check-points, though on this occasion, given that the road-blocks were set up to catch animals, as long as you didn't bleat you'd probably have got through OK. It was a relief, though.

At dusk we stopped the car and solemnly observed a minute's silence in anticipation. This was the time they usually sat around the fire beside the steaming pot. They would start eating shortly and they would be dead within a couple of hours. When I got back to London, once everything was over, I looked it up in the library. There is a name for death by strychnine. Strychninomania or nightshade madness. The British Poison Rules of 1935 restricted the sale of strychnine, but I was reliably informed it is still used in small doses as a stomachic and stimulant for the central nervous system and the circulation. Homeopaths prescribe it for hangovers. Not at the dosage we administered, though, obviously. What we administered was certain death. Nightshade madness makes it sound almost romantic, doesn't it? But it's a hell of a way to go. $C_{21}H_{22}N_2O_2$, obtained from the seeds of *nux vomica* – deadly nightshade.

It was dark as we drove into Belfast and made for the

Malone Road. Moyra and Professor Jackson had already had dinner. When we arrived they were arguing about whether the British Government should make an official apology to the Irish nation for its behaviour during the Great Famine. It was kind of topical. It was something which had recently been suggested as a way to appease the IRA into reinstating the ceasefire. It just goes to show you how far back Republicans aren't prepared to forget. But I was past all that. I had my revenge and I was no longer involved. Professor Jackson looked particularly pleased to see us, though, and Moyra made us some soup, which we ate gratefully, then we both had a shower upstairs. We made up the details of our little holiday, staying with the real story as far as Galway town, but saying we had spent the last three days camping in Sligo, rather than Connemara. Moyra made us cocoa and tucked us up in bed. We waited until the Jacksons finally went to bed themselves, then we burnt the bottle and the syringe in the tin wastepaper bin in Jake Jackson's bedroom. It made a hell of a lot of smoke and it smelt revolting. We had to open the window and put the bin right underneath the draught, while we squatted uncomfortably near the doorway. They took ages to burn, but once they were melted together and blackened and unrecognisable, we sneaked downstairs and outside into the back garden and buried them there in a hole too deep for ordinary gardening to reach. We figured that they would only ever be found if the Jacksons decided to plant a tree on that spot. Then we got back into bed, where we slept for twelve hours straight. I can honestly say I have never slept so well. The next day Becka arranged for Moyra to lend us some money, to be underwritten by Professor MacIntosh.

The last thing I said to Moyra was this: 'You know there aren't any political solutions without personal solutions too, and they are both subject to negotiation.'

Not that negotiation was the path I had chosen, but I figured that it might help her. We ordered a cab to take us to the City Airport and from there we flew to London.

Twenty-seven

Becka knew of a squat in Kilburn. Squats weren't supposed to happen any more, but this one had escaped the Nineties purge and lived on. She had stayed there before. So we agreed to go there – besides, I really wanted to get my hands on some newspapers and Kilburn was a good place for that. The Irish community there is so enormous that the local news-agents sell the *Irish Times* and even *An Phoblacht*, which is the *Republican News*. The British Govern-ment were engaged in organising the compromise which suited nobody – elections in the North. More bombs had been planted and the Unionists were fuming editorial comment all over the political pages of British newspapers. The Orange March in Belfast had caused fighting in the streets round the Ormeau Bridge and the leaders, the MPs for the Unionist areas concerned, had helped to man the many makeshift barricades set up to stop the RUC policing the area effectively. Catholics had been told to stay at home for days. The RUC had blocked off the nearby Catholic streets and wouldn't let people out. Even to the shops. It was crazy. And they weren't even organised yet. Once the marching season got into full swing the barricades were manned by people who had mobile phones and fax machines. They knew exactly what was coming. Already, though, the place was in uproar.

I wanted to do my research before confronting David Curran. Becka was all for taking the tube directly to the mews where he lived, but I absolutely insisted that we planned exactly what we were going to do before we did it. Becka said that as we had both seen *Reservoir Dogs*, there could be nothing more that we would need to know. I pointed out that we didn't have any weapons and thereby won David Curran a short reprieve. Murder on the deserted hillsides of the Gaeltacht is one thing, but murder in central London is quite another. We still had three days before I was due to start work.

'I wonder how much money it is,' Becka mused, as we walked from the tube station on Kilburn High Street down towards the main row of shops.

'Well it's got to be a tidy sum if they are intending to buy arms with it,' I said. Though I felt I had to point out that we might not be able to get our hands on any of it. I braced myself for that. 'Becka,' I started, 'it might not even still be there. They might have spent it, you know. We've been away for ten days. They are involved in a bombing campaign. They might have bought arms with it. Anything could have happened.'

'Nonsense,' said Becka. 'They'd have to know it had arrived safely before they could set up the deal. That could easily take more than a few days. And it hadn't even arrived when we left. He was prepared to do it this one time – to go ahead and do it, remember. Future tense. No, I can feel it. It's here. I know it is.'

Thus forearmed against any financial disaster, we entered the newsagents and bought tabloid and broadsheet newspapers to cover the whole political spectrum. The Irish papers were a day out of date. But still, they would be useful enough. I wondered when the bodies of the Currans might be found. It could take weeks. I wondered if the poison had really worked. I wondered if they had all eaten the stew, or if, at the last minute, one of them had changed his mind or lost his appetite. I wonder that still. Strange, isn't it, but I still don't know to this day if we really did kill them. I bought the newspapers every day for a year afterwards, but nothing was ever mentioned about their bodies. Not one word. From time to time I still ask myself if there are to this day skeletons beside that deserted lough to the south of Ballynahinch.

David Curran was a different matter, though. I know for sure that he died. Becka killed him.

We left the shops and made our way back under the grey iron bridge and towards the tube station, where Becka led me across the main road and into a maze of residential side-streets away from the busier area where the shops were. The squat was five minutes from the main road, two blocks back. The front door and all the windows on the ground floor were boarded up, but Becka pushed open the grubby green gate to the back garden and we wandered around to the other side of the house. The back door was open. As squats go, it wasn't a bad place. It wasn't filthy, though it could have done with a good clean right enough. We walked in through the kitchen. The whole place was engulfed in gloom – there were no windows downstairs. It was quite bright outside and this made the ground floor seem stuffy, and to make matters worse the carpets and furniture and walls were dark – shades of burgundy it looked like, or maybe deep brown. Becka called out but there was no reply. We carried on through the living-room and into the hallway, where light cascaded down from the large arch-shaped window half-way up the stairs. The hallway was a dull moss-coloured green. Whoever had decorated the place had been one sombre son of a bitch. She called again. Silence. We made our way upwards. Becka checked each of the bedrooms. The place was deserted. 'Strange,' she said, 'it's not as if anyone has a job.'

In the end we settled in the bedroom which Becka said had previously been hers. We changed into the clothes which were lying strewn around the floor, and Becka disappeared downstairs and made mugs of tea while I opened the window to air the room and settled down to look at the papers.

About an hour after we arrived we heard some movement downstairs and Becka went off to see who was there. She resurfaced proudly, with a guy on her arm. 'This is Eddie,' she said. Eddie was about our age. He had a mass of dreadlocks and wore combat trousers and layers and layers of T-shirts. When he smiled I noticed that he had the bluest eyes I have ever seen. They were so blue that they were almost fluorescent.

'Hi,' he said.

I nodded.

Becka hugged him tight and kissed his cheek with fervour. 'We're only going to stay for a few days,' she said. 'Promise.'

'As long as you like,' Eddie replied generously, though I suppose it wasn't his house.

'Who's in this room now?' asked Becka.

'Lisa,' Eddie said. 'You don't know her. She's new. She'll share. No problems. She's dead decent. Though she might not like you wearing her clothes.'

'Had to,' Becka explained. 'We were filthy.'

I cast a sideways glance at the outermost layers of Eddie's T-shirts. We hadn't been as dirty as that.

'You can square it with her when she gets back tonight. She's working in the pub round the corner.'

'Wow!' Becka gaped.

We went out, though, before Lisa came home. We had decided to go and case David Curran's mews flat and we set off across town by bus. We had made up our minds, after some discussion, that travelling by bus was a good way to get a feel for the city again. It took ages to get to Chelsea from Kilburn, though by the time we got there we had the stirrings of a plan in our communal pot. These were the facts. David Curran had access to Republican money, which he, presumably, was responsible for laundering. Previously he had been dealing with his brothers, but now – and again, we assumed this – he must have been given another contact. He would be bringing the money into the country (after all, foreign exchange was his expertise) and handing it over – most likely in cash so that it would be untraceable. But to hand it over he would have to get it from somewhere. If we got to him at home, he wouldn't have it on him. He would have to get it from the bank. Therefore we had either to scare him into not pulling the plug on us in between the bank and handing over the money to us, or get him at the bank. And we had to kill him. If we didn't kill him the IRA would. That part was not negotiable. And before they killed him they would interrogate him. And before he died he would tell them everything he knew about us – and he knew names and what we looked like. He knew plenty. So we couldn't let him live and we couldn't go to the bank. We'd be captured on film. Security guards (reliable witnesses in court) would see us and perhaps even recognise us. We had to get him at home and make him do our bidding. It was like a game of chess.

And we had options. Not very good ones, perhaps, but at least we had something to decide on:

1. We could pretend to be from the IRA to collect the money. This would only work if he hadn't already established contact with someone else. Unlikely.
2. We could pretend to be from the UVF. This was, we immediately decided, a bad idea. However much he disliked what the IRA was doing, he probably sympathised more with the Republicans than with the Unionists.
3. We could tell him the truth. Bad move. Never tell

the truth when you are engaged in murdering someone. Especially if that means they will be more scared of the other guys than they are of you.

4. We could pretend to be from the police. This was, surprisingly, a more promising option. Not that we knew David Curran well, but we did know that he didn't particularly want to be doing what he was doing. We could let him off the hook of his own conscience and tell him we'd protect him. As long as he handed over the money. This would also put him off his guard. He wouldn't be expecting the police to murder him. That's quite surprising. The police and army are responsible for over ten per cent of the deaths in the conflict. But there you are, it's not what you expect.

So in the end we went for the police option. I was Detective Inspector Louise Galt of Scotland Yard. Becka was my able assistant, Detective Sergeant Tina Peel. Good, solid British names from the Anti-Terrorist Squad. The plan emboldened us. We were willing to wing it a little.

We stopped off on the King's Road and nipped into a second-hand shop where we bought two plain black suits and two horrible polyester white blouses. Then we bought lipstick and sheer black tights in Boots the Chemists and tied our hair back with five-penny hair ties from the cosmetics counter. Becka rubbed talcum powder into her hair to tone down the brashness of her newly blonde locks. She looked a bit older. I followed suit. We bought lined leather gloves. We didn't want to leave prints anywhere. Then, transformed, we walked nonchalantly along to David Curran's mews.

Becka laughed. 'We are criminals,' she said delightedly, wheeling round and round along the pavement.

'No,' I said. 'We're the law. Focus on that.'

We had played a lot of games in our lives, I suppose.

Everyone does. Playing at being someone else, some-one similar, but entirely other. It's what makes you attractive to other people, your ability to become what they need you to become. This time, though, it was professional. There was money involved and we didn't give a shit whether David Curran liked us or not.

We broke in as soon as we got to the mews and settled down to wait for him to come home. He hadn't put the alarm on. He'd lapsed. I wandered around, getting a feel for the place. Becka checked out his kitchen knives. There was a full set of Sabatier chef's blades in the kitchen. A full set of twelve sharpened weapons with which to devise different deaths for David Curran – a little vegetable knife for cutting arteries and a great heavy blade, the size of a small wood axe, for hacking off limbs or a head. Crime is easy once you get started, you know. It's the initial break with respectability which is difficult.

Twenty-Eight

I never knew much about money. I always thought that money was traceable, containable and solid. The scheme that David Curran had devised for bringing the money into the country, though, liquefied currency to the point where it almost evaporated. When the time came, he told us everything. He had moved the money from one medium to another to make it difficult to trace. Money, shares, bonds, goods which hadn't ever existed but were bought and sold none the less. He spilt the beans good style. He thought we were the police, after all. It was late. He had had a busy day. He wasn't to know. He recognised us both, of course. But that only convinced him that we had been on to him all along. He made us promise to protect his mother and we had no qualms about that.

After our initial perusal of the flat, we had settled ourselves down in the comfortable velour-covered armchairs in his sitting-room. Becka had switched on the table lamps, which cast a gentle light all around the room. I drew the curtains and we waited for what seemed like for ever. Until after it was dark.

'Who gets to be the good cop?' asked Becka.

'You.'

'No, I'd rather be the bad cop,' she said.

'Do you think that really works, that good cop/bad cop thing?'

Becka shrugged her shoulders. 'Well, we're going to see, aren't we.' She smiled.

We practised phrases, coached each other and agreed to leg it if necessary.

The Prevention of Terrorism Act.

Resettlement Schemes.

We've rumbled you, son.

You're going to need one helluva brief to get you off here, Mr Curran.

Surveillance.

You have been surveilled.

You have been surveilled?

Under observation.

We've rumbled you, Mr Curran, Sir.

David. David. Can I call you David?

David Curran.

Inspector Galt.

Sergeant Peel.

Looking at twenty years to life, you know.

We've rumbled you, but we'll cut a deal.

If you'll help us.

Because you aren't the scum we're after.

It flowed from us for a while. It really did. We had practised for ages. Then Becka had fetched us a little snack from the kitchen and after we had eaten it we just waited in silence for a long, long time. It's strange that we weren't nervous. The last time I'd been in the mews I had been paralysed with fear and now I wasn't nervous at all. I suppose the circumstances had changed. We had just murdered four people and were fully intent on murdering another. For money. We were on a roll. We knew how serious it was. Well, I did, anyway. If we were found out the IRA would be after us and so would the police. But we weren't nervous at all. We just sat there, impersonating police officers, ready to take money for menaces, poised to murder him. We were ready because we had practised.

Though in the end we were nicer to him than we'd imagined we would be.

We heard him open the door and climb the stairs. We stood up. He started as he walked into the room. I stepped forward and all the play left my mind. All the rhymes and the joking. It was for real and I was in charge.

The words came naturally. That time back in Ireland had restored me. I could talk fluent and convincing nonsense with the best of them. 'Mr Curran,' I said, 'we have been watching you for some time. I am Detective Inspector Louise Galt. Anti-Terrorist Squad. This is Detective Sergeant Tina Peel. We have come to ask for your help.'

'Oh, God,' said David Curran. 'Oh, shit.'

He was so scared he didn't even ask to see any identification. Thank God. For a moment he looked like he might bolt, but he didn't have the nerve for that. I think, you know, he wanted to stay. He wanted to purge himself. We were relying on it.

'Mr Curran, we are here to make a deal with you. It's not you we are really interested in, you see. We want to get the terrorists. You're not a terrorist. We know that. We know about your brothers. We know about everything. Yes, we even know about your girlfriend. We've been holding off the boys from CID for over a week now. We've had this place bugged for quite a while. And your office. The Prevention of Terrorism Act lets us do more or less what we want to in these cases. It even lets us plea bargain. Did you know that? Sit down, Mr Curran.'

David rested himself shakily on the sofa. Poor bastard had never read the Prevention of Terrorism Act. He didn't know shit. Any more than we did. 'Do I have a choice?' he asked.

Silly question.

I continued. 'I'll be frank, if you don't help us you

231

are going to prison. And you'll be there a long time. But I have a good gut feeling about you, David. Can I call you David? Good. Well, I have a good gut feeling about you. You didn't want to do this in the first place, did you?'

David shook his head.

'We can protect you. We are going to protect you. And your mother. It's your mother that they used, isn't it?'

He nodded.

'You recognise us, of course,' I said nonchalantly. 'You'd be surprised how many of our people you'll recognise. We will protect you, David. It's them that we are after. Them and the money. That money is due to the Treasury. Will you talk to us?'

He nodded again. It was so easy. Years of watching cop movies had trained us. It probably isn't like this in real life. Not one bit like it. But that doesn't matter. If you've seen the movies you believe it's like that, and as long as you believe, that's the main thing.

Becka shot him a nasty look. 'You might not consider him a terrorist,' she said to me, 'but I do. Turned over his girlfriend. Money for arms. Money to kill people.'

'Calm down,' I snapped at her. Just like they do in the movies.

We turned to David Curran. It worked like a charm.

'What do you want to know?' he asked humbly.

'The money first. We'll start with the money.'

'I laundered it. A pyramid.'

I sat down in the armchair again. Becka leant forward to listen as if she was really interested in the details, instead of just wanting to know if we could get our hands on it.

'It was easy,' he said. 'I'll tell you everything. But my mother. You've got to keep her safe.'

'Don't worry, Mr Curran. We have had her under surveillance for some time. We co-operate with the

Gardaí, you know. We work very closely. We are going to move her. After this is over we will move you. We'll hide you somewhere safe. Don't worry about that. It's something everyone worries about. But we're the best in the world at this. We're going to protect you.'

David nodded. He was a big coward, really. Just the kind of big coward I had been before. Wanting someone else to save me.

'I'll draw it for you,' he said.

He went over to a small desk in the corner of the room and came back to the sofa with a paper and pen. He started to draw a flow chart. Becka and I gazed at each other. We couldn't quite believe it was working. He scribbled for a couple of minutes and then he turned the paper round. 'This is how I did it,' he said and hesitated, with the paper still held up, delicately, between his thumb and forefinger, so we couldn't quite see it.

Becka broke in on his thoughts, like the bad cops always do. 'I don't want to push the point, but you're as good as dead if you don't co-operate, Mr Curran. We're talking about you going to prison, but to be quite frank you'll be lucky to get there and stay alive. We find it difficult to protect people in prison. Strange, isn't it? But that is one of the most difficult places for us. The odds aren't good. You're entitled to call your lawyer now and consult him. Before we arrest you. He'll advise you to co-operate. If he's any good, that is.'

We just had to go on being nasty to him from time to time and he'd co-operate. Amazing.

David Curran cast his green eyes to the carpet and took a deep breath. How Becka knew that he wouldn't call his lawyer I'll never know. 'It's OK,' he said. 'I know. I know all about it. I'll tell you how it works. Here.' He motioned towards the paper that he still held in his hands and started to talk us through the notes — the flow chart that he had drawn.

'They are responsible for getting the money to an account in New York. The money starts in America. That's where it comes from. Right, they have to deposit it over a period of a few weeks, deposits of less than $10,000. The Securities and Exchange Commission don't trace it then. It doesn't have to be reported. The money all starts in that one account in New York. It's our New York branch. First Caledonian, I mean. I'll get you the number. I don't know it offhand. It's 1.2 million. Dollars. Everything works in dollars. Then I arranged to buy Tesso Bonos with it. Those are Mexican Government securities. They are under-written by the US Treasury. It's a good way to move money in the short term. In the Seventies and Eighties all the countries which defaulted on loans – you know, Brazil, Argentina, Mexico, Costa Rica, Paraguay, Poland, Nigeria – they were all insolvent. The Foreign Secretary or whatever, the guy in the White House at the time, renegotiated the loans with them. Nicholas Brady. They are called Brady Bonds. I bought Mexican ones and I routed those through an account in Turks and Caicos. I bought an off-the-shelf company there. The company is supposed to do business with other companies in the Far East. So the money goes to Hong Kong. By transfer. This time as Brazilian coffee bonds. The instructions come through Hong Kong. I set up an account there. The main thing is that I used a respectable bank. That way the Stock Exchange Council don't ask any questions. Provided you don't do anything outrageous, that is. Anything stupid. It doesn't arouse any suspicions. That's the main thing. The money's on its way to being clean by the time it gets to Hong Kong. Right. Are you with me?'

We nodded furiously. One point two million dollars. Wow.

'Then I used the money to buy securities which are routed through another account in Macau. The dummy company in Macau does business with a dummy company here. That's the account at First Caledonian in London. I opened a trade letter of credit in London. It's supposed to buy leather or something from the company in Macau. There are Bills of Lading for all the ghost goods. No goods, obviously.'

'Where is the money now?' asked Becka.

'It's here. It's been here for two days. They want to get it at the end of the week. I'm to deliver it to them. In cash. They will ring me and give me an address. You'll want to wire me, won't you? You'll want to catch them that way.'

'Yes,' I said. 'We will. But we want the money first. We're going to look after you for the next two days. You won't be going in to work. You're going to call in sick. We're going to look after you.'

'But they'll be suspicious if they find out I'm not going in to the Bank,' David stuttered.

'They aren't watching you, David. Trust us. We're the only ones watching you. They trust you with their money. But we want you to give us the money.'

'You can just seize the money, can't you?'

'We want a bearer bond,' said Becka very definitely. She stood up and walked to the window. 'We want a bearer bond from you, Mr Curran. Drawn on the London account.'

'Why?' asked David. Fair question. Fair comment.

'Because it takes time to seize money. We don't have that time. Besides, we are going to issue you with counterfeit money. Marked notes to take to the terrorists. A case of it. That way, if anything goes wrong, we can trace it. It's misuse of Government funds if we give that money to you for nothing. They are good fakes, you know. We wouldn't give you that without the real money as security. Use your head.'

Thank God Becka thinks fast on her feet. That stuff made sense to David Curran. He was a banker at heart. I think he was actually glad to see us. Glad he wasn't going to get away with it, I mean. There was something in his eyes that betrayed him as a quitter. Quitter Curran. At least the others were fighters. I didn't feel so bad about killing him any more.

He agreed to everything. He said he would go back to the Bank and fetch us a money order. We arranged to meet him back at his place in a couple of hours.

'Mr Curran, I want you to know that we will trace you. If you bolt on us, there is no way you will get out of the country. You have nowhere to go. We have been following you for some weeks now. We have men on you twenty-four hours a day. There are officers outside right now. They will tail you to First Caledonian and back. You are not to go anywhere else. If you do, they will pull you in. You understand that, don't you?' Becka gave him a hard time. 'We'll meet you back here. We were sure that you were going to co-operate. When you get back we will start taking details about your contacts. Your new contacts. We know everything we need to about your brothers. We'll take a statement about them later. It's the new contacts that we are interested in.'

David nodded. 'Don't worry,' he said.

We left the mews together. He got into his car and drove off. We made as if we were walking to our car, up the road a bit.

'Whatcha reckon?' asked Becka.

'Hook, line and sinker,' I said.

'Yeah, one born every minute.'

We didn't want to be seen hanging around outside the mews. After all, it was about to be the site of an horrific crime. So we decided to walk off for a while and come back at the appointed time. We went up to the river and sat there on a bench.

'One point two million dollars. Oh, my God,' said Becka.

'We can buy a house,' I said.

'We can buy whatever we want,' she pointed out.

'Not quite,' I realised all at once. 'We can buy things that aren't traceable. Holidays, clothes, food, stuff like that. On second thoughts, we won't be able to buy a house. Six hundred thousand dollars each. That's about £450,000.'

'I hadn't thought about it like that,' said Becka. 'I mean, as individual money. I hadn't thought about it like that at all. I thought we were sharing it. Like a communal fund.'

'Of course,' I said. 'But you know what I mean, don't you?'

We sat in silence and watched the river. I was worried because I wasn't doing it for the money really, and I was worried because Becka *was* doing it for the money. That was when we made the break.

'Becka,' I said. 'I trust you, absolutely.'

'Yeah,' she replied. 'Me too.'

I wonder if she was lying as well. I mean, I wonder if she knew she was lying.

After a while it was time to go back to the mews. We reapplied our lipstick and then walked away from the water, nonchalantly, up the cobbled lane. He wasn't back yet. We nipped in through the back window, as we had done before.

Becka ripped her tights. 'Bollocks,' she said, inspecting the damage.

I thought for a moment. Then I spoke. 'If he comes back with the lads, you make a break for it. I'll try and hold them off. If you hear gunshots, just get away as fast as you can. If you don't hear gunshots, go to the police.' I figured that was only fair. I had got her into all this, after all.

Becka looked at me with incredulity. I don't think she had realised how serious the whole thing could potentially be. I had, of course, but she hadn't realised that we could get killed. Not really. I understood then how separate we are. She stared in incomprehension at the thought of being shot. Or maybe she just couldn't quite believe that I'd have laid down my life for her. We needn't have worried anyway. After five minutes we heard him at the door. Becka had taken the large cleaver from the set of kitchen knives. She was still in the kitchen when David Curran came into the living-room. The curtains were still closed so nothing could be seen from the street.

'You get it?' I asked.

He nodded. 'Your guys are good,' he said. 'I didn't see anyone.'

I smiled a great, beaming smile at him. 'Practice makes perfect,' I said and held out my hand for the cheque. It was a bearer bond.

'It always unsettles me. All that money in my hands. There must be a bit of the criminal in me. Makes me want to leg it to Switzerland and open an account,' I said.

He smiled. He thought I was warming to him. I suppose people warmed to him a lot of the time. He was used to it. But to me he was just a carcass. He was already dead.

'Well,' he said, 'just in case you ever do, they don't ask many questions on the Swiss–Italian border. Lugano. Places like that.'

'Thanks,' I said. 'I'll bear that in mind.'

Then Becka struck him on the head with the cleaver.

I always remember that part in *Macbeth* when Lady Macbeth goes on about all the blood. When she is trying to wash her hands. You know: *Out, out, damned spot . . . who would have thought the old man to have had so much blood in him?* I suppose that Becka didn't go for the fleshy parts of David Curran. But still, there wasn't much blood. He didn't die at that first blow – he shrieked instead – so she slit his throat with a paring knife and that's what really did it. A skinny little stream of blood trickled down his neck to the collar of his blue shirt. David Curran just stared in disbelief for less than a couple of seconds, then he collapsed.

I went into the kitchen and fetched a pastry brush. I painted 'IRA SCUM' in blood on the living-room wall. I wanted the police to know, when they found him. I wanted them to look into it. It was only then that it occurred to me that the IRA might never know the money was missing. After all, if they had left the whole thing to David, it was conceivable that they wouldn't know the bank account numbers or the names of any of the companies. They wouldn't know exactly how he had done it. They might just assume that the money was still in a bank account somewhere. They wouldn't be able to get to it.

We put the weapons and the pastry brush into a plastic bag. I pushed the money order into my pocket and we left the mews flat. We walked for ten minutes along the main road, until the streets became busier. Then we got a cab back to Kilburn High Street. We had got away with it.

Twenty-nine

The appeal for information went on for ages. There were pictures of David Curran on the news; pictures of a moist-cheeked Mrs Curran arriving at Heathrow to assist the police with their enquiries. They probably went looking for the other Curran brothers. Maybe that's how their deaths never did get reported. Maybe they ordered a news black-out while they investigated it all. Strange phrase that, news black-out. In a country where liberty and freedom of speech are valued and where people care about knowing exactly what is going on, right down to seedy details about the sex lives of MPs. You'd be amazed how much doesn't hit the TV or the newspapers. I mean stuff on the mainland. Not just stuff in Ireland. I met this guy once who was a TV cameraman and he said that it happens all the time. Drugs shootings, fights between gangsters, all sorts of stuff doesn't get reported. They get down there with the cameras and they are just told to go away. The film is taken off them. It's a news black-out. Free press, my arse.

Two days after we killed him, Becka and I took a little trip to the south coast and we joyfully threw the cleaver, the knife and the pastry brush off the cliffs at Dover. We had taken a picnic and lazed in the spring sunshine, our hair golden and our eyes hidden behind newly purchased sun-glasses which we had bought ourselves as a special treat.

It was while we were there, after lunch, that we decided to take David Curran's very last piece of advice about Lugano. He had been a consummate professional at the money business. He had really done the IRA proud. You'd never have traced it all through conventional means. So we agreed to open a little bank account in Switzerland. They are famous there for being discreet, just the way we wanted them to be. I had to start work. I knew that I wanted to get back to a normal life. I had rung Charlie Campbell and confirmed that I'd be starting with him at the firm. He had asked me for lunch again, at the Tate. The second lunch of many, and the start of being fond of Charlie Campbell – the way I now am. There's something about the colour of him – something that can't be camouflaged. I like that in people now. You know what you're getting. Anyhow, I couldn't go to Lugano, so Becka said she'd go and do it herself. The next day we took the tube to Heathrow. It was a really sunny spring day when I waved her off, the kind of day which felt like the first day of summer. Full of hope. She was going to fly to Pisa and Eurorail it north up to the Swiss border. It seemed like a good idea. A good cover – the tourist season was just beginning. We held each other tight at the airport and said our goodbyes. As she disappeared into the departure lounge I realised that my sun-glasses were missing. That was when I knew that I would never see her again. Her last reason for hanging around was gone. After all, now she had the money.

A month later, the day, in fact, that I paid off most of my loan at First Caledonian with the proceeds of my first pay packet, she sent me a little key for one of the left-luggage boxes at Paddington station. It arrived at the office, by DHL. After work I went to the station and opened the box. There was £75,000 in cash in it and a little note. It just said, 'Don't come after me.' I wonder if she was afraid of that. I wonder if she's scared I'll follow her; whether she looks over her shoulder in the bus queue or wakes up hot-faced after nightmares of me. If she is scared, then it's because she'll be stuck with me liking her and caring about her in her own personal, unrelenting kind of living hell. I think that's what would panic her most. She had to do something awful, you see. She had to do something unforgivable. Or I'd like her.

I didn't want to go after Becka, though. I could have gone to Glasgow. I know. I could have kicked up a stink. But I wanted to start something new. A new life, I suppose. The job at Charlie Campbell's has worked out well. I knew it would the very day I started. I felt like I belonged there. I sold the house in Belfast. I got £6,500 for it in the end. An atrocity can surely depreciate your capital assets. After I had paid all the fees and shipped the furniture over to London, I still had a little under £5,000 left. A little nest-egg to add to my windfall. I put Ma's ring in a safety deposit box at the bank, then I made my decisions.

I rang Trish at Pagan McSwain and told her I wanted to buy a little flat. Something small but groovy. Somewhere industrial. Maybe somewhere near the East End. She fixed me up, though in the end I had to stay for three months in the Kilburn squat. Lisa was OK. She didn't ask questions and I kept myself to myself. It took a while to sort things out, but I'm settled now. They'll never find me. I'm sure of it. Though sometimes I do get paranoid. The other day I could have sworn I was followed from the tube station on my way home from work. There was a guy and his clothes were too clean, and he just seemed to be tailing me. Well, you know, I face that sort of thing now. Head on. I turned round in the street and stared at him hard and he tried to brush past me, but I caught hold of him. 'Have you any idea how intimidating it is for a woman on her own to be followed?' I shouted.

Loads of people heard. Heads turned. I don't give a shit about that now. It's only a weapon to use against people like him. People who get in your way. Creep. He mumbled his apologies. That's something a policeman wouldn't have done. He definitely wasn't a policeman. They won't find me. They wouldn't know where to start. And the lads. The IRA. Well, they wouldn't just follow me. Not their style at all. I'll never be scared again, you know. I'll never be scared again.

So. I told you Becka's story, I suppose, as well as my own. The story of two girls who went in search of four men and found them. Two stories. And, as they say in Belfast, that's great value, because one of them is even true.

RECKLESS DRIVER

Lisa Vice

Concise, resonant prose . . . From the first propulsive words of Lisa Vice's debut novel, readers know they're in for a breathtaking ride with a powerful stylist. Sometimes sweetly lyrical, at others quietly foreboding, *Reckless Driver* is always fascinating'
San Francisco Chronicle

Lana Franklin's house is full of mysteries: Why does 'remodelling the house' involve her father tearing it apart yet never doing it up? What do her mother and sister find so exciting about boys? What's it like being dead? The adults around her don't seem to have the answers, nor the time to listen to her questions. As Lana grows up, she has to seek her own solutions.

Told in Lana's piercingly honest and lyrical voice, *Reckless Driver* hauntingly captures a young girl's struggle to make sense of the chaos of her world. Unsparing and yet deeply compassionate, this highly acclaimed novel is beautifully written, moving and insightful. It is a novel you will not forget.

May 1998

NAMEDROPPER

Emma Forrest

I don't see what's so good about being genuine. Clog dancing is genuine. Isn't being fake more of an achievement? At least it take some inspiration.

At the start of the summer, sixteen-year-old Viva Cohen has a blissful home life with her gay uncle Manny, a best friend who eats a pound of lettuce a day because she likes the taste, a tune she can't get out of her head and a lot of Elizabeth Taylor posters. At the end of the summer she has a lot of Elizabeth Taylor posters. When Viva rejects a happy successful rock star for a miserable, unsuccessful one, Elizabeth is there. When she runs away with a sickly celebrity who wears an anorak in ninety-degree heat, Ava and Marilyn help out. Follow them all, from Edinburgh to Brighton, from L.A. to Vegas, as Viva uncovers the icon in everyone.

Witty, insightful and fresh, *Namedropper* is a must for anyone who's ever felt nostalgic for something they've never experienced.

SEESAW

Deborah Moggach

Take an ordinary, well-off family like the Prices. Watch what happens when one Sunday seventeen-year-old Hannah disappears without a trace. See how the family rallies when a ransom note demands half a million pounds for Hannah's safe return.

But it's when Hannah comes home that the story really begins.

Now observe what happens to a family when they lose their house, their status, all their wealth. Note how they disintegrate under the pressure of guilt and poverty and are forced to confront their true selves.

And finally, wait to hear all about Hannah, who has the most shocking surprise in store of all.

'Provocative, enthralling, bang-up-to-the-minute . . . truly, Moggach gets better and better'
Val Hennessy, *Daily Mail*

'A delight to read'
Daily Telegraph

STRAIGHT TALKING

Jane Green

This could be about your best friend.

Or your girlfriend. Or it might be about you.

Are you Tasha – single and still searching? Are you one of her three best friends? Andy, hooked on passion; Mel, stuck in a steady relationship with a bastard; or Emma, endlessly waiting for her other half to propose?

Do you know an Andrew – suave goodlooking and head over heels in love . . . with himself? Or a Simon – allergic to commitment and dangerously treacherous? Or an Adam – handsome, kind and humorous, but too nice to be sexy?

Follow them all in their odyssey to find fulfillment and the RIGHT kind of love in this novel that is very funny, painfully honest, sometimes sad but always on the button.

CHLOË

Freya North

Chloë Cadwaller is in a quandary.

Jocelyn, her godmother, has died leaving Chloë a letter instructing her to give up her job (lousy) and her boyfriend (awful) to travel the four countries of the United Kingdom during the four seasons of the year.

Heavens. How can Chloë deny a godmother's last wish?

Off she goes, with a tremor of doubt and a letter marked Wales, to a farm deep in the Black Mountains where she finds an assortment of animals in varying states of mental health and the best looking man she's ever laid eyes on.

As the seasons unfold, so does Chloë's journey. From Abergavenny to St Ives, from the Giant's Causeway to the shores of Loch Lomond, with sex, sculpture, ice-cream, egg sandwiches and a potter called William thrown in on the way, Chloë encounters love, lust – and a man for each season. Travel with her in the warm and witty story of one girl's quest for a place to call home.

OTHER TITLES AVAILABLE IN ARROW

ALL ARROW BOOKS ARE AVAILABLE THROUGH MAIL ORDER OR FROM YOUR LOCAL BOOKSHOP AND NEWSAGENT.

PLEASE SEND CHEQUE / EUROCHEQUE / POSTAL ORDER (STERLING ONLY) ACCESS, VISA, MASTERCARD, DINERS CARD, SWITCH OR AMEX.

EXPIRY DATE .... SIGNATURE ....

PLEASE ALLOW 75 PENCE PER BOOK FOR POST AND PACKING U.K.

OVERSEAS CUSTOMERS PLEASE ALLOW £1.00 PER COPY FOR POST AND PACKING.

ALL ORDERS TO:

ARROW BOOKS, BOOKS BY POST, TBS LIMITED, THE BOOK SERVICE, COLCHESTER ROAD, FRATING GREEN, COLCHESTER, ESSEX CO7 7DW.

NAME..

ADDRESS..

....

Please allow 28 days for delivery. Please tick box if you do not wish to receive any additional information ☐

Prices and availability subject to change without notice.